CARING FOR YOUR CLOWN

BOOK TWO

Trial And Error

OLEANDER BLUME

Disclaimer:
This is a work of fiction. All characters, locations, and businesses are purely products of the author's imagination and are entirely fictitious. Any resemblance to actual people, living or dead, or to businesses, places, or events is completely coincidental.

Warning: The content of this book involves mature themes, graphic violence, and abuse against minors.

It's Official

Generally, and especially on weekends, alarm clocks are the most annoying, god-awful things in the world.

This Saturday morning, though, was different.

The moment Oliver's alarm started screaming, his eyes popped open, and he began vibrating with quiet ecstatic energy.

The kid practically leapt from his bed, turning off his alarm in an excited little twist as he bounced on the balls of his feet, still trying to figure out what he should do first.

It was an important day, a really important one. Probably the most important day of his life.

He was gonna get his name changed.

First, he tiptoe-ran out of his room, crossing the balcony to the attic where his father slept. Halfway there, before a different idea popped into his head and he halted, swinging back around and racing down the stairs to the back porch.

It was barely light out, and the sun cast a pinkish-orange glow over all the frost and the light powder of snow on the ground. And an alien clown sat on the porch frozen stiff.

"Dindet!" Oliver jogged in place, trying to keep his bare feet from freezing in the snow on the porch. She didn't answer. Probably because there was a solid two centimeters of ice caking her entire body.

He grabbed her head, cracking and twisting until it popped clean off.

"I need your help with something," he said, turning her around to face him. The alien blinked at him. Slowly, she leaked oozing black and sparkly slime out of the hole around where her neck had been, pooling in the ice and snow until she was a separate being from the perfect shell on the porch.

"I need your help making something for my dad," Oliver repeated with an enthusiastic smile. She hadn't seen that before. The boy grabbed her by the hand and dragged her into the cabin with nary a clue to how much his unabashed joy infected her and turned her bright with sunny colors.

"What are we doing?" The clown hardly had time to ask the question before Oliver shoved a bowl into her arms and began digging through the pantry.

"Making Gujarati Tikha Pudla." He pulled out mustard oil and chickpea flour and then set them on the island. "It's like his favorite breakfast."

"Whose?" Dindet inspected the green chillies Oliver had grabbed from the fridge.

"My dad's."

The clown could barely keep up with the boy's overzealous haste. He darted all around the kitchen, shoving the ingredients he needed onto the island at the center before he let out a breath and stared at the big mess of his unprepared Thank You Breakfast.

"Since Matthew's gone and Dad won the court case, he said that we could officially change my name." Oliver smiled, taking the ingredients he needed to make the pancake-like part of the breakfast.

"Mom wanted me to wait until I was eighteen," he said, "But now that I'm legally his kid, I don't have to."

Oliver took the bowl from Dindet and started mixing in his spices and flour with water to turn it into a paste. "I wanna make sure he knows how much it means to me."

It was more than that. So much more. Dindet could see the genuine appreciation and love that emanated from Oliver as he quietly focused on creating something he knew his father would like. It radiated in creamy warm tones around the tiny black part of him that believed he didn't deserve to be loved at all.

"What can I do?" Dindet butted lightly into him, pulling his attention away with the noise of her static. Oliver blinked and turned his gaze toward the vegetables he had yet to chop.

"Can you cut up those, and the garlic and chillies? I gotta mix them with this." He tilted his bowl toward her so she could see the paste he had made. "And then cook it in a pan."

She nodded and promptly began doing as he directed, following his orders as the two of them turned the entire kitchen into a fragrant war zone.

Once they were done, Oliver set a glass cover over the dish he put an insane amount of effort into and pulled Dindet up the stairs with him to wake up his father.

"Did he stay up all night?" He whispered to her at the door, creeping it open just enough to peek and make sure his father wasn't still awake.

"I think he stopped moving around when the sky circle got to the other side?" Dindet answered, taking note of Oliver's hushed voice and mimicking the way he spoke.

Oliver pushed the door open the rest of the way, making sure not to accidentally slam it into any of the mouse cages that lay on the floor.

The two of them rounded the half-built interdimensional portal at the center of the room to get to his still-snoring father.

"Dad," Oliver whispered loudly, picking up the blueprint that had stuck to the man's face from dried drool. "Wake up. It's Saturday."

"Nā, mēṁ vāyarō…badalyā nathī." Jon mumbled something

about wires. Oliver wasn't so great with Gujarati. He was only marginally passable with his Hindi, thanks to spending months in Surat with Manpreet.

"Please? I made you something," he replied, shaking his father just enough to make him snort and peel his eyes open.

"Oliverissstillearly..." Jon mumbled, and his eyes fluttered closed again, prompting Oliver to give up on keeping the gift a surprise.

"I made Gujju Tikha Pudla," he finally said, "just like how Baba and Dādā make it."

That made his father's eyes pop open. He heaved in a semi-reluctant grunt and sat up. "With the panchamrit and everything?"

Oliver nodded, grabbing his dad's hand and pulling him out of the futon so he could show him.

"You said it was your favorite, so last night I called Manpreet to ask for the recipe," Oliver led his still-very-tired father down the stairs as he went on. "Dindet helped and everything!"

He stopped at the kitchen, plopping his dad down at the table and quickly shoving old court papers and hospital records to the far corner of it so Dindet could set down the sizable plate in front of him.

"Oliver, you really didn't have to—"

"I know," he cut in, allowing Dindet to place the covered plate in front of his father. Oliver pulled the cover away to show off what the two of them had made. "I just really wanted to."

Jon blinked, his tired eyes slowly coming to focus on the pancake-like meal his son had made. It smelled wonderful, the aromatic spices commingling in the kitchen with the subtle sweetness of the panchamrit, immediately making his mouth water.

"You do a lot...for me." Oliver smiled, dropping his gaze down to the gift he had made so he wouldn't see the look on his dad's face.

"It's probably not exactly the same...." he hesitated, watching intently as Jon took a bite. "I did my best."

"Oliver," Jon spoke through his chews, drawing the kid's attention from the plate back to him. "It's delicious. I love it."

"Really?" The boy let out a soft sigh of relief. "You think so?"

"Of course! You did a good job." Jon scarfed more of it down, offering a bite to him. "Baba and Dādā would be proud."

***

"There you are." The nasally voiced court secretary wheezed as she pushed a small and most wonderful pile of papers to the edge of her marble counter.

Oliver bounced on the balls of his feet, brimming with near nauseating excitement as he watched his new and official father straighten the stack of forms, birth certificates, social cards, and a whole lot of particularly important paperwork generally needed to arrange sole custody. On all of which Oliver now shared Jon's last name.

"Did they change the gender marker also?" He asked, taking a peek at the papers. Jon lowered the stack for him to sift through, and his bright smile faded just slightly as he caught a glance at what he was looking for.

"Sorry, the judge ordered a deferment until you're of age," Jon answered, offering a consoling smile to lift whatever hopes had been dashed. Oliver pulled the papers from his hands to read in full, providing a slow and distracted nod of understanding.

"I guess that makes sense…" he trailed off, choking down some of that nausea. "Since I can't go on testosterone 'til I'm sixteen and all. That's all right."

"Only two more years. Well"—his father cocked his head—"more like one and a half."

Oliver swiveled on his heel to face the big glass window that separated the waiting room from the secretary's office and waved his papers at Dindet to draw the alien's attention.

Her head popped up at the movement, and she stared at him

with dumbfounded confusion. Probably because he looked like a happy baboon, waving around a bunch of paper in the middle of a mostly empty room. She offered a vacant smile in return, clearly more occupied with her own thoughts than whatever was occurring behind the glass wall.

"Would you make it so you can adopt her too?" Oliver asked distractedly, his gaze still focused on the clown that sat on a bench, entirely deaf to what he'd said. He glanced back at his father to gauge his reaction. "I mean, 'cause she's been here a while and I figured maybe, I mean—after we get mom back?"

Jon's face creased with subtle worry at the mention of Marie, but he hid it well with his smile and patted his son on the back, gently pushing him toward the door. "That's not really up to me, Ols. Dindet has a home too, and she might want to go back to it once our project is complete…but, afterward, I can ask her."

"Yeah?"

"If she says yes, I might have to invest in another attachment to the cabin. That thing was built for a family of one, not four."

***

"Oliver." Dindet hovered over Oliver's spinning head, and he peeled an eye open to stare at her and her dopey grin. She was little more than a few inches away from his face, leaning over the back side of the living room couch like a colorful bat and kicking her legs to keep from falling face-first into him.

"What?"

"Wanna go somewhere really fun?"

"Last time you said that, we almost got killed," he replied softly, not bothering to sit up. His stomach curdled. *Did the milk expire?*

Dindet shook him a bit, a meager effort to get him to at least look at her.

"I promise this time it'll be different—it's like those, uh, the lines?" She doodled something in the air, trying to find the right word to say. "The ones on tree slices?"

6

"Drawings?" he corrected, shaking the hair from his eyes as he sat up.

"Yeah, but when you make them, they turn real!" She bounced a little, hoping his moment of contemplation would come to an eventual 'yes'.

Oliver sat there, mulling over the idea. *It would be pretty cool to draw something and have it come to life, actually....but I have a better idea.*

"Actually," he paused, glancing out the back porch toward a small shed near the tree line. "I want to do something else—show you something else."

The boy stood up and pulled Dindet over the back of the couch until she flopped onto the cushion in abject confusion.

"Show me what?" She watched as he paced around in thought.

"You know how you make things? I wanna make something but not in the uh—" Oliver gestured at the air, at a loss for whatever word he intended to say. "Not in the same sort of way you do. Just, stay put. I'll be right back."

Dindet stared at him for a couple of seconds, then twisted and contorted herself to where she sat on the couch like a normal person usually would, and nodded, prompting Oliver to head up to his room to grab whatever it was he needed to do whatever it was he was planning to do.

He returned a few minutes later, arms full of perfectly rectangular, thick blocks of wood and some leather pack that was folded up in his elbow and dropped it all on the coffee table in front of her, situating the wooden blocks on her end and then rolling out the leather pack to reveal a host of different, and incredibly sharp tools.

"What is—"

"It's for sculpting—well, *carving* specifically. I don't have any soapstone anymore, so I grabbed some wood blocks I hadn't messed around with. Here." He pulled out a chunky wooden tool with a sharp rectangular edge. "This is a chisel; it's for scraping off thin pieces of the wood so you can make different shapes, like balls or ovals or even animals and stuff."

Oliver held out the tools for Dindet to take, and she politely plucked it out of his hand to inspect. "That one is my dad's. He gave it to me after I sort of broke Lord Ganesh."

Dindet hesitantly poked the sharp edge, causing little droplets of her starry matter to spill out of the puncture she'd made.

Oliver stared at it, some soft smile creeping across his lips in his nostalgia. "You can—you can use it if you want."

At that, the alien's eyes flickered back to him, and she raised her head. "But I don't need any of this to make things."

Yeah, no duh. That's not the point. Oliver bit his tongue and reached to take the precious tool back.

"I know, but *I* do, if I wanna make something. I can't do it like you, and I thought maybe you'd wanna see how human people make things."

Dindet blinked, clearly at a loss on just exactly what he was trying to accomplish.

"Look." Oliver shrugged off her indifference. "I just—I'm in a really good mood and I wanted to show you something that *I* like to do instead of just running off to some other dimension for the night. I haven't made anything in…in a really long time. And I'm actually in the mood to make something again."

The alien's mouth dropped open slightly in a silent 'oh,' and her gaze fell to the kit of tools he had laid out in front of her and was already starting to put away in quiet regret.

"You made all the ones in your room?" She asked softly, prompting Oliver to stop.

"Yeah, like, a year or so ago?" He answered, glancing back at her. She was still staring at the tools, then her gaze slowly shifted from them to him, and her eyes widened in what looked like realization.

"Okay. I'll do it your way," she said, taking one of the blocks of wood in her palm. She gave one of those soft, knowing smiles. The kind that Oliver recognized meant she was looking straight through him and probably eating whatever jumble of emotions he had that was making his guts roll up with bile. "It's something that makes you happy."

"Y-yeah," Oliver pulled away from the coffee table, his intestines already forming knots that were far too much for him to handle at the moment. *What did I eat??*

His mouth watered at the thought, and he promptly jumped to his feet, startling the clown back onto the couch.

"I—" he gulped, that horrific flavor rising up in his throat almost unfettered. "I'll be right back."

Oliver bolted up the stairs and into the bathroom, making it just in time to expel all the contents of his stomach into the toilet and plop back on the tile floor in a nauseous haze.

He sat there for a moment, still reeling from the rush and the sting of acid in his throat. And trying to run through the catalog of his brain to figure out what made his insides want to murder him so much.

***

Dindet sat on the couch, patiently waiting for her friend to return from his emergency bathroom trip. Eventually, that patience wore thin, and she was overcome with intrigue.

She glanced back up the stairs, watching the bright colors wisp out the bedroom door in a gentle ebb and flow until they turned very ugly very quickly, and she stood up.

"Oliver?" she called, moving from the edge of the couch toward the stairs. He didn't answer, aside from a horrendous retching sound. Dindet popped to the threshold of his bedroom and leaned in, peering straight down the narrow crack of his bathroom door where the colors radiated with intermingling brown and nasty shadows. It tasted horrific.

Dindet took a small step inside and shuffled toward the bathroom, making it just close enough that she would have phased straight through if Oliver hadn't abruptly pulled the door open and slid out before she could even react.

"Is everything okay?"

"Oh, yeah"—he strayed away from her touch and moved to the balcony—"I just ate something bad, I'm pretty sure."

"Oh? You can eat bad things?" She turned on her heel to follow him down and into the kitchen, where he clambered over the countertop and began digging through the cabinets.

"Yeah, sometimes. If you eat something that's expired, or moldy, or whatever. It can make you really sick, or sometimes just being around people." He spoke very casually and moved exactly the same way. But the flavor of him still made the alien nearly gag.

"Like the empty?"

Oliver paused, pulling out a half-empty box of fancy-looking, chopped-up leaves as he turned to stare at her.

"Uhm…I guess? If that's the best thing you can compare it to?" He dropped down from the counter and began turning the leaves over into a thin baggie with a string on it.

Dindet watched him intently until her gaze made him uncomfortable enough to follow up.

"It's tea. Back during the divorce, I usually got really sick after I stayed with Matthew, so my mom made this tea to help me feel better. Probably because he smokes and drinks a lot around me— that sort of stuff can make you sick too," he explained, dipping the small bag into a mug full of water and shoving it into the microwave, prompting Dindet to take a solid five steps back from the kitchen altogether. "Go ahead and pull out the rest of my kit. I'll be there in a second to show you how carving works."

Back on the couch much later in the evening and already on his third mug of hot tea, Oliver held up his block of wood in the lamplight, scrutinizing it for notches and blemishes. It had gone from a boring rectangle to something more akin to a weird, misshapen blob with a flat bottom. It was *going* to be a figurine of Dindet, but that would likely take another several days.

Dindet's attempt at carving was just as ugly as his, though with a lot more nocks in the wood where she hit the edges a little too hard. Somehow, she'd also managed to wedge a three-inch crack down the side of the solid oak. He had absolutely no idea what she was trying to make.

Oliver took a sip of his tea and sat forward on the couch to set down his tools. "It's all right if it looks really bad at first. I was *really* bad when I first tried it. And I was working with stone."

He gestured loosely at the Mandira in the corner of the room. "It took my dad and me like seven weeks to figure out how to make an elephant. With nothing but those sped-up videos on the internet."

Dindet tossed her block in her hands, judging its ugliness in comparison to Oliver's. They both looked almost identical. Aside from the crack. "How do you know what you're making? If you've never unmade it before?"

Oliver shrugged, adding on an 'I don't know' noise to boot. "I just see it in my head, and then you just break it up into little pieces until it looks like whatever you were trying to make."

Dindet let out an exasperated groan and melted off the couch into a half-puddle of herself on the floor. "But that takes *forever.*"

She rolled over and set her block on the coffee table before getting to her feet. "I thought you liked going to other places with me. Why can't we do that?"

"Well, next time, you can take me to the Cornucopia," he suggested half-mindedly, stopping Dindet from heading off to the attic. The alien froze for a moment, tensing up as a bit of her seemed to jerk and ripple under her skin.

"No."

Oliver frowned and looked at her.

"Why not? That's where you're from, isn't it?" He hunched forward, sizing up her opposition. "We let you hang around here all the time, so why can't I get to see where you're from?"

Dindet bubbled a bit longer and shrugged him off with deliberate dismissal. "You wouldn't like it. It's really boring."

"A place full of clowns. *Like you.* Is boring." *She's making this way harder than it needs to be.*

"I bet you're lying," he said, prodding her in the side until his finger poked through the surface of her skin. "I bet it's just as weird as you, and if you just—"

"I said NO!" Dindet barked, turning bright red when she swatted his hand away.

Oliver withdrew, clamping his mouth shut at her obvious displeasure with the topic. He shifted further back in his seat to create some idle distance between them.

"*Geeze*, forget I asked," he muttered, letting her go to help his dad. She lingered for a moment, though, uncomfortably changing colors until she looked positively regretful of her outburst.

"I..." she swayed, knotting her fingers up in her jester hat until they tore off and floated in the air around her head.

"Just forget it." Oliver shot a glare at her, which quickly faded when he caught how distraught the subject made her. She stared at him a tad longer, as if she were expecting him to say something else, but he didn't.

Rumors

Cassidy meandered at the edge of the fire line at the school bus drop-off, pacing quietly back and forth as her thoughts began to pile up on top of each other. She had been deliberately avoiding the topic, but it wholly consumed her mind now, and she simply had to get it out.

Dindet isn't human.

Finally, the bus Douglass and Oliver rode pulled into the lane, harkening their arrival. She watched as all the other students filed off, patiently waiting for the grumpy kid to trudge down the steps with his not-human housemate bouncing behind him.

She wanted to confront the monster first—if she was that. She could have been anything, honestly. Monster was just the first thing that came to Cassidy's mind when she watched whatever Dindet was explode and consume Oliver completely.

That was nearly a month ago, though. And Oliver had yet to come back to school since. So hopefully, he would today.

As she watched Douglass stumble out of the bus, a small breath of relief blew out her lips when Oliver followed shortly after. *Okay, cool. Not eaten.*

Cassidy waited for the colorful entity to hop out next, but the boys drew closer to the school entrance, and she quickly realized that Dindet was nowhere to be seen.

"Uh—" the girl hesitated. It wasn't a secret that Oliver wasn't particularly fond of her, but she attempted to get his attention anyway. "Hey, um, Oliver?"

Cassidy waved, cringing at the look of absolute disinterest he gave her.

"Dindet didn't come to school today," he answered blandly through a fortifying gulp from the thermos he'd brought, already leaving her to head off toward the cafeteria.

The girl clamped her mouth shut and adjusted her glasses, preparing to chase after him and Douglass.

"Actually, I wanted to talk to *you* about something." She caught up with him, and he quickly veered off to the breakfast line.

"If it's about the Poe project, I already rewrote my essay," Oliver muttered, picking through different kinds of juices to find the last orange. "Mrs. Hargreaves said because Ma—I missed school, I had extra time."

"Yeah, uhm…about that." Cassidy followed him through the line, opting not to get any sort of breakfast. "I, uh, I saw something—and, well, I wanted to talk to you about it?"

Oliver nearly slammed his tray into the metal conveyor and drew in a quick gasp. "It wasn't what you think it was, so just drop it."

Cassidy blinked, then furrowed her brow.

"What am I *supposed* to think?" She countered, watching the boy begin to curl in on himself at his own reply. She wasn't entirely sure if they were talking about the same thing, but Oliver was definitely hiding something. *Or he's at least trying to.*

"Oh my god, Cas, we've been waiting for literally ever!" Hailey interrupted, wrapping her arm around Cassidy's neck and tipping her away from the person she was actually trying to talk to. "What are you doing talking to Olivia?"

"That's not my name," Oliver remarked, not even putting in the effort to look at the two girls.

"Right, sorry. *Oliver.*" Hailey replied, "I just figured you changed your mind again—since you were wearing that dress and all."

Oliver let out a grunt, muttering something under his breath before leaving the line for a table.

"Hailey." Cassidy dipped out from under the girl's arm. "That really wasn't nice to say."

Hailey merely gave her a shrug and toted her off to their own designated table.

"You know, I'm just worried," she stated, sitting Cassidy down and dropping into the chair next to her. "You've been hanging out with that clown girl so much, and you barely even talk to Saoirse or me anymore."

Cassidy offered a weak smile and twisted around in her seat to figure out where Oliver had gone to sit. "I was trying to talk to him about something important, though."

"And *I'm* trying to talk to *you* about something important," Hailey argued, placing her hand on the girl's head and turning it back to face her. "You really shouldn't be hanging out with them."

"Why not?"

"'Cause they are all, you know, they're all *weird.*" Hailey's eyes flickered off toward the table that Oliver and Douglass sat at, and she lowered her voice. "I just heard some stuff recently."

"Why? Is it bad?" Cassidy narrowed her eyes, finally placing her focus on the girl in front of her and not the overwhelming and genuine strangeness that Oliver was somehow harboring a non-human, clown-shaped entity in his home. "Do you think he's hiding something?"

"Well," Hailey gave pause, as though she were contemplating what she was about to say. "I just think they're a bad influence. I don't want you to end up like *that.*"

"And what is *that?*" Cassidy folded her arms expectantly, mimicking the way the girl phrased her words. *Doesn't sound like a compliment.*

15

"Look, Cas." Hailey bit her lip. "I know you got like a huge thing for broken kids and stuff, but Cleo and Anika on the soccer team told me Olivia—"

"Oliver."

"It doesn't matter," Hailey continued, "they told me they thought they saw them with this person, and—and you know what Markus said last week, right? How they, *you know*—"

"I don't pay attention to rumors." Cassidy cut in. "So no. *I don't know.*"

Hailey rolled her eyes at her remark and scoffed, "Whatever, just forget it."

***

Douglass plopped down in the seat next to Oliver as he quietly doodled in his sketchbook at the lunch table.

"What's up?"

"My entire reputation is blowing up in smoke around me cause of that stupid freaking dress," he answered, not glancing up from his sketch of the more terrifying version of Dindet.

"Oh." Douglass fiddled with his breakfast burrito, tearing bits of it off while he tried to come up with some kind of reply that Oliver genuinely didn't want to hear. "I was kind of hoping that me wearing it instead of you would have made that, uh…not happen?"

"That's super great of you, but you're not the one who's trans." Oliver pulled away from his drawing for a second and let out a disenchanted sigh. "There are already people that think I changed my mind." *And worse, people who probably saw me with Matthew.*

"You don't know that for sure, though. It wasn't even for the whole day," Douglass argued gently.

"Doesn't matter," Oliver retorted, throwing his pens and pencils into his bag. "People talk, and right now, I'm apparently a really interesting topic to talk about."

"I don't think so."

Was that meant to be a compliment? Oliver rolled his eyes and finally looked at the kid directly. "Everyone knows my mom is dead, I have a weird clown girl living with me, I'm always in and out of the hospital, and I'm basically the *only* trans kid in the entire school—and I showed up in a dress four weeks ago, then *disappeared* for another two weeks…I'm not an idiot, Douglass."

Oliver gathered his things and stood up, opting to ignore any further contest his friend had to offer. It didn't matter; he wouldn't let anything like that get to him. *It isn't important, and it doesn't hurt.*

The boy made his way back to class, hoping no worse rumors floated around the halls about him than that. It was already hard enough getting a handle on Dindet, and Matthew showing up threw a wrench into everything. In more than one way.

He couldn't help but think about it, the way his biological father nearly killed him…again. But more than that, in the front of his mind, he thought about Dindet and the way she so effortlessly stopped Matthew from succeeding.

She was terrifying. If not for being completely inhuman, it was the way she fed off his thoughts and feelings. *My memories. The way she used them to fuel her rage-filled frenzy.* Part of him thought it was remarkable, and another part, tucked deep and away in his mind, feared that power and ability. What she could truly do with it—if she wanted.

The clown had decided not to come to school today. He figured it was because he hurt her in some way. She was quiet in the morning, and every time he glanced in her direction, she phased into ugly and uncomfortable colors. As though seeing him reminded her of something awful.

He hoped her not being here was why Cassidy was so unbelievably antsy throughout the entirety of class. The girl fidgeted and twirled her dreadlocks, spinning the little metal rings in them as a brief and pointless distraction.

He *particularly* hoped she wasn't antsy because she possibly saw him and Matthew.

***

"Oliver." Cassidy's voice pulled his attention away from the tiles on the floor as he walked toward the lunchroom after the bell rang. "I *really* need to talk to you about something."

"And I *really* don't want to talk right now," Oliver replied, turning in the opposite direction. She bobbed and weaved around other students, quickly catching up to him and tugging at the sleeve of his shirt.

"It's important—I was gonna talk to Dindet about it, but she's not here. And I really, *really* need to say something," she urged, trying to get the kid to come to a halt and actually listen to her.

"If you need to talk to Dindet, you should be patient enough to wait for her to come back tomorrow," he retorted, dread-fueled frustration pricking at his skin. He quickly turned heel once more to evade her.

"But—"

"Cassidy," Hailey's stern voice cut the girl off, and both Oliver's and Cassidy's attention turned to her friend. "Are you gonna go sit with *them* or with us today?"

Cassidy blinked, caught entirely off guard by the malice of her friend's voice. "I haven't decided yet?"

"Well, you have to now, 'cause if you don't, Saoirse and I aren't gonna hang out with you anymore," Hailey stated, prompting Oliver to let out a stifled laugh. *That was her ultimatum? For what? Honestly, that's the most childish thing I've ever heard. 'We won't be your friends anymore if you don't sit with us!'*

"That is literally—"

"Oh my god, *IT*, no one asked your opinion." Hailey cut Oliver off, turning her attention back to Cassidy. "It's either us or those freaks."

Cassidy stared at her, dumbfounded by such a ridiculous notion. "Well, honestly, I don't think I want to be friends with someone who talks to people like you just did."

Hailey bit her lip, as if she genuinely contemplated apologizing, but instead, she dug into her completely forced indifferent demeanor and scoffed.

"Well then, you should know that the school *tranny* is also the school *slut*," she spat, turning her nose up at Oliver's utterly baffled expression.

"You're an awful person! How could you even say something like that?!" Cassidy pulled herself in front of the boy, glaring back at Hailey with contempt. "You can't just call people that!"

Oliver blinked, trying to get some sort of grip on whatever it was he just walked into, but his mind stood stark still on the slur that so effortlessly rolled off that girl's tongue.

"It's true." Hailey flipped her hair over her shoulder and glanced back at the redhead next to her. "Saoirse and I saw *it* with some older guy. They were all close and cuddly in the corner by the counselor's office. Right, *Olivia?* By the fire doors? I think I even saw his hand up that *pretty white dress.*"

Oliver's breath hitched, and he couldn't help but stare at the girl as she described Matthew, all with a sadistic smile on her face. It was something she truly knew would get under his skin. All to deter Cassidy from him. Like it even mattered at all.

"Hailey, *stop.*" Cassidy's voice was cold, and her eyes only briefly flickered back to look at how horrified and pale Oliver had become.

"Why?" she retorted.

"*You* know what I'm talking about, don't you?" Hailey addressed Oliver now, forcing him to stumble back as she invaded his personal space. "Or are you gonna lie about it? Gonna lie about what Markus saw at his dad's motel? We all know your favorite hobby is *choking.*"

"I—I..." Oliver drew in a staggered breath, struggling to come up with words to string together that would compel this girl to stop talking. But instead, small tears bubbled in his eyes, and he blinked them away in an effort to hide them.

"Does it feel good?" Hailey's voice was low and quiet as she circled around the two of them. "Knowing everyone in school knows you're just a big joke? Pretending you're something you're not to get pity points 'cause your mommy's dead and you like to screw crusty old men?"

The girl's next words dripped like poison from her lips, quiet and sweet in the disjointed ringing of his ears as Oliver processed them.

"I bet you *like* the attention. *Jailbait.*"

Hailey stared at him, taking awful joy in the stupor of shock he was locked in, until Cassidy's palm slapped across her face and smacked into Oliver's neck, sending him stumbling back.

"Oh!" Cassidy lunged forward in an attempt to catch him, her hand latching around his wrist to keep him from hitting the ground. "I didn't mean—"

He cut her off with some silent, visceral look of terror, digging his fingers between hers and forcing her grip away before she could properly take hold.

Out of the Bag

Oliver ran, not entirely sure how far or exactly where he was going. Just away.

He didn't stop until he was forced to by two large doors at the end of the hall that he promptly shoved open to dip into the darkness of whatever room he'd made it to.

He stumbled, out of breath, and desperate to get air back into his lungs. His bones ached like broken glass crunching under his feet, and he dropped down with a startled shriek into a pit, landing hard on old music stands and chairs that broke his fall in the worst way possible. It hurt. *It hurts.*

The boy drew in an ugly gasp and scrambled onto the carpet in the shadows of the orchestra pit, staring in the dark at the nothing that felt so loud. Overbearing. Screaming. *I can't breathe.*

Oliver dug his fingers into the grimy carpet, haphazardly attempting to calm himself down before that awful surge of clenching catatonia pulled his hand up to brace for something that only existed in a memory. It hurt. So much.

Stop. It's fine. I'm fine. It's not real. It's fine.

He reached and kicked. That pounding, breaking. Twisting bones. Tearing skin. So much screaming.

Make it stop!!

"Aghk—" Forced into silence by the sudden noise of the theater doors bursting open, Oliver clapped his trembling hands over his mouth.

"Dude, dude, no, you gotta do it like this!" a boy's voice called, followed by some loud coughing and a soft thud from the stage above.

Oliver jerked back into the shadow of the pit as the lights were flipped on, casting a bright and hot yellow haze on the stage above him.

"No, no," another voice announced, "Mr. Kirkpatrick said hemlock is like—what was it, Tye??"

"Asphyxiant or something," the first voice answered.

Oliver held his breath, shaking and holding so tight to himself that it made his muscles ache in his quiet terror.

How many are there?? They can't see me. No one can—

"Cody, what are you doing?! That shit's vintage, you're gonna break it—" the second voice barked, prompting Oliver to tighten his grip further, despite how much effort it took to calm his frantic breathing.

There was a shuffling overhead, thudding and thumping that grew closer until something small clacked and skittered against the floor above Oliver, launching over the edge of the stage and straight into the orchestra pit.

Whatever it was, it clattered against the stacked chairs and music stands, and Oliver stared with wide eyes as it hit the orchestra pit carpet a mere four feet from his shoes.

"Way to go, Mulligan!" The second boy's voice chided, followed by the thwack of what Oliver knew in his bones was a smack upside the head. The footsteps on the stage grew closer, shuffling in discordant rhythms.

Three? Four? Four guys?

Oliver held his breath and kept his mouth shut tight as he scooted further along the wall toward the shadows. Someone large with long legs dropped down directly in front of him, causing the boy to yelp and close in on himself.

The silhouette swiveled around and stumbled back in shock, catching himself on the nearest music stand as his eyes met Oliver's, and the two of them stared at each other in silence.

Short-lived silence.

"BRO. THERE'S A GUY DOWN HERE!" the clumsy boy's voice boomed. He sounded older, like a junior or maybe senior, but Oliver couldn't recognize him in the dark pit. The moment he spoke, three other pairs of feet dropped down.

Oliver scrambled, attempting to make a break for the orchestra pit door. But he was blocked off by what he could only guess was another upperclassman who held his arms wide in an effort to catch him.

"Woah! Chill!" The lanky blond one reached for Oliver's shirt to catch and stop him from stumbling back, straight into another guy's chest.

"Don't—" Oliver choked on his demand. Before he could act, that stifled terror and panic reached its peak, and he dropped down on the ground in a tight ball, nails clawing into his head to try to make it go away. *They can't see me. Not like this. Please.*

Be better. Get better now. NOW.

"Hey," one of the boys murmured in confusion. Oliver heard him crouch down. He was so close that Oliver could almost feel his hands before the boy even reached him. He flinched.

"Stop!" He wheezed out the word, desperate to cease his terrible shaking. "Don't—don't touch me! Just leave me alone! I'm fine!"

"You don't look fine—"

"I *am!*" he lied.

"Hey, isn't that—" one of them was cut off by a soft noise, someone smacking his leg to get him to shut up.

"Guys, back the fuck up. Go! Get out!" the boy closest to

Oliver ordered. "I got this. The tape is over there. I'll just meet back at Kirkpatrick's."

Oliver shoved his face deep into his knees like some small animal that couldn't burrow any further into the hole it had dug for protection. There was more noise, and it made the shaking worse. The broken glass. Bleeding. It hurt.

The strangers shuffled.

"Mark—"

"Mulligan, I swear to god. You're lucky you're my stepbrother. Get the fuck out. And don't break my fucking tape recorder!"

The shuffling faded until the creak of the stage door sounded the other boy's departure, and the only noise in the room was Oliver's uneven breaths. It was rhythmic, in a weird way, growing louder and more frantic every couple of increasingly long seconds until he choked it back down. *It's fine. You're fine! Be fine. They're gone—*

"It's just us now," the older boy said, prompting Oliver to dig further into his skin. He'd thought he left as well.

"Here, can I help you? I think I can help." The senior's voice was creaky and deep, but calm. He reached his hand up, hovering over Oliver's trembling self and causing that aching convulsion to tighten its grip on his stomach and make the child cough in an effort to force himself to relax. He was so close. So close that Oliver could feel the heat of his palms before they landed over his hands and pried them away from his head.

Oliver reared back in a sobbing and terrified effort to flee and shake and jerk his hands back to himself, but the older boy held him fast and stared right at him.

"I-I can't—please! I need you to stop! *Please!*" Oliver gulped, and his gaze focused back on the things only he could see. He attempted another pull to free himself. To clasp his hands around his arms. He shook his head for a second or two before an awful shudder rippled up through him and he clenched his eyes shut. "Please stop. Please stop. Please stop."

"I'm not gonna hurt you. Just tell me what's wrong—"

"NOTHING!!" Oliver ripped his hand out of the older boy's grasp and clambered backward in his second break for escape. "Just, just, just leave me alone!"

He twisted around to gain a better footing. To stand up or get his legs to move despite the fact that they felt like they'd been lodged into the ground and he was trying to carry the entire weight of the earth along with him.

And then something very heavy and very hot landed on top of him, cramming his face into the dirt and grime of the carpet as arms wrapped around his torso and forced him back into the senior's lap.

"LET GO OF ME!" Oliver kicked and clawed into the boy's hands, only getting them to lift up for a brief second before they dug under his ribs, and he let out a curdled yelp of pain. Then the boy's hand planted itself over his forehead, pressing into the stitches over Oliver's brow and stinging it with his sweat.

"CALM DOWN," he barked. It was the same loud and commanding voice he'd used to chastise his brother. Oliver stilled himself.

"Don't...please, don't."

"Don't what?" The senior breathed, his voice hoarse from the yell. The tension of his muscles eased. "I'm not gonna hurt you. I'm not gonna do anything. You're safe. I just need you to breathe."

The boy drew in a deep breath, the kind that lifted against Oliver's back, prompting him to mimic the exercise. He exhaled.

"Again?" He requested, this time much softer and Oliver did as he was told. The reward was the senior's grip loosening further.

"One more time. In...and out..."

Oliver gulped down the bile in his throat with one last inhale, and he felt the older boy's hands lift and hold themselves above him, as if they were enticing the idea of escape. But he was far too exhausted to commit. So he just sat there, sinking into this stranger's lap like a heavy, aching blanket.

"You...did that...in the *worst* way...possible..." Oliver muttered through soft gasps.

"Well," the senior dropped his hands to his sides, allowing Oliver to crawl to his knees away from his well-meaning, but incredibly ignorant captor. "You didn't exactly make it easy."

"Well, I'm good now. So you can leave. I don't need your help anymore—not that I needed it in the first place," Oliver retorted gruffly, still thoroughly struggling to get his legs back underneath him.

The senior stood and held out his hand to help him up, which he made a point to refuse.

"Kind of a dick move, considering *you* were the one losing your shit," the older boy remarked, pulling his hand back. "What are you even doing here? The stage was reserved for our short film."

"*Clearly*—" Oliver drew in a deep breath and brushed the dust and dirt off himself. "I was having a party. If I knew it was *reserved,* I wouldn't have come in the first place. But people don't exactly think straight when they're *'losing their shit.'*"

"*Mrow!*" The senior mimicked the sound of an angry cat and hissed. "Damn. Kinda wished I didn't help you. What's your name? Grade?"

Oliver shot a glare back at the boy, trying to discern details of his appearance in the shadow of the once again dark auditorium. He was tall and somewhat lanky and had dark hair. But that's all he could really guess. "Sorry, I don't talk to strangers."

"I don't think I really count as a stranger anymore—considering."

Wow. One moment of weakness is all it really takes, huh? Oliver huffed in disgruntlement at the thought.

"Ah!" the senior snapped, and Oliver forced himself not to jump at the echo of it. "You gotta be what, a freshman? Shortest freshman I've ever seen...lemme guess...AP English is your homeroom? Whattabet it's Hargreaves?"

Oliver rolled his eyes and climbed over the pit gate and back into the rows of seats. "Oh boy, a real genius. She's like, one of three AP homerooms. And *all* the English classes take B lunch. Props for effort, though."

"I'll walk you back to class if you want? Kirk's not gonna care if I'm late." The older boy followed him toward the auditorium doors, despite Oliver's increasing pace and look of disdain.

"I know the way. I don't need a babysitter—"

"Oliver!" Cassidy's voice cut the conversation short as she threw the auditorium doors open with an exasperated sigh of relief. "Oh, my god. I've been looking for you *everywhere!* Is everything okay?! You just ran off, and I know Hailey said all those awful things, and I really, *honestly*, don't blame you for running off, but principal Balboa is under the impression that *you* hit her and not me, and they aren't listening to me, and I'm pretty sure you might get suspen...dedwhoisthat??"

The girl's gaze flickered past Oliver straight to the older boy a few feet behind him.

"Just some guy." Oliver shrugged, filing his way between her and the door before the senior could catch up.

Cassidy swiveled around, her mouth hanging open in confusion as Oliver trudged onward without a second thought.

"You're sure you're okay? You looked—well, I don't really know how to describe it, but you looked really—"

"I'm fine. Everything is fine. And I honestly couldn't care less what your stupid friends think of me," he cut in, gesturing in dismissal of the whole event. *It doesn't matter. It can't matter.* "What did you want to tell me anyways? Since you've been so dead set on trying to talk *all day.*"

"I—well..." Cassidy stopped at the cafeteria entrance, the lunch hall still buzzing with the chatter of students to drown out her much softer words. "I wanted to talk to you about Dindet."

Oliver stopped, and for half a second, the thrill of relief trickled down his spine until it settled in his curdled stomach alongside his apprehension.

"What about Dindet?"

Cassidy didn't immediately answer, instead shuffling her weight hesitantly. Oliver turned, bringing his gaze up to look her in the eye and watching as she averted her eyes and grappled with words to describe what he knew was something not easily described.

He let out a long and tired sigh, brushing his fingers through his hair to fix the mats that had tangled from his struggle. An uncontrollable shiver still lingered in his bones, despite his attempt to hide it.

"So you know."

Cassidy lifted her gaze in the subtlest of nods, prompting Oliver to keep walking and hope she wouldn't follow. Except she did.

"I didn't mean to find out! I mean, it wasn't particularly hard, but I saw you in the courtyard on the day—"

"I wore a dress?" He finished, twisting on his heel to face her with an accusatory finger. "Listen. *You can't tell anyone.* Not your mom, or your *other* mom. Not Douglass, your dumb friends. *No one.* If people find out she's an alien then it's gonna be like a whole *thing.* And I already have a lot of other *things* to deal with, so you have to *keep your mouth shut.*"

"She's an...alien?" Cassidy leaned away from him with a dumbfounded look on her face that quickly turned into absolute glee. "She's an *alien. Clown??*"

Oliver's brow furrowed. "Yes."

Cassidy pushed his finger out of her face and immediately

caught pace with him. "Do you know what kind?!"

"The clown kind?"

"But what does that *mean?* Do they all look like clowns? Or only some?! Do you know what planet she's from?"

"She's not from a planet," Oliver hesitated, "…I think."

"No planet? Oh! Oh! Do you know why she changes color? And the—the thing with her face. Do you know how that works? You have to have notes! You *have* notes, right?!" Cassidy jumped in front of him, forcing the boy to halt in his tracks with a stern glower. "I have to know! Are they humanoid—well, yeah, 'cause she looks like a regular girl, *but what about the inside!* What kind of biology does she have? You have to tell me!"

"My god. Look." Oliver sidestepped the girls' blockade with a gracious eye roll. "If I take the fall for you hitting what's-her-face. You have to *swear* you won't tell anyone…and…I'll let you hang out with my clown, and you can ask her all those questions yourself."

"You'd really—wait." Cassidy took a step back and placed her hands on her hips in skeptical contemplation. "What exactly are you getting out of this? You'll get suspended for like a week."

"Yeah. Exactly."

"And you *want* that?"

Oliver groaned. "I don't know if you noticed, but I don't exactly have perfect attendance. What's another week? So, deal?"

Cassidy shifted her weight in thought, pressing her thumb to her lips as she murmured in a tangent of French only she could understand.

"So, *deal?*"

"Okay. Deal."

Sleep Eater

Oliver stood at the edge of the curb, teetering on his feet as he flipped from one app to the next in order to waste his time while Douglass was in the bathroom.

"Hey, Oliver, right?" Some voice called his attention, and he flicked his gaze toward the caller. A guy probably two or three years older than him was strolling up along with two other kids his age.

Oliver decidedly didn't give any indication he noticed them, hoping that they were trying to get the attention of some *other* Oliver around. At least until that same boy's shadow dropped over him and made him draw his gaze away from his phone again.

"Clown kid, right?"

Clown kid?

"Yeah?" Oliver grunted, raising a brow at the stupid title. *If anything, Dindet is the clown kid. Not me.* "She doesn't do birthday parties if you're asking."

"What? No." The older boy chuckled, brushing his fingers through his hair as he glanced back at his two friends near the flagpole. "Actually, I just wanted to talk to you."

Why?

Oliver looked up at him, trying to read the look on his face. He wasn't familiar in the slightest. Just some tall dude with dark brown hair and freckles. Acne scars covered them up on his cheeks.

"I don't even know you," he answered blandly, watching the guy curl up in what looked like embarrassment.

"Right, yeah—that makes sense. The theater *was* pretty dark."

Oliver nodded slowly. *Oh. It's you. Bad with panic attacks guy.*

"I just see you around school between classes and lunch, and you seem interesting." The boy added, "Isn't your dad like a super famous scientist at the lab?"

"He's on leave right now," Oliver answered, thoroughly avoiding addressing the compliment. "I'm not as smart as him, so I can't do your homework…what's your deal?"

The senior's eyes widened for a split second, and he forced out an anxious little laugh at Oliver's blunt tone.

"Damn, dude." He offered a smile and pulled his phone out of his pocket. "Don't bite my head off. I was just gonna ask for your number. I wanna hang out sometime."

At that, Oliver blinked, trying to wrap his mind around such a concept. The only person who ever approached him with such an intention was Douglass. Cassidy sort of fell into his very tiny circle because she hung around Dindet—and knew she was an alien.

"S—sorry," he mumbled dumbly, turning his phone screen over to make the exchange possible. "I don't make a lot of friends."

"I can tell," the senior remarked, once again glancing back at his friends while Oliver was busy attempting to be personable. "For someone with a walking rainbow, you gotta open up more. That shit draws attention."

Oliver gave a little huff through his nose at his words, taking the boy's phone and typing in his number. "She doesn't follow me *everywhere*."

"Yeah, figured that out the hard—"

"I'm back," Douglass interrupted, half jogging up with a form in his hand. He glanced from Oliver back to the older kid for a second or two, quickly gathering what was going on. "You know him?"

31

"Nope," Oliver answered, handing the senior back his phone. The boy quickly thanked him and ducked out of the conversation to head back to his friends.

Douglass eyed the senior incredulously as he left before turning his full attention back to Oliver. "And you just let him have your number?"

"You really think I'm gonna talk to him?" Oliver retorted bluntly, "I barely even talk to you, Douglass. Besides, I'll probably string him around for, I dunno, a week or two if I get bored."

Douglass made a face at his remark, something akin to the look one would make when they were more consumed by pointless jealousy than concern, but he let it go and gave a short nod. "Sorry I took so long. There was a huge line for the Driver's Ed course."

"That's what you were doing?" Oliver glanced down at the papers in his friend's hand. "You don't even have a car."

"Well, we still have Jojo's old one. My dad found out about me working at old lady Deauxtree's, and I feel kind of bad that Theo's mom has to cart me and her back and forth," he explained, following Oliver as he climbed onto the bus and made his way to one of the furthest seats from the front.

Oliver plopped down into the window seat and scooted aside so Douglass could fall in next to him. "Bet that's not awkward at all."

"You have no idea, dude." Douglass gave a somewhat exaggerated shudder. "But money's been kind of tight, so I figured if I go through the school's courtesy classes, he won't have to pay for it. Plus, I can pick up more shifts."

"I've got a ton of money if you need it," Oliver stated, thinking back on the enormous settlement Jon had halved for him and his family in Surat. "My dad had it locked up in a bank, and I can't mess with it anyway—was gonna use it for top surgery, but I can ask about it?"

"No, it's cool." Douglass waved away the offer. "It's not really that he doesn't make enough. It's just all the alimony on top of my sister's old hospital bills. I'm pretty sure your dad already offered. And—well, I know how much getting that surgery means, and I don't wanna make you wait or anything."

Oliver stared at him and cocked his brow at such an idiotic notion. "I was just saying I'd ask, but I'm pretty sure it's in a trust fund or something…are the classes after school?"

"Yeah, I gotta take the activity bus home after today."

There was a tone to Oliver's question that Douglass didn't quite catch when he answered. It made him force out a reluctant little sigh. It's not like he'd miss him or their walks home. *It's fine. Dindet would always be there anyways.*

She opted to skip class today for almost no reason, and when Oliver asked about it, she simply said everything was fine and she was just trying to finish the machine faster. It didn't fit with the way she avoided his probing about the Cornucopia, though. *Must have really hit a nerve.*

***

The alien silently crept from the attic toward Oliver's room, peeking in to see that he was for certain asleep—which apparently took just about as long as it did for his father to do. When he did manage to sleep, oftentimes, he tossed and turned with little whimpers from nightmares she preferred not to digest.

She pressed through the dark, teetering at the edge of his bed, keeping low so she wouldn't be noticed.

Dindet lingered here, usually when he was asleep, because he didn't particularly like her being in his room while he was awake.

Eventually, after fiddling with knickknacks and thumbing through pages of scribbles and drawings that were significantly better than anything she could do, she turned to the thing she was most intrigued by.

She rounded his bed, only pausing when the kid rolled over with a tired groan, and stood at the edge of his night desk, staring at the photo he seemed to care very much about.

Quietly, Dindet picked it up, gazing into the still little memory. Not for sentimentality—no, there was something terribly familiar in it, *someone* terribly familiar. And for a very subtle, tiny moment, an ache filled her at the thought of it.

She knew her.

***

"You have to learn how to sleep," Oliver said rather frankly the next evening. "I know you creep into my room at night, and it's freaky, so let me teach you so you can stop being so weird."

Dindet cocked her head, staring at him like some dumb animal while she slowly parsed out what could constitute as sleep for her.

"I would just get all gooey."

"No, I mean—not like when you're knocked out. It's a different kind of thing."

The alien looked around his room for a moment, gauging whether or not this was a good idea. "I've never slept before."

"I know." Oliver waved her forward, allowing her up onto his bed so he could pull out some regular sleepover supplies. "That's why we're gonna practice tonight."

"Why?"

"Because I told Cassidy you would hang out with her, and if she's like me—"

"Cassidy is not like you."

"I *mean,* if she sleeps like most human people do, you standing in the corner of her room all night is gonna probably creep her out." He finished, throwing a couple of extra blankets on the floor in case she needed them.

As far as he knew, though, she didn't seem to care for comfort.

"All right, so, lay down, close your eyes and just think about nothing," Oliver directed, pointing at the place he made for her next to his bed. The clown dropped down to her knees, keeping her eyes on him as she navigated the new territory with intrigue.

"Nothing at all?" She questioned, lying on her stomach with her head resting in her palms as she stared up at him. He rolled his eyes and gave a small nod.

"Well, you can also just think about whatever. It helps if it's not something you really care about." He grabbed the other blanket and threw it over her before changing into his pajamas. "I'll keep an eye on you if you start to turn all gross."

Immediately, Dindet sat back up, eyeing him with incredulity and perhaps a hint of worry. "I've never not thought about things, though."

Really now? That's hard to believe.

"Don't worry about it—it's just sleep." Oliver peeked over the edge of his bed, then rolled onto his other side. "The worst that can happen is a nightmare, and those don't really hurt you."

Dindet sat back again, mimicking the way Oliver laid down and staring up at the little stars on his ceiling. She lay there for a few hours, hearing him toss and turn with soft little breaths. He had managed to go to sleep, but it seemed to be an arduous thing for the both of them.

It was sort of boring.

The alien relaxed, as best she could manage, and allowed her thoughts to commingle elsewhere. Somewhere between her body and the rest of the world.

Oliver said she could think about anything, really. And she thought about a lot.

Mostly the way things seemed to ~~crash together~~ around her.

Pictures of cracks and broken worlds mixed with things that were real and also not.

Like a bunch of thin strings braided together ~~over and over until the whole thing~~ burst in her head and she saw some semblance of what could have been—quite possibly even,

***

Oliver brushed a hand over his face in his sleep and startled himself awake from his nightmare with a jagged, broken grasp. Another remnant of Matthew...

He peered over the edge of his bed to see if the clown succeeded in sleeping.

She wasn't there, though. In fact, she was nowhere to be seen. He panicked, some small part of him realizing that she could be *anywhere*.

"Dindet?" He glanced around the dark room, trying to gather up something in the shadows to prove she was still around.

Oliver leaned over, pulling up the sheets to see if she might have hidden under the bed. The only thing there was the music box toy she'd gotten from old lady Deauxtree. He got up and slid out of bed, circling around his room for a second before checking his bathroom and closet and heading downstairs to see if she opted to return to the porch.

She hadn't.

Oliver slid close the back door curtains, let out a beleaguered sigh and turned heel.

"Holy—" He jumped back, throwing his arms up instinctively in defense from the sudden appearance of the alien.

She didn't do anything, though, and she looked just about the same way she did when she was unconscious, starry black and gooey, floating around like a ghost with blank white eyes.

Oliver relaxed and eyed her, expecting her to snap out of her supposed slumber at any moment.

"Okay, I get it, *really* sleeping probably isn't the best idea—"

"I'm hungry." She cut in.

Oliver cocked his head, hesitant to reply. *She is still asleep, right?*

He held up a finger and moved to poke her in the head to see if it did anything.

But the moment he touched her, she caught his hand and yanked it down, staring at him with empty eyes as she bubbled and grew twice her size.

For a second, maybe two, he could hear her thoughts. Unconscious or not, they raged on about some insurmountable hunger, growing louder and louder in his head.

His heart skipped a beat, and he drew in a fragile, broken breath. *This is like—*

"O-okay! It's time to wake up now!" Oliver tugged his hand back, pulling her viscous tendrils along with him.

The alien stared at him, then slowly leaned closer, dripping parts of herself on his face as she blindly inspected him, as though he were some fresh meal.

There was a small, guttural clicking noise that grew from her.

"D-Dindet, stop." He took a step backward, and she took another step toward him.

"Afraid." It was gurgled and obtuse, the way she said it, like there was little control to the word at all. "What are you afraid of?"

Oliver's breath caught in his throat, and he felt his heel hit the foot of the stairs, causing him to stumble back and hit the steps.

The alien bent forward, losing almost all silhouette of what human form it had, and hovered over him, keeping those blank, wide eyes on him as it closed in on its prey.

Long clawed fingers spread out over him, and ever so briefly, those white eyes widened, and the creature morphed into something far, *far* worse.

"This," Dindet answered herself, twisting the empty expression on her face into Matthew's visage.

Oliver's blood ran cold, and the breath in his lungs grew shallow and quick under the false gaze. Every muscle he had tensed, and he froze up, swallowed by the terror she inflicted.

It isn't real. He isn't really there. He's gone. Stop freaking out! Stop being scared.

"S-st..st-hhop." He breathed, pressing back into the stairs and forcing himself to crawl backward up them. He only got one or two steps, though, when the alien pressed a firm hand into the plank, catching his hair and preventing any feeble attempt to escape.

Oliver winced from the pull and let out a small whimper.

There were gentle murmurs in the back of his head, tiny words of worry, fear? No, concern. That undoubtedly belonged to her.

He clenched his eyes shut and focused only on that, far past that groaning, terrible hunger and under the layer of static Dindet always seemed to barricade herself with.

"You have to."

"Mom?" Oliver drew in a quick gasp, nearly losing what small attention he had on the irrefutable sound of her voice.

His eyes shot open, and the alien changed shape again, long, blond hair fanned over her shoulders, tickling Oliver's nose, and he blinked in astonishment at the new face she wore.

It was like she was there, real, and for a moment or two, he felt so incredibly safe.

Until Dindet's eyes widened, and she snapped awake with a look of absolute horror.

A terrible shriek rattled through him from her head, and she reared up.

The alien whipped back, relinquishing any touch she had on him and immediately retreated, returning to some hideous creature before he could even object.

Oliver scrambled to his feet, dropping all pretense as he clambered up the stairs, only stopping when he heard soft murmurs from the clown.

"No, no, no, no, *no.*"

He hesitated, twisting back in a moment of contemplation but she was gone. Popped off to some other plane of existence to hide away from the confusion of all his twisted-up thoughts...probably.

Very Important Things

There was a substantial silence between the two of them the following morning. Oliver stared at the clown in no small loathing, and she kept her eyes away from him, squirming uncomfortably in an effort to stay whole under his gaze.

"Oliv—"

"Don't." He cut her off, taking a swig from his Thermos as opposed to his usual morning cereal. "Don't say anything. Don't apologize. Just shut up and sit there…please."

Dindet dropped her head, closing in on herself in terrible shame. She deserved it, honestly. Some control, whatever it was, was gone, and she remembered what a horrific creature she was.

"Come on." His voice cut through their boiling silence, and she glanced up at his red-hot hatred.

She slid off the stool and followed him outside, trailing much further behind him as he met up with Douglass.

Oliver's head spun with everything he previously knew about the alien. He hated her, or wanted to, but he also felt some soft longing—a stupid thing, really, to have her look like his mother again. And he questioned, yearned, to know why she dreamt of her voice.

"Are you all right?" Douglass's voice caught him off guard, and Oliver tripped on his feet, stumbling forward and forcing the kid to grab him by the arm to keep him from falling face-first into the pavement.

Douglass pulled him back, a twinge of concern on his face when he noticed how red and watery Oliver's eyes had gotten in just a couple of seconds. His face burned up with quiet blush, and he quickly let go of him.

"I'm fine," Oliver answered, retracting from him so he could pick up his pace. Regardless of what he preferred, though, Douglass increased his stride, easily catching up with him.

"Is it because of—"

"*Please.*" There was a break in Oliver's voice, and even from afar, Dindet noticed his anger completely dissipate as he spoke.

His eyes flickered up toward Douglass's, and, for such a brief moment, there was a pleading so familiar in them that the boy immediately wrapped an arm around Oliver and pulled him into a small and very short embrace.

"S-sorry." Douglass strayed off, putting a couple of feet more between the two of them, though he kept a watchful eye on his friend.

There was a jitteriness about him, and it would have been a lie to say Douglass didn't notice the kid tense up at a loud noise or a stray touch, like a simple hug.

He pressed his lips together, an active attempt to not say anything that would set him off, and decided to question Dindet about it later—if she would talk to him at all, that is.

***

"Dindet—" Douglass tapped on the alien's shoulder, filling her up with his concern and embarrassment the moment he touched her.

He pulled back just as she twisted around and dropped his

gaze to the floor. "I was just wondering if something happened. At home—Oliver's home, house, I mean...I won't tell anyone, like, the teachers or anything cause I know—"

Douglass glanced around a moment and dropped his voice into a whisper. "I know about his other dad."

For a split second, the clown turned a deep purple, not long enough for the kid to notice, or if he did, he didn't comment on it.

"No, I—uh, nothing happened!" Dindet shook her head vigorously, donning a terribly unconvincing smile as she let out a small, nervous laugh. "I didn't do anything!"

Douglass raised an eyebrow, "I didn't say...you did?"

He shook his head and shrugged, indicating that her terrible save face had somehow miraculously worked. "I was just wondering because he's acting sort of—I don't know if you knew, but his other dad—"

Dindet stopped him, placing a hand on his and squeezing just a bit to make him stop talking.

"I know," she answered softly, tasting his worry turn to vile embarrassment once he noticed she still held his hand.

"I'm not mad at you," she said cheerily, and immediately the boy deflated with sincere relief at the statement.

He slumped back in his chair and fiddled with his pencil for a moment. "I'm sorry that I freaked you out so bad, then kind of totally ignored you. I—I wouldn't blame you if you hated me."

"Why would I hate you?" Dindet stared at him until he looked like he was about to crinkle up if he tried to answer. Eventually, he let out a tired, almost melancholy sigh.

"Because I'm pretty stupid when it comes to people," he mumbled even more quietly.

"Hmm...so am I," she replied rather matter of factly, "that's why I'm gonna maybe try harder at it? Oliver says I'm really bad, though."

Douglass held back a snicker. "Oliver doesn't know the first thing about people."

"He knows more than me!" she retorted, loud enough that their subject of conversation snapped his head around with a short glare.

"Does he?" Douglass whispered, prodding her lightly in the arm, "What's he say about you then?"

"I'm"—she stopped herself, and a look of puzzlement crossed her face for a bit while she tried to figure out what to say—"Not very good at it."

Douglass furrowed his brow, and she waved off her answer with a nervous laugh. "I'm happy to be that, though. I can be what anyone wants—"

"You shouldn't think like that," he interrupted, "you're not obligated to be something just 'cause it's what everyone else says, you know? There's no reason to bend over backward like that if it doesn't make you happy."

***

"Class." Mr. Chavez tapped his marker on the whiteboard, pulling the students' attention away from their classwork as principal Balboa and a young, twenty-something-looking red-headed woman entered the room. "Principal Balboa has an announcement to make."

Oliver let out a genuinely disinterested grumble and reluctantly forced himself to stop working on his doodling to look up.

The somewhat plump principal stood at the center of the class, going on about the outside stressors of life or whatnot.

"So, I believe that having a helping hand like Miss Popiviolli's is going to provide an outlet for students going through tough times. I know some of us have lost relatives and friends from the recent incident surrounding AKAN labs, and some of us from…other events that have impacted our lives." Principal Balboa gave a moment of pause, his eyes flickering to a corkboard in the classroom with the most recent image of the girl that had gone missing a few weeks prior.

"Anyway." He cleared his throat, gesturing for the pale young woman to introduce herself. "Miss Popiviolli?"

"Oh, right." The young woman nodded and smiled brightly, moving to the front and center of the classroom. "My name is Pamela Popiviolli. I'm a licensed child psychologist and therapist."

Oliver blinked, and his full attention placed itself on the woman as she spoke.

"Your school recently hired me to provide a sort of…outlet for students to talk about any issues you guys might have."

Cassidy's hand shot up, drawing the therapist's gaze. "Do you still follow the rules of confidentiality?"

"Absolutely," she answered with a nod. "Nothing leaves my office unless there is a risk to you or the people around you. I'm required by law to divulge information that involves the harm of minors as well."

"What kind of therapy do you do?" The words fell out of Oliver's mouth before he even realized it, and almost immediately, other students turned to stare at him.

"I mean, like…cognitive-behavioral and stuff? Or just…" He drew back into himself. "The regular…kind…"

"That's a really good question," the lady answered cheerfully, inadvertently pulling all the unwanted attention back onto herself. "I do five types of therapy: cognitive and behavioral, interpersonal, psychotherapy, and on occasion, I've even done EMDR. But that one is usually reserved for patients I help at Amelis."

Oliver dropped his gaze, moving it toward Dindet to see what she may have been thinking. She was stiff in her seat, though, pressed so far back into it that she would have become flat if it weren't for the fact that she had hardened herself so much.

Dindet's eyes were planted on the therapist as she spoke, flitting to the door as if she were readying herself to escape at the next possible opportunity.

"So, I'm sure many of you probably don't feel my presence here is entirely necessary," the therapist continued, "but I'd hope that one or two of you at least drop by my office in your free periods?"

"Thank you, Miss Popiviolli." Principal Balboa nodded and gestured back to the class, taking one good once-over of the students for good measure. At least until his eyes landed on the bright purple jester hat that Dindet wore.

"Young lady," he said, forcing the clown's attention back into this dimension. "I'm afraid I'm going to have to confiscate your hat. Headwear is only permissible for religious purposes."

Dindet blinked and forced herself to relax just enough that she could look at the principal as he shimmied haphazardly through the column of desks to hers.

"But—"

"No buts," he interrupted, holding out his hand. "You can retrieve it from the front office at the end of the day."

Principal Balboa crinkled his fingers up as a gesture for her to hand it over. The clown's eyes flickered back to Oliver, and he meekly nodded, prompting her to very reluctantly pull the precious gift off and place it in the stranger's grasp.

She let out a soft little whimper, and her kinky-curly bright teal hair poofed and frizzed out in an unruly mess on her head, making it nearly impossible for anyone to see her face above her orange nose.

"I promise I will keep it very safe." The principal added sweetly. Though he still backed away and walked out of the classroom, taking with him the thing she desperately wanted to keep.

She was upset. More upset than Oliver had ever seen the clown before. He couldn't even see most of her face, but the black marks around her eyes bled down as tears over her cheeks.

For nearly the entire duration of the day, she stayed incomparably quiet, despite Douglass and Cassidy offering small condolences to cheer her up.

"You'll get it back at the end of the day," Douglass said once the teacher stepped out for a period switch. He pulled the clown's attention away from the desk she stared at.

"No one usually steals from the principal's office, so I'm sure it will still be there." Cassidy offered a gentle smile, digging in her bag for some hair ties. "Plus, your hair is really pretty. I can style it for you if you want?"

Dindet shook her head, letting out the tiniest of sobs before she face-planted dramatically on her desk.

"But—but it was—"

"I'll go get it for you," Oliver interrupted her before she could lose herself to her distress. Dindet stopped and lifted her head, turning to face him with a little sniffle.

"But they said I have to wait?"

"So?" he argued casually. "It was a gift, right? From before you—you...moved here. It's important."

Oliver stood up from his desk, glancing back at the classroom door to make sure the next teacher wasn't already on their way in. "It's a dumb rule anyways."

It was a pretty stupid rule, and as much as he would have previously liked to see Dindet in a tizzy over a dumb hat. He really didn't want to risk her melting from the stress of it.

And seeing her so bent up and out of shape about it made him increasingly uncomfortable.

"I'll just be gone for a couple of minutes. Balboa never usually comes to the classrooms, so he won't even notice you got it back," he said, rounding his desk and heading toward the door.

Oliver slipped out into the hall, checking once or twice to make sure all the teachers were still running around trying to get to their classes before the bell rang again. This was an opportune time to leave class, mostly because both teachers and students roamed around between bells, trying to get bathroom breaks in before the next period started.

He made his way down the hallway toward the cafeteria, taking a left by the trophy case to the front office, and snuck inside while Mrs. Deauxtree was busy not doing her job and painting her nails instead.

Oliver casually moved toward the office aid room, where seniors usually hung out during their free period. That also happened to be next to the teacher's lounge as well as Balboa's office.

The room was big and empty, outfitted with a makeshift kitchenette and a leftover cafeteria table serving as the lunch table. In the back left corner was Balboa's office, and inside that, a big wooden box.

He sifted through the confiscated clothes, most of it gym stuff, some of them purses and skirts from when the school still used uniforms and pulled out the bright purple jester hat, marveling at how much smaller it was than what it appeared to be when Dindet wore it.

"Excuse me?"

Oliver jumped and spun around, quietly tucking the hat into his pocket as he met eyes with the new school therapist.

She smiled at him and lightly tossed a blue stress ball from hand to hand, casually setting it in her pocket before she continued. "Did you lose something earlier?"

"Well, no—my friend did," Oliver stuttered, forcing himself to calm his stupid nerves. *She's just a therapist, or teacher, or whatever. You're being dumb. There's no reason to be so scared.* "I was just getting it for her, is all."

Miss Popiviolli's smile wavered ever so slightly as if she were trying to recall something. "You're the one who asked me about what kind of services I provide, aren't you?"

"Yeah—" Oliver filed between the woman and the office door in an effort to get around her. "I was just wondering. I've been to

"Not in the mood."

"You're never in any mood," He retorted, softening his tone once he noticed the blotchiness under his friend's eyes. "What's going on?"

It wasn't a question. Oliver looked away from him, stubbornly fiddling with his tray of food but not eating any of it.

"Nothing."

"Last time you said that—"

"I know what happened last time I said that, Douglass," he snapped back, though it didn't cause him to retreat like he wanted. The boy only buckled down harder, going so far as to attempt to console him.

Douglass reached out. "It's your—"

"It's a lot of things!" Oliver pushed his hand back and stood up, nearly knocking over his chair in his hurry, and trudged out of the cafeteria.

Nothing, nothing makes sense! And it built up in a pile in his head and at the center of it was that stupid clown.

With her dumb, stupid smile, saying, doing—looking just like her! And isn't it convenient? Right? To pop around just before all hell breaks loose—to scoop me up out of the clutches of my own personal nightmare and—and the GALL.

She's tricking me! Playing some sick joke like she knew her!

Oliver paced the halls for a moment, finding a spot at the corner adjacent to the restrooms, and tucked himself between a break in the fire doors. He dropped down, sliding against the cold, scratchy brick wall until he sat on the floor like a dumb rag doll, waiting to trip some unfortunate soul.

The best option would probably have been to go to the counselor. *Call Dad—if he isn't asleep.*

Which he probably is. Go home. But she would still be there. Dad would still be there. The machine, that house, that ghost would still be there.

57

Everything reminded him of her. And when he wasn't being reminded of her, he was reminded of everything else.

"Yo, clown kid?" The vaguely familiar voice pulled Oliver from his thoughts, and he brought his gaze up to stare at the bad-at-panic-attacks guy that gave him his number. "You good?"

Does it seriously look like I'm good?

"What do you want?" He croaked, glaring at the boy and hoping he would go bother some other kid instead of him. The senior glanced around a bit before looking back at Oliver and offering a soft smile, the kind that made you drop your guard after realizing it meant no harm.

"Skipping, same as you," he said, prompting Oliver to let out a small huff.

"It's not skipping if it's my lunch period, idiot."

"Rowr!" The boy mimicked a cat's hiss and chuckled to himself at the look Oliver gave him in return. "I know a place. If you don't wanna get caught."

"I'm already waiting for the ball to drop on my suspension," Oliver retorted, turning his attention back to the cafeteria to see if Dindet had followed him out. "I don't exactly care if I get caught."

The boy shrugged. "In that case, nothing to lose?"

Oliver stared at him, trying to make something of this guy that was apparently adamant about getting his attention. *What does he want?*

"Fine." Oliver pulled himself to his feet and sized up the boy for a few more seconds. "Show me this—"

"Oliver...?" Dindet's voice cut him off, and he turned to face the alien.

She stood a few meters back, looking almost as dumb as usual, but the marks on her face resembled some amalgamation of all the ones she'd previously gone through.

"What?"

She wavered, rippling with a meager effort to stay whole. If it were a ploy for his heart—it mostly worked. "Are—are you busy?"

Oliver's look softened, and his eyes flickered back at the boy before returning to Dindet's fraught face. "I mean—I was gonna hang out with—with…"

"Markus."

"With Markus." *Why does that sound familiar?* Oliver gave an uncomfortable nod, watching the alien register so terribly slowly that he didn't know how to be around her. That he didn't really want to. *Not right now.*

"Okay," she murmured, donning a placid, fake smile to boot. She still struggled to stay whole in front of him, though. *Maybe this is better? She shouldn't really want to be around me anyways, after last night.*

***

Oliver followed a decent distance behind Markus as he led him out the back entrance of the school toward the football field and adjacent enclosed pool.

"You do sports?"

"Not allowed." Oliver stepped up on the bleachers so he stayed above Markus as he walked.

"Why not?" The senior spun on his heel, walking backward as he watched Oliver balance on what was supposed to be a place you sat.

Oliver's eyes flickered back at him, searching for some kind of indication that proved he wasn't being played. *Everyone knows why I can't do sports.*

Markus just looked up at him, patiently waiting for an answer and prompting Oliver to let out a forced laugh of nonchalance.

"You're dead serious. You don't know?" He said after a second, "School won't let me, duh…on account of me possibly 'making the other students uncomfortable' or 'giving the teams an unfair advantage'."

Markus chuckled at his mocking tone of Principal Balboa's

lecture at the start of school. "Wait, that whole assembly was about you?"

Oliver snorted and jumped up a bleacher to increase his distance from the conversation.

"*Behold*, the trans blight of Pineton High," he drawled, rolling his eyes at such an ugly self-descriptor. *It's better than school slut.* "I prefer Clown Kid."

"No way! I wouldn't have even guessed!" Markus hopped onto the bleacher below him, and Oliver promptly turned in the opposite direction to head back to the other end. He wasn't entirely sure if that was meant to be a compliment or not. "So, uh, which way?"

Oliver made a face at the objectively innocent tone of the question and plopped down on the bleachers with a huff. "Which way do you think?"

Markus followed suit, sensing the change in Oliver's demeanor and falling in one bleacher up and slightly behind him. "Am I being an asshole?"

"Yeah, kinda." *It's not like I pass, so you're just rubbing it in.* Oliver overheard a reluctant little hum from behind him, and he twisted around to stare up at Markus.

The senior looked down at him with an unreadable expression, or maybe the kind one made when they were trying to figure out if someone was a girl or a boy. Either way, it made Oliver anxious and uncomfortable.

"Do you have a boyfriend?" *What?* "Or—or girlfriend? I guess?"

Oliver blinked, dropping his gaze away from Markus, who thoroughly stumbled over all the stupid words that just came out of his mouth. It made him kind of want to punch him. Or sink beneath the bleachers into the dirt and never come back out.

"People don't really *like* people like me," Oliver stated, trying incredibly hard not to let the thought sink in. "From my experience…most of them just want me dead."

Matthew wanted me dead.

"Is that why you were freaking out so bad?" Markus answered, garnering a forced sarcastic laugh from the boy.

"Hah, yeah, that's a great joke," Oliver retorted, though regardless of his dismissal, the senior's words dug under his skin and made him quiet with thought. "You haven't…told anyone about that, right?"

"Dude, no. Course not." Markus slid down onto the bench next to Oliver, prompting the boy to draw his attention back to him and simultaneously scoot away. "You're cool. You're smart, I mean—it probably takes a lot of mental mapping to figure out all the places you can hide to, you know…"

"'Lose my shit?'"

"Heh, yeah."

Oliver stared at him for a second or two, trying to wrap his mind around why he was being so nice. Why Markus was looking at him like he lit up the world with bright, colorful lights.

"You're probably not half as bad as you think you are. Or—at least not to me. You're smart, and I don't think I've met anyone with as smart a mouth either…Plus you're pretty mature for a freshman." Markus leaned in, trapping Oliver in his gaze as he continued. "For what it's worth."

"Hmmmm—he, hah—" Oliver choked on whatever it was he was trying to articulate. It felt so nice being told such lovely things. He didn't believe them at all, but the way this older boy spoke made his insides tumble over and his face get so hot he couldn't come up with words. He couldn't tell if it was brief infatuation or unbridled fear.

"You—" Oliver gulped, his eyes trained on where Markus's hand pressed into the inside of his thigh. "You're touching me."

How'd I not notice that?

Markus's eyes fluttered down and back up to Oliver, and he

promptly removed his hand. "Oh, my bad."

Oliver made some horrible little sound, and all the words he wanted to say were caught like rocks in his chest. He pulled in on himself, closing off in an effort to hide his sudden nausea. "You— you don't even know me."

"I know enough," Markus replied, "and I sort of always see you walking around in the halls."

"Only cause Dindet makes me stick out like a sore thumb," Oliver retorted, scooting a bit to the side to maintain his distance. "Makes me easy to clock...Is *that* why you're talking to me?"

Markus averted his eyes from Oliver's glower, taking a poignant moment to tap his fingers anxiously on his knee, something the boy picked up on immediately.

"Actually," he said hesitantly, "I kind of wanted to do a sort of interview-documentary thing. For AV class."

"*A what.*" Oliver's whole face scrunched up at the thought. The senior heaved an awkward sigh and rubbed his neck, looking positively nervous about the idea.

"Well, I mean, you're the only trans kid in school, and I know that's gotta be weird or, I dunno, hard? I figured it would be cool to do something to spread awareness?"

"Yeah—no." Oliver got up from the bleachers and started hopping down one step at a time. "I'm good. I don't do cameras. Plus, my whole goal this year is to be as invisible as possible."

And I'm already struggling with that.

***

Oliver meandered through the school halls until he found Dindet idly standing in the same place he had left her, looking slightly less distraught the moment she saw him.

"Oliver! Douglass wanted me to tell you that he saved some sticky buns for you?" She fell in step with him, watching as he slowly turned over in his thoughts. "Is everything okay?"

"What?" Oliver blinked and offered a mild grumble of dazed

discomfort, "yeah—no, yeah, uh, everything is fine. I just—"

"Watch where you're going!" Theo barked, shoving the boy to the side with her shoulder as she pushed past. Dindet swiveled around to stare at her, almost as if to ask why she felt the need to be so angry all the time, but the girl merely gave her a look equivalent to a death sentence and kept walking.

For a second or two, her thoughts turned to Theo as opposed to how discombobulated her friend was, and she tapped Oliver on the shoulder lightly.

"She likes you," she said, shortly catching his attention so she could point out that unmistakable flavor of affection and infatuation that permeated the room like warm, fresh cinnamon candies. Oliver's face twisted up in absolute disbelief, and he shook the whole idea from his head.

"No, she doesn't. Theo freaking *hates* me," He retorted gruffly, not even contemplating the idea. "She's mean anyways."

"Cassidy says you're mean too."

"I'm not mean, I'm honest," he argued, casting an obligatory look at Cassidy that she no doubt didn't even notice. "Theo is just mean."

"Also, I'm pretty sure she doesn't consider me a person," He followed up, far more quietly. The clown cocked her head but didn't reply.

Oliver halted, nearly causing the alien to tear in half as she kept walking. He made some kind of noise, a mix between a groan and an uncomfortable, pitiful whimper, and his face twisted up in discomfort.

"Are you okay?" Dindet slowed her pace to match his, circling around him to better gauge whatever sudden thing created a swirl of unease in him.

"I'm all right." He dragged on a bit longer, then promptly bent over and vomited right there in the hallway.

Organs are Stupid

For a second, Oliver just stared at the ground, and Dindet panicked next to him, doing an abhorrent job of not falling apart from the pure shock of it.

"I don't think that's good—that's not good, is it? Stuff is supposed to stay inside you, right?!" She bent down to look at the puke, then back at Oliver, who looked just about as though he would've dived headfirst into it if he teetered long enough.

"Okay," he mumbled, "maybe not as all right as I could be."

The kid wrapped his arms around his stomach, rolling his eyes up at the ever-worsening pain, and crouched down for a brief moment. Dindet, however, was frantic, weaving around him, raising and flailing her hands in the air until he eventually snapped at her to stop freaking out so much.

"It's just puke. It's not that bad!" He grumbled, clutching his upturned stomach a little harder as a spike of agony rippled up. "I just need to get through the rest of the day and…."

He trailed off, holding back another upchuck of vomit so the poor janitor didn't have to deal with him twice.

Eventually, they made it back to the classroom, and regardless of whatever schoolwork was to be done, Oliver relegated himself to the corner of the room.

He stayed lying on the ground and doing his utmost to be as

quiet as possible through what amounted to a never-ending, twisting, aching, and piercing suffering that made him really, *really* want to scream.

"Poor dude," Douglass remarked, nudging Dindet with his elbow to get her attention off of the boy moaning and whimpering in the corner while the rest of the class enjoyed a movie. "He'll be all right."

She didn't believe him for a second, though, and with every passing moment, the taste of her panic and concern gradually enveloped her.

"Is this normal?" she murmured, peeling her eyes away from Oliver to look at his friend. Douglass shrugged a bit, half nodding and also shaking his head.

"Sort of—it's not ever supposed to be so bad, though, which is why he usually skips school." He lowered his head, resting it in his arms, and glanced up at her. "Guess he forgot."

***

To save Oliver the effort—or most of it at least—Dindet carried him home since it didn't look like he could manage walking or standing up without getting horrendously nauseous and buckling over again with little choked-up whimpers. Or risking vomiting up whatever had long since stopped existing in his stomach. He meekly crawled onto the couch and planted himself face-first into the cushions to drown out some of his mewling.

"Dindet…cabinet…drugs, please."

She promptly obliged, popping into the kitchen in search of whatever thing he hopefully deemed helpful. She gathered up several little bottles of miscellaneous pills and carted them back for him to inspect, handing him one after another as he threw them aside in search of what he needed.

"Is it gonna make it stop?" she asked softly, taking the bottle and opening it for him once he got too frustrated in his agony to try anymore.

65

"NO!" Oliver let out a stifled howl and immediately dropped back onto the couch to moan and turn and cry about how awful his insides hurt. "Hhhhhgggrrrrrhggijustwantittostooop!"

"I can unmake them if you want?"

"No, no, no, *no*!" He rolled over and curled up into a tiny little ball, waving her off with his hand. "The last time you did anything with *my* body, it almost killed me!"

"It wasn't on purpose!" she retorted.

He simply pointed a finger at her, though, and kept the rest of himself buried in the couch cushions. "I don't wanna be coughing up confetti because *you* don't know how people work. You stay right there—don't do anything, don't touch anything, don't touch *me*. Just…let me lie here and die for a while, okay?"

"Do you want me to get Mr. Your Dad?"

Oliver smacked the couch repeatedly in frustration and gave a little half shriek into the pillow.

"YES!! *GO!* DO WHATEVER YOU WANT! I DON'T CARE RIGHT NOW!" He yelled, writhing and rocking uncomfortably until she was positive he wasn't going to improve anytime soon.

The clown retreated off to the attic to see if his father might have been asleep up there. That was somewhat hard to believe, though, because Oliver was very loud. When she looked, he wasn't—*he must have gone off to get more parts.*

For lack of knowledge and ever-increasing worry, she went out on a limb and scrambled over to Douglass just as he got off the activity bus.

"Oliver says he's dying, and I don't know what to do!" She rambled, not bothering to listen to any objection as she tugged the kid away from his house, "I went to look for Mr. His Dad, and I think he went to go get things for…for…dinner? And I don't know how to make him feel better. Also, he's making a lot of noise, and it's scary, please?"

"C-calm down!" Douglass pulled back, forcing the frantic alien to halt and twist around to look at him. "He's just being a drama queen about it. All he wants is some pain medication and a hot blanket or something."

Douglass rolled his eyes up a moment in thought, "I think I have something that might work."

He waved her back toward his house and headed around the back to the garage door. "My sister used to have this thing that you plugged in. It gets really hot, but it helped her feel better after chemo, and I think it'll make him feel better, too."

Douglass moved to turn on the light, and a small flicker of disappointment flashed across his face when it didn't work. He quickly shrugged it off, tore some boxes down from the back shelves and dusted off the heating pad with his hand before giving it over to Dindet.

The room itself was dark and musty, and wires laid out everywhere on the ground, but the small corner of the garage he led her to had several boxes full of clothes, machines, and grimy little toys with sharpie marks over them.

"What are—"

"Jojo's," Douglass interrupted, standing up tall so he could restock the shelves with humidifiers and old bedpans. "She passed away a couple of years ago."

He smiled softly, and the unmistakable bitter taste of sorrow filled the air.

"Uh—anyway." Douglass broke the small silence between the two of them and patted the heating pad gently. "Give this to Oliver and tell him I'll come by to take it back later."

Dindet nodded and offered a quaint smile before he led her back out of the garage toward the road.

When she got back to the cabin, Oliver wasn't yelling so much anymore as he was simply groaning at the air. For a brief while, he stopped crying altogether and was lolling about in the kitchen, doing his absolute best just to remain upright.

"Douglass let me borrow a thing," Dindet said, offering the heating pad to him with a more than nervous smile.

The kid stared at it for a second, maybe a few too long, then reached for it only to miss entirely.

"Dindet...ca–call 911." He teetered, and as the world shrank away, Oliver very quickly lost all color to him and crumpled to the floor in front of her.

Dindet shrieked, dropping to her knees to see whatever horrible thing just happened to make him stop feeling anything at all.

"Oliver?!" She poked and prodded him, turning over his head in desperation as parts of her struggled to stay intact with her sudden and terrible distress.

"Oliver, wake up!"

He didn't, though, and felt limp in her hands.

"Oliver! Whe–where are your colors??" The alien glanced around frantically and teleported from place to place in search of the phone thing he had taught her about. *It wasn't here! It wasn't— or if it was, she didn't know where. She needed—she had to make it better.*

"DOUGLASS!!" The desperate shriek of her voice made him jerk up from his homework. In a near instant, before he even realized she was outside at first, Dindet was dragging him through his own home out toward the door.

"I–I need your help. Oliver stopped moving! He...he fell and said to call 911, but I can't find the phone, and Mr. His Dad isn't—he isn't here, please!" She didn't give him any opportunity to reject and promptly shoved him into the cabin in the desperate hope that he could make something out of whatever very awful and very scary thing was happening.

The second he caught sight of his neighbor, though, Douglass grew pallid, and the worry in Dindet infected him as well. He didn't say anything and only fumbled to fish his phone out of his pocket to call an ambulance.

"My friend is unconscious—his dad's not home yet…yeah—no, uh, he got really sick earlier today, and I thought—I think he needs to go to the hospital." Douglass hung up the phone and sat down on the floor next to Oliver's unconscious body.

"There's an ambulance on the way. They're gonna take him to the hospital to figure out what's going on," he said numbly. It was a poor attempt to comfort the clown, who had gone almost entirely silent.

She only stared at her friend, murmuring little nothings to herself about how horrendously stupid she was to leave him alone for so long.

This was surely her fault, right? He was fine before—she must have done something, moved something to the wrong place when she remade him. How many times did she do that? Three? Four?

Stupid, stupid! How could she be so dumb and thoughtless, and bad and wrong, if he were—No…absolutely not. Not like last time.

Last time?

"He's gonna be okay." Douglass offered his hand for her to take, and while she flinched back at first, eventually, she gave it to him. "They'll fix him up, and he'll be all right."

He didn't know that, though. And the doubt and fear in his head made it so verifiably clear to Dindet that neither of them really, truly understood what was going to happen.

At some point, indiscriminate to the thread of time, the siren of the ambulance grew around the corner stop sign, and the bright lights snaked up against the walls and windows as Jon came bursting through the door with bloodshot, teary eyes. The paramedics followed, carting Oliver away on a metal bed into the back of a square, screaming car. And Dindet still didn't understand what was happening.

***

Douglass sat in the waiting chairs outside Oliver's hospital room.

They were the kind that had almost no stuffing and were made with that thick oak railing that dug into your skin and made it impossible to get comfortable. Especially after the several hours he sat there, waiting for the doctors to give him, Jon, and Dindet any information.

Jon sat next to him on his left, his legs bouncing in silent anticipation. He'd been doing that for a while now, and every thirty minutes or so, right before Douglass could begin nodding off, the scientist would get up and pace around or ask about Oliver.

Dindet, on the other hand, sat perfectly still, staring at the door like she were depending on her life for when it opened.

"Jariwala?" A young nurse poked her head out of the door, and Jon immediately stood, inadvertently shoving Douglass back into reality when he kicked the chair on his way up.

"Is he awake? Is everything all right??" Jon took a long step forward and reached for the door to Oliver's hospital room, prompting Douglass to sit up straight in his chair to try to catch a glimpse of his friend behind it, though the nurse blocked most of the view.

She offered a small, almost-forced smile. "He's fully recovered. There's just something we wanted to address. With you present."

The scientist's agape mouth closed, and Douglass watched his shoulders stiffen with anxiety before he nodded. *Address?*

He had little time to contemplate the thought as the nurse pulled the door open wide enough to allow a view of his friend.

Oliver sat in a gown at the edge of his hospital bed, fists clenched tight on the thin mattress with his head turned down. It dipped slightly as the door creaked, and he looked up.

He wasn't looking at Douglass, though. Instead, his eyes were trained firmly on Dindet, and the exhausted stare he gave her made Douglass instinctively turn to look at the girl.

She was staring right back at him, and maybe it was his sleepy head that made it hard to understand, but it looked like the paint on her face wavered. Stretching and pulling and writhing into long and jagged lines despite her absolute stillness.

Then the door closed, pulling Douglass's eyes away from her long enough that when he looked back, she looked completely normal.

Talk to Me

Jon fiddled silently on the molecular transporter in the attic, holding his hand out to take the pieces and components Dindet fabricated from his blueprints. The house had been eerily quiet for hours after they returned from their stay at the hospital.

I'm gonna have to talk to him…eventually.

He blew out a reluctant breath at the thought and moved to work on microengineering the computer chips in the control panel.

Dindet was thumbing through the blueprints on the table and trying very hard not to knock over any of the mouse cages as she reached for the stack on the other side of them. Then she stopped short. Both of them did. Forced by the quiet sound of the boy's bedroom door opening and closing and his light footsteps creaking down the stairwell.

Jon sat straight, stretched, and cracked his back with a soft groan and met eyes with the alien.

"We're almost done," he mumbled, searching the room for something he could use as a distraction. He preferred her not be present for the conversation that needed to be had. *She probably wouldn't even understand it.*

"There's just a few more things I need. Could you find me

a...uhm...ah—" he snapped his fingers, offering the clown a bright smile to lighten the shadow of her silence. "A MacGuffin?"

Dindet cocked her head and did a small rotation in her spot in search of whatever he was talking about. "A what?"

"A MacGuffin," Jon repeated, pulling himself to his feet. He reached for the table and scribbled a shotty sketch of an absolutely made-up electronic doohicky he had no purpose for whatsoever—other than making sure Dindet had something to do for the time being. "It's...it's a *very important* component for my machine. *The most important*, actually. It runs on...on uranium chloride, and I *can't* get my machine to function long enough to safely de-atomize matter without it. It might be in—in one of those places? What did you call it? The Peace Zone?"

He handed her the roughly made sketch of what looked a whole lot more like a rainbow disco Rubik's cube than a legitimate component for his machine and gently nudged her toward the door.

"But I don't know where to find something like this?" Dindet eyed the paper. "Is it really that important? It's not in any of the blueprints—"

"It is, absolutely. Marie never put them in her notes because she was never able to calculate how to make one." *Because it doesn't exist. Please just take the bait, Dindet.* "I'm sure you can find it."

Dindet held the paper up once again, her skepticism worn plainly on her face. "Okay—"

"Fantastic!" Jon filed between the alien and the door, keeping his hand on the knob until he watched her vanish from sight. "I really appreciate it!"

Now.

The scientist peeked the door open and peered down the small loft balcony to the living room below. Oliver sat on the couch, huddled up with Douglass's heating pad wedged between a pillow he'd pressed over his stomach. He was quiet and hadn't even turned on the television.

He knows we have to talk about it...

Jon drew in a preparative breath and wiped his hand down his mouth to straighten his beard and calm his thoughts. *Be casual...it's...I'm not upset. He has to know I'm not upset.*

"Hey, Ols," he called, donning a smile that he very much hoped hid his concern as he glided down the stairs and pressed a hand into the back of the couch. "How're you feeling?"

Oliver's eyes flickered back at him for a moment. It looked like he was contemplating his reply. Then he slung his head back on the couch and let out a most exasperated groan.

"I'm pretty sure my cervix is out for blood," he answered, re-situating to make himself slightly more comfortable as his father moved in next to him.

Jon gave a nod of understanding, still trying to work his way around to the topic he wanted to discuss. "Yeah—"

"I'm scared it's gonna mess with my blockers, mostly...the birth control," Oliver added, much softer. "The lady said it wouldn't, but...I still worry..."

Jon pressed his thumb to his lip and leaned forward, hesitant to look back at his son. It was a rightful worry to have, but a part of him wanted so badly just to skip to the real topic. *Be patient. Let him go at his own pace...he'll say it if he wants to.*

"Douglass came by earlier today." Jon changed the subject because, of course, he couldn't think of a tangible reply, and his thoughts were consumed by other, far more horrific implications than Oliver's access to hormone blockers. "He's worried sick about you, and well...he's gonna wanna know what happened."

Jon watched as his son shifted uncomfortably, pressing the pillow harder against his stomach with a slight wince.

"He's a good kid. He cares a lot about you...we all do." *We have to talk about it.*

Jon lifted his chin momentarily and only long enough to gather the words he needed. Then he looked back at his child, reading the shame on his downturned face.

"Oliver...how—how long had Matthew been...hurting you like that?"

The boy shrank back, clutching his pillow taught in his arms.

"You can tell me," Jon added softly, reaching to console his child. Oliver shifted away from him, though, and kept his eyes on the floor. "I'm not mad at you, and you're not in trouble." *Please, Oliver. Just talk to me.*

The boy didn't answer, only curled further in on himself.

"A...a long time then..." Jon whispered in conclusion. "Did he...make you promise not to tell anyone?"

"I'm sorry..." The words were soft and light, and Oliver buried his chin into his pillow.

Jon eased his eyes, trying to hide his boiling rage so his child felt safe, if he even could feel safe. He reached again, and this time the boy allowed his comfort, albeit hesitantly. "I want to know because...because it's important, *you* are important to me...and you have nothing to be sorry for."

You never think you're important. But this—it's important. It is so important.

He pressed his palm into the boy's back, rubbing gently in an effort to coax a reply out of him. His insides burned like fire in his chest that bloomed around his core and into his arms and legs. But Jon kept his composure, or did so to the best of his ability. "I'd like for you to talk to me...if you can? I know it's hard, but I want to help. Can you say something?"

Oliver drew in a heavy breath that raised his back and fell with his long and tired exhale.

"I know it's not okay," he finally said, "that...parents aren't supposed to do that."

"I'm glad," Jon answered, letting his boy sink further into his arms. "I'm glad you know that, Oliver. I just...I just wish I had known sooner...that he'd done that. I wish you had told me you were—"

"I didn't know..." Oliver cut in, so quiet his father could barely hear him. "I didn't know that's how it worked. I just thought—I thought I was sick..."

Jon's soft petting stopped, and his focus faded in and out as he stared at the fireplace, jaw clenched just slightly at his child's words. "You...what?"

The boy's whole face crinkled with despair, and he quickly raised his hands to wipe the tears from his eyes. "I thought I was just sick because—because I used to get sick *so much* whenever before— when they were getting divorced, because I still stayed with him sometimes and I didn't think anything of it because you—you know Matthew smokes a lot and he drinks and that stuff makes you sick so I thought that I just got sick again because I *always* got sick after I was around him and no one ever told me—she never told me so *I didn't know.*"

Jon clamped his mouth shut and dropped his gaze in confusion and shame at the way his son curled up with pained sobs. *I could have prevented this...all of it.*

"Oliver—"

"I didn't know, I *promise*," he repeated through his choked-up breaths.

Jon reached forward, hesitant with his son's uncontrolled flinch away from him, and pressed his hand over the boy's back.

"I believe you..." he breathed, allowing the child to relax and fall into his embrace if he so chose. "I'm not mad, and you're not in trouble. It's not your fault—and we...we were able to take care of it and make it so that it doesn't happen again. I am *so sorry* it happened at all."

Oliver's ragged gasps settled for some tender moment, and he raised his gaze, meeting his father's gentle and terribly weighted face. It made him sputter and whimper, caught up in that awful emptiness until he let out a mournful little wail and pressed himself into Jon's chest, wrapping shaking arms around him to keep himself steady as he tried to control his upturned thoughts.

It was heartbreaking, holding him. And Jon could barely muster the conviction to not shed a tear in solidarity. *He needs you to be strong right now. Always. He needs something good. Someone good.*

The man wrapped his arms around his boy and pulled him close, covering him up like a big, warm blanket that rocked so steadily on the couch until Oliver was curled up and his crying had turned into raw and uneven gasps and, eventually, calm and rhythmic breaths.

They were the only noise in the room, aside from Jon's gentle cooing and hushing or the sound of the refrigerator ice machine loosing its load into the freezer.

I could have been more present. He wanted to be...for his son. But Jon's thoughts had turned toward some horrific secret. Told only in roundabout through Oliver's rambling.

He really had no idea...and Marie...never taught him?

"Hey." Jon patted his son's back, drawing his attention from the soft and self-soothing humming he was making. Oliver lifted his chin, pressing his forehead into the scraggly bottom of his father's beard.

"I just have one more question, if you're okay answering?" he leaned back to look at his son, giving a soft smile and pressing him just slightly into his chest. "Where did you get the tea?"

The boy stared up at him, his blotchy eyes flickering down and back up as he registered the words. "Momma used to make it for me...but...I don't think she knew it could do that."

Jon nodded, struggling not to show how quickly his heart fell deep into his stomach and made his lips quiver. He pressed his hand over his mouth to hide it. "I—I'm sure she didn't."

***

Jon edged Oliver's bedroom door closed after making sure he was most definitely sacked out and comfortable in his bed. He was more surprised that he didn't wake up in his arms during the very awkward trip up the stairs. Apparently, the hydrocodone had kicked in somewhere between their talk and his hyperventilating. Though the latter was known to take a lot out of him.

He pulled the door shut with a soft click and felt the silence of the house in stark and terrifying contrast to the few and haunting words Oliver had said. Words left echoing in his thoughts.

Jon dragged down a breath, or more of a gasp, as the effort of maintaining his own composure in the wake of his unfortunate education.

Quietly, as if searching for some momentary escape, he twisted around where he stood. Useless steps that he tried to keep so quiet as not to wake his child. *My child. And he—*

His eyes watered, blurring the shadows of the night, and he shook his head—hard like it would remove reality from him. But it didn't. It couldn't.

Jon fell back, the soft thud of his weight against the wall just outside his boy's door, shaking the shiplap panels as he dropped down and crumpled with that all-consuming sob he'd been shoving down for so many hours. He was angry. So full of rage and anguish and exhaustion and he didn't—

I don't know what to do…what I'm doing. How—how can I fix this, Marie? You must have known. You must have…right? He's your son. My son…

And this whole time, he was being—

"I got it!" Dindet's shrill squeal of excitement cut the scientist's thoughts short as she splattered into the living room, getting mucky star goo and some preferably unknown bright green liquid all over the floor as she dripped. Jon scrambled to his feet, wiping his eyes and doing his utmost to remove any trace of his worry and exhaustion from the alien's view.

She twisted around, holding up, miraculously, a MacGuffin. How she got it and how it existed in the first place, he was entirely unaware.

"Shh!" He held his finger to his lips and pointed at the door. Dindet's eyes flickered from him to Oliver's door, and she lowered her trophy with a nod.

"I got your MacGuffin!" she repeated, this time in a loud whisper as Jon made his way down the stairs.

"Thank you," he gave an honest smile and pressed his hand into her head, unprepared for it to sink much further into it than he anticipated. The alien shuddered, and bits of her boiled up in response to his thoughts, and Jon pulled back, bringing that sticky, stringy matter with his hand as he raised it and gave an unconscious grimace. "I…appreciate it."

He moved into the kitchen to start on his coffee, expecting Dindet to trot her way up to the attic, but instead, when he turned to grab the coffee pot, she stood directly in his path with a dead stare. Until the petals around her eyes streaked out and her brow furrowed.

"You didn't really need that, did you?" She called him out. "You just wanted me to leave."

Jon held the coffee pot close to his chest, his eyes flickering down at the massive puddle of clown matter growing at the bottom of Dindet's feet and dripping off the rest of her like slick oil.

"I…well…to be honest, I didn't think it really existed," he admitted, hoping the laugh in his voice calmed whatever frustration she had with him.

"Anything that can be thought of exists—somewhere."

He averted his eyes, moving his gaze up through the kitchen ceiling. "I just needed to talk to Oliver about something… important—something you wouldn't understand."

"He lost his colors."

What?

"I'm sorry?"

Dindet's streaks of frustration shifted into something more like tears, and she ran through several colors before they settled on some mismatched blotchy orange and purple.

"I saw it. His colors were gone..." she repeated, bending down to scoop up the bits of her that had congealed on the floor and shoving them back into her body. "It happens when something dies. I think I might have... broken him."

Jon stared at the alien, trying to figure out where she got the idea that any of this was her doing.

He set the coffee pot under the maker and let out a soft sigh.

"No, Dindet," he corrected. "That wasn't your fault. You couldn't have known...none of us knew—even Oliver. Don't blame yourself for things you have no control over."

The alien glanced back at him, her expression unreadable as she continued to attempt to shove her matter back into her body, despite it seeming to want to stay very much away from her.

"Is...is everything all right?" Jon cocked his head, gesturing at the sheer amount of slime that seeped from the alien without her control. "I mean—is that a normal thing? For you?"

At that, Dindet grew some slight look of distress before she saved face with a smile. "It, uh, yeah. It happens all the time. Totally normal. Regular—regular Clown thing."

Jon lifted his chin with skepticism. "Uh-huh...well, whenever you're ready, I'd love your help with the microchips—*not* the same thing as a microwave, by the way."

"Right," Dindet nodded, shoveling the last bit of herself back together. "I'll—I'll be right up."

The Partial Truth

Douglass wandered around the back of Oliver's porch, trying to find out where exactly he was. He had invited him over via text a couple of hours prior, something about needing a reason to get Dindet out of the house and getting suspended from school.

"You can come through the front door too, you know." Oliver's muffled voice startled him from his search. The kid stood behind the sliding glass door in his pajamas, quizzically raising an eyebrow. He slid it open and beckoned Douglass inside.

"Why did you need Dindet gone?" Douglass asked, following Oliver as he made his way into the kitchen.

"Cassidy really wanted to hang out with her, and she won't leave me alone about the hospital trip. It's getting on my nerves," he answered, gingerly pulling out a large gumbo pot from the bottom cabinets. "So I told her we were having a guy day to make her feel better about not being around."

Douglass held back a small chuckle. "You didn't actually have to invite me over if you didn't really wanna hang out."

At that, Oliver grumbled, murmuring something inaudible under his breath. Of course, Douglass didn't know that if the alien so much as wanted to, she could easily pop in on them. And if he weren't actually there, she'd catch Oliver red-handed in a lie. Which would probably make her feel worse.

"I don't mind it. You're not all boring," he remarked, fetching a carton of coconut milk from the cabinet. "Plus, I can't really go back to school yet."

"Right, uh—did you really hit that girl?" Douglass casually helped him arrange his ingredients into the center of the kitchen island. "Theo was talking about it in class earlier today. She said you punched Hailey in the face for no reason."

"Hailey called me a—it doesn't matter." Oliver forced himself to remain nonchalant as he dug through the fridge for chives. "Cassidy was the one who hit her, though. I just took the fall for it 'cause I wanted a day off…didn't really plan on the week, though."

"Oh…so…what are you making?" Douglass stepped around the kitchen island, eyeing the array of ingredients Oliver had pulled out. *What do you even use fish sauce for?*

"Coconut chicken curry noodles," he answered. "My dad usually makes it when I'm sick, but he's out for some reason. I figured emergency rooms still count as being sick. Plus, it's my favorite."

"Yeah, you mentioned you had a really bad infection or something, right?"

"Sepsis, actually. I had a, uh—a piece of glass stuck in me from when Matthew stabbed me."

Douglass's quaint smile dropped, and his breath hitched. "W-what?"

"Yeah." Oliver turned, pushing away his concern with an inordinately casual shrug. "I guess they didn't see it the first time and sewed it up in there or something."

"But—wait, you said he *stabbed* you??" Douglass stared at him, trying to make something of the look Oliver gave him.

"With a broken bottle. I thought you already knew that?" Oliver began throwing in more ingredients for his soup like the conversation hadn't suddenly taken a left turn. "It was like three years ago? Around the time I moved here. Actually, that's mostly why we moved in the first place."

Douglass's eyes flickered down, averting his gaze as he recollected that night. *There were a lot of police cars. And an ambulance.*

Oliver licked some curry powder from his fingers and slid past Douglass toward the pantry for some rice noodles.

"He *stabbed* you, though," Douglass repeated, providing a little more emphasis to get the kid to somewhat understand the gravity of what he was talking about.

"Just forget I said anything, okay?" Oliver chucked the noodles at Douglass, gesturing for him to drop them in the boiling pot. "It's not that big a deal."

"Why? But it is." He fumbled, accidentally dropping the plastic bag into the pot along with the noodles. "How can you say it's not a big deal?"

"Well," Oliver pushed him aside and pulled the half-melted bag out with a pair of tongs, "I was kind of hoping you wouldn't *make* a big deal about it."

He spoke so casually, but as Douglass moved back behind him, he could see the tremors that ran up and down Oliver's arms. This was not something he was comfortable with in the slightest, and Douglass, for the life of him, couldn't figure out what compelled the kid to talk about it.

"Are you telling me 'cause he came back?"

"What? No!" Oliver spun on his heel, sliding himself between the stove and his friend in an effort to gather a more culpable lie. "I just figured you deserved to know since the whole hospital stuff."

"Yeah, but you never once said anything—I figured it was bad but...how come you decided now?"

"Didn't wanna tell Dindet about it," his voice was quieter

now, and he stirred the pot thoughtfully. "She kept asking, thinking the trip's got something to do with her, but I don't want to see that look again."

This time Douglass leaned in, glancing down at Oliver as he sprinkled bits of garlic and chives into the mixture. "What look?"

"The same one you have right now."

Douglass stepped back from the stovetop, allowing Oliver to turn around. That casual demeanor he had, had dropped, and he stared past him. "I don't talk about it because every time I do, I get the same look. Like it's this awful, terrible thing that happened, and it makes everyone uncomfortable. Like I make them uncomfortable."

Oliver shrugged, putting on that forced air of nonchalance once more. "It's all right, though. I mean, I get it. Who wants to hear about stuff like that, right?"

He pushed past Douglass and grabbed a couple of bowls from the counter, "It's just something you don't—"

Oliver stopped, feeling something brush against his shoulder. He turned, and Douglass stood a few inches away, staring at him and holding back tears in his eyes. The boys stood there for a moment, and before Oliver could reasonably object, Douglass wrapped him tight in a hug, squeezing the breath out of him and causing him to squeal with tiny shock.

"What...are you doing?" Oliver grunted, shifting his weight.

"You needed a hug." Douglass tightened his hold slightly, burying his face in the boy's shirt collar to wipe his unwanted tears. He was so stupid. So stupid and sad and silly. And he knew that he likely looked too desperate in this particular moment, but all be damned if Oliver didn't deserve a hug.

"Come on," Oliver patted Douglass on the shoulder in an effort to make him loosen his bear hug, "it's not like it's still going on. I don't need you to make me feel better."

"Who else is going to, though?" The boy's voice was soft and riddled with a sob he failed to hold in. It made Oliver hesitate. So he simply stood there, at a loss for an answer.

It was dumb of him to even mention it. Douglass had a gentle little heart, and Oliver was stupid to think that the kid wouldn't freak out. But Dindet already knew on some level what kind of person Matthew was, the things he did. She already looked at him like some fragile, broken thing. It just got worse after he was in the hospital because Jon knew too now.

Douglass was only slightly different. He didn't know, at least all of it. So he looked at Oliver like he was a person, no matter how rudely he treated him. Just a regular person, and that's all he wanted. He couldn't lose that now.

"Douglass," Oliver filed his hands between the two of them, forcing the kid to take a step back. "My curry!"

Douglass blinked, befuddled by his remark, until Oliver sprinted over to his pot and slammed down a lid on the overboiling soup.

"S-sorry!" He stammered, turning heel as he watched Oliver wince and turn down the eye. The kid grabbed a couple of kitchen towels and began soaking up the scalding water, shaking his hands every few seconds as he carried and chucked the sopping wet towels into the sink.

"It's all right!" Oliver let out a relieved sigh. "I think I saved most of it."

He watched closely as the boiling soup died down, and after a few more minutes, he ladled two decent-sized servings into bowls.

***

Dindet stood in Cassidy's room, trying so very hard not to burst from the strength of the girl's excitement as she softly closed her door and turned around.

Her colors were bright and yellow, like a sun that radiated out of her and made it hard to focus on anything else. She stood, leaning against the door, vibrating with her barely contained energy and staring at the alien with all the marvel that could be contained in her comparatively tiny human body.

Dindet opened her mouth to speak.

"I KNOW YOU'RE AN ALIEN!!" Cassidy cut in, quickly slamming her hand over her mouth to subdue her squeal of excitement. She pulled away from the door. "I know you're an alien. I'm sorry! I didn't mean to yell. I just—*you're an alien.* I have a *real alien* in my room!"

The girl circled around Dindet, thoroughly engrossed in her own thoughts as she rambled on with little care.

"I had suspected a bit, 'cause I've never heard of any countries or indigenous peoples who dress up like clowns—and I do *a lot* of research," she reached behind the alien, prompting her to evade as she grabbed the small sample of hair she'd snagged from her during school. "But I knew *something* was up cause I've never seen—well…"

Cassidy spun on her heel, opening up her glasses case to show off the tiny sample she'd stolen, which had now turned into a mere drop of black goop on the plastic. "I don't know what you did that day in the courtyard, but it was—I've *never* seen anything like that before."

Dindet's whole face crunched with regret at the memory and a small ripple of discomfort rose through her. Her eyes flickered down to stare at it, still trying to wrap her mind around the course of events that led her to be standing in this girl's room, reeling with the flowery taste of Cassidy's joy on her tongue and just how she managed to get Oliver to spill their secret.

"What *are* you?" Cassidy drew out the question and the alien's gaze lifted to meet hers. Then she made the most uncomfortable of faces, the kind that would make any statement afterward fallible beyond belief.

"I…don't know what you're talking about?"

Dindet watched as Cassidy blew through her lips in dismissal and rolled her eyes. She didn't believe it for an ounce.

"It's okay," the girl shrugged, setting her glasses case down on her bed. "You don't have to lie anymore. I'm not gonna, like, report you to the government or anything—I'm fourteen. They wouldn't even believe me. *I* barely believe me."

Cassidy's eyes rose above her glasses, donning that perfect pouty face as her sunny ball of light wavered and flickered with pastel blue hues. Dindet cringed at it, dreading the potentially fleeting flavor of joy.

Cassidy huffed softly, and the colors turned darker, garnering a hushed groan from the clown as the girl dropped her gaze and twiddled her thumbs.

"Well..." the girl tilted her head, pushing her glasses case further away from her with a horribly dejected tone. "I guess I was just—"

"Okay! I'll tell you!" Dindet cut in, and Cassidy immediately dropped her weak sorrows.

"Really?!"

Dindet blinked and offered a terribly anxious smile.

"Really."

***

"Actually," Oliver said as he handed Douglass his bowl and moved to the couch. "I *did* sort of want to talk to you."

"About what?" Douglass followed, sensing the tension between Oliver and himself rise as the kid anxiously attempted to remain casual. "Is it about Matth—"

"Do you still love Jojo?" Oliver interrupted, plopping down on the couch and flipping on something to watch for background noise and hopefully use it as an idle distraction from the conversation.

Douglass slowed and dropped his gaze, numbly stirring the noodles in his bowl as he thought about the question.

"Of course I do," he finally answered, bringing his eyes back up to Oliver. The boy let out a soft sigh and looked away from him, mulling over the response.

"What if you found out something about her that you...you didn't like?" Oliver asked.

Douglass took a meager bite from his still piping hot meal, using his long and slow chews to really think about whatever it was Oliver was getting at.

He must have found something out. Or maybe, for once, he started really thinking about...the kind of life he had before this one.

"I find out new things about my sister all the time," Douglass offered, hoping the lightness of his response would ease the visible discomfort of his friend. "Did...did you find out something about your mom?"

He hated that he had to ask, but Oliver probably wouldn't have said anything if he didn't.

"The whole custody case was because..." Oliver hesitated, trying to rework the words over in his head so they didn't hurt nearly as much as they did. "...She lied..."

An unpleasant silence fell between them, only broken by the deep breath Oliver drew in from anticipation.

"Oh..." Douglass finally mumbled. He sat down next to him, quietly whirling up inside as his thoughts moved toward the subject of their conversation.

Oliver's mother. Marie.

She was nice, to Douglass at least. But as kind and sweet as she was on the outside, he could never quite understand what she wanted, what she was doing.

He knew only a little, from the way his father talked about her or the fleeting moments he saw her at his Bar Mitzvah. To him, she looked like an empty person. But Oliver idolized her.

"When..." Douglass almost stopped himself, anxious to tread on the subject at all. "When Matthew...stabbed you, why did she bring you here?"

Oliver blinked, shifting in his seat and glancing back at the boy with confusion. "What do you mean?"

"She brought you *here*," Douglass attempted to clarify, "instead of straight to the hospital."

"I don't know," Oliver answered almost defensively. "Long drive? Why does that even matter? She still saved me. It took longer, and I had to—"

He paused, cutting off his thoughts and words with a small huff of indignance. "It was my fault that it happened in the first place anyway."

Douglass's face screwed up with dissatisfaction, and he stared at him as he continued, oblivious to the words falling out of his mouth.

"I was being stupid, trying to stop them from hitting each other, and I got in the way. That's all. He didn't usually hit me before then. Mostly it was—" Oliver stopped himself, choking on the words before he could say them aloud. "It really wasn't as bad as it sounds."

He shakily brushed his hands through his hair and set his bowl down. "She was doing her best, all the time. And we were a team, you know?"

Oliver's eyes flickered back to Douglass, avoiding the look of bafflement on his face. "We protected each other."

Douglass's agape mouth clamped shut, and he looked away from him. The growing unease of Oliver's excuses made him want to force the boy's eyes open so he could see just how deluded he sounded. But he didn't. And only sunk into the couch with a quiet and idle sentence.

"It shouldn't have been your job to protect her."

Suspended Disbelief

Oliver milled about the cabin, trying to find something that would occupy his mind for the some odd seventy-two-odd hours he still had to wait before he could go back to school. Dindet was there right now, probably having her not-ears talked off by Cassidy or Douglass.

The boy plopped down on his couch and flipped on the television, surfing through the crappy free satellite channels he got until he made a full circle and realized nothing was on but news channels and boring educational stuff.

He wanted to be home, but this was awful. *So bored.*

Oliver had forgotten how much quiet there was in the house. He'd gotten so used to Dindet scampering about or his dad coming down from the attic to refuel on coffee, that being here alone was eerily similar to how he felt before he even lived here.

That silence was always dotted with yelling and fighting, though.

She lied.

Oliver grunted softly, forcing the thought out of his mind by way of turning the T.V. volume too far up. He didn't want to think about it. *Mom lied about what he did, what Matthew did.*

That's why he was able to take me—because she lied.

He didn't like the idea. He didn't like the way it made him feel, compounded on top of Dindet knowing exactly what his mother looked like, exactly what she sounded like. *What else has she lied about? Her job? Matthew? What if—what if Theo was right? What if she really couldn't stand me anymore and just—*

Oliver shifted and stood up, trying to pace out his anxiety at the notion of such an awful thing. *What if she really wasn't gone? What if she just left? Did I—did I make her leave? Did I do something wrong? It's not—it's not my fault, right? Because of the way I am?*

He drew in a shaky breath, and his gaze flitted back to his parent's room. He almost moved to enter but was stopped by the soft buzz of his phone on the end table.

Oliver turned and snatched it up, hoping that it was Douglass providing his daily check-in to see how he was doing. *I could ask him about it, if it was my fault she was gone, right? Douglass is good about proving me wrong like that.*

Instead, it was a message from Markus

He felt his stomach roll at the notification. He'd gotten lucky with the convenience of suspension on top of having his organs poked around. It made avoiding the senior easier.

Oliver stared at the message, reading it over and over again in an effort to figure out if there was something hidden and extra in the words.

'Wanna hang?'

Instead of answering, he called his father.

"Ols, what's up? How you feeling?" Jon's voice settled his nerves almost immediately, and Oliver sunk back into the couch with a slightly uncomfortable grunt.

"I'm bored," he lied.

"Well, you're also the one who got suspended after lying about hitting that girl. Dug your own grave there, kiddo," Jon remarked with a hint of playful sarcasm. Some noise sounded in the background, and he cursed under his breath at the following crash.

"Where are you?" Oliver changed the subject, glancing at the clock to check the time. It was only eight or so in the morning, not a normal time for his dad to be awake at all, let alone out of the house. *This is the second day in a row...*

"AKAN called me in," he answered, and Oliver rolled his eyes.

"But you said you were on leave 'til next year?" There was another sound, and Jon cursed again, much louder, followed by him chastising Dr. Abadi for leaving his samples in the wrong section again.

"Chris and I have to join in on a meeting with the Head Director. I'm sure it's nothing. I'll be home later today." His father paused, and Oliver could tell he pulled the phone away to talk to someone else. "Ols, what do you think of Bajra Khichdi for dinner?"

"Am I making it or you?" Oliver questioned, glancing back at the pantry and trying to recall if they had enough ingredients.

"My treat ah—uh, I gotta run. See you tonight?"

"Wait," Oliver interjected before his father could end the call, "is it cool if I hang out with a friend?"

There was a pause and the sound of snapping on the other end of Jon's line.

"I thought you mentioned Douglass had that driver's ed stuff going on? Or did your circle of two grow in the last six weeks?" His dad asked. Oliver could hear the smile in his voice.

"Well, I mean—it really didn't. This guy from school just wants to do a sort of interview thing—about being trans," he answered. "He asked if I could hang out, but I wanted to check with you first?"

"Uh-uh, are you cool with it?"

Oliver pulled his phone down to check the second message he'd received from Markus, asking if he wanted to ditch school and go to his place. Oliver didn't really want to do that. But he *did* want a distraction.

"I mean—I haven't really thought about it, but I figure maybe if he posts it online other kids like me can, I dunno, feel less alone?"

He heard his father hum, and then that hum got interrupted by what was definitely Chris's voice urging Jon to get off the phone.

"If you're comfortable with it, I don't mind. Now—I, I really gotta go. Be safe. I love you!"

"Love you too—" the call ended before Oliver could finish, and he was once again greeted by the silence of his home.

Markus seemed nice. *Said I was mature and cool... He could tell me that it wasn't really my fault mom is gone.* Or provide enough of a distraction to get Oliver's mind off the topic altogether.

***

"I'm here. What's going on?" Jon burst through the back door of the laboratory just as Chris met up with him, placing a hand on his shoulder as he tried to slow the man down.

"The security tapes from last year. The government is doing an investigation—"

"Dr. Jariwala, Furkin. It's a pleasure you could come." The woman's voice cut into their conversation, and the two scientists came to an abrupt halt in front of the head director of the lab. She was escorted by two burly men in black suits, as well as a much younger, paler-looking red-headed woman, who eyed them quizzically. The director held a compact tablet in her hand that replayed aerial footage of the incident with Marie's machine.

"Dr. Hausman." Jon nodded, donning his best poker face. "What can I do for you?"

It wasn't a real question—not in the sense that he could be willing to do anything for the woman. But a tactic to figure out as discreetly as possible what was really going on. They wouldn't have called him in otherwise.

The woman nodded briskly and gestured toward the roped-off lab room where the incident occurred. Now, though, a simple round table and cafeteria chairs sat in its center.

Jon and his colleague obliged and sat down in the chairs as the director moved to sit across from them.

There was a heavy moment of silence between all of them as the doors swung shut and the two burly men stood just behind the comparatively scrawny scientists.

Dr. Hausman leaned forward, pressing play on the video she had obtained before sliding it toward the two men to see.

It was grainy, and static interfered greatly, but clear as day, they could see the alien creature in the stilled frame. Just before the explosion that had taken Marie.

"I don't—"

"Don't give me that shit, Furkin. You know damn well what that is." Dr. Hausman interrupted, cocking her head to the side as she eyed Jon now. "And I know that your wife's the one who brought it here, Jon."

"Look, we here at AKAN value our scientific minds, especially when they come across extant interdimensional life forms." She continued, clicking her nails across the table. "You know what we have been striving for. Your wife—bless her soul—gave her life for it."

Jon dropped his gaze, clenching his fist until the knuckles turned light. "She—"

"Uh-uh-uh, I'm not done, Jon." Dr. Hausman peered up at one of the men in black, and he wrapped large, muscular hands around Jon's shoulders, digging his fingers in to not so subtly get the message across.

"The Arthur Knowles-Anne Newman Laboratory is going in a new direction," she said, stopping her fingernails from clacking. "You could say we've been bought out—partnered with a government entity. And in the process, I've been moved down the totem pole to your direct supervisor. The new head of the company has a program in need of bright minds like yours."

"As in?" Chris glanced back at the door in an effort not to look her in the eye.

"They want you to rebuild the molecular transporter." Dr. Hausman held up a hand, and one of the men handed over the unmodified blueprints Marie had created. "And I want you to find that *thing* so we can study it."

"I don't know what, or where, it is," Jon answered. He watched the no-longer-head director contemplate his words, almost as though he convinced her.

"I think you do, but if I were you, I'd be more worried about the repercussions of continuing to hide your work from us, Dr. Jariwala." She clasped her hands together and offered a slightly uncomfortable smile. Her steely facade flickered, revealing some genuine concern in the midst of her blackmail. "You both have people to take care of."

Dr. Hausman leaned forward, her eyes shifting back to the pale woman that stood next to her before she spoke. "You've broken a lot of laws, boys, and I don't want to see the consequences of that. So I suggest you play along."

Jon and Chris exchanged a glance, forcing themselves to nod, despite the urge to object.

"So, you will begin work on this molecular transporter, rebuilding it from scratch. The scale has increased by twenty-four as well. We have a deadline of one year for the prototype, and once we reveal the possibility of interdimensional travel, our…federal problem will be forgiven. According to Director Miles." Dr. Hausman stood up, pressing her palms into the cold table as if to keep herself grounded in the severity of the situation.

"You start work tonight, and I wouldn't expect to leave this facility until the same time tomorrow…I think you will find the terms agreeable, and as always, we are doing this for science. For progress." She nodded at the men in black, and they silently opened the doors.

Jon stood, briskly heading toward the door just as the director's voice halted him.

"Oh, and boys?"

He paused, relinquishing his hand from the knob as he gave Chris a grave look. The woman came up behind him and wrapped her fingers around his hand tightly, drawing his attention away from his colleague and to her eyes.

"I'd be particularly worried about the well-being of your families." Dr. Hausman's gaze lingered for a moment, flicking back toward the pale woman once more, almost like some kind of secret message. Things had spiraled out of control now, and on some level, Jon knew she had done all she could to protect them. Regardless of how cruel she sounded.

Positive Attention

Oliver answered Markus's text and paced back and forth in the living room, then up and down the stairs, waiting for a reply. But, instead, what he got was a phone call.

"Dude, texting is a thing," He jeered at the inconvenience of verbal communication. He did a decent job at hiding the shake in his voice.

"Yeah, but I'm driving right now and not really in the mood to die," Markus answered, prompting Oliver to listen a little closer to the background noise of his turn signal clicking.

"Did you already get out of class?"

"LOL, no," Markus chuckled, "I left to grab lunch 'cause I'm cool like that. I was gonna ask if you wanted anything since you no-showed."

Just how visible am I? Oliver scrunched his nose up at the idea. "I got suspended, remember? *And* I had to go to the hospital. I'm at home right now."

"Badass, you gotta show me your battle scars."

"There are very few people I take my clothes off for," Oliver deadpanned. The first person that came to mind was Douglass, who just happened to be in the right place at the worst time. *It was still cool of him to trade clothes. Maybe I can talk about that in the video?* "Did—do you maybe wanna try some interview stuff?"

The turn signal stopped before Markus answered. "Totally! Are you really in? I can bring my camera over and everything. I'd like to see your house."

"R—really?" Oliver felt his whole face start to heat up at such a silly notion. "I mean, I'm here alone. You don't plan on bringing anyone else, right? My dad said we could hang out, 'cause—'cause I asked him. But, like, it's no big deal or anything. It's chill. I'm chill."

"Right," There was a soft laugh in Markus's voice, and it made Oliver's heart drop at the thought of it being directed at him. "I'll drop by?"

Oliver hadn't expected Markus to roll up in his shoddy, half-working coupe after thirty minutes of having his address, but the senior sauntered up to the door with a nonchalance as though he'd already been to his house several times over.

"Hey, uh, hi—welcome," Oliver stammered the moment he opened the door.

The older boy's wandering eyes dropped down, and his whole face paled with shock.

"You're a girl?"

Oliver blinked. And then, with all the grace of an anvil written with the words 'you have titties!' falling on the top of his head, it dawned on him, and he promptly shoved his hands into his armpits to cover his chest.

"I practice *safe* binding!" He shot, despite his whole face burning with embarrassment.

"Besides"—he stepped aside to allow Markus in, and all of a sudden his nervous jittering doubled as he watched him pass the threshold—"I-I've been at home all day. I don't normally bind when I'm at home."

"It's cool, dude." Markus offered a semi-distracted nod. "Just surprised me."

Okay…it's cool. He doesn't care. That's good! He's in my house. That's fine. It's fine! My territory.

"Cool place! Eclectic." Markus glanced around the cabin to get a good look at the decor in the living room. "Your mom into that hippy stuff?"

He gestured at a few decorations and wall tapestries that didn't exactly fit the theme of a cabin in the middle of the woods.

"My—those are actually from my dad." Oliver corrected, casually dusting off the mandir that took up the whole northeastern corner of the living room. "We're Hindu, but there are not a whole lot of temples nearby. That's the Puja Mandir."

Markus nodded for a second and moved to poke one of the murtis before Oliver stopped him.

"Don't touch Ugly Ganesh," Oliver chided softly, watching the boy fiddle with the camera strapped over his shoulder as his attention moved toward other things.

"I think the printer might have run out of ink." He gestured at the framed photo of Jon and Marie's wedding. Particularly how both Oliver and his mother stood out among the rest of Jon's family. "Is that the lady who discovered that new particle? I heard AKAN shelled out a ton of cash to patent it and everything. Didn't she—"

"My mom, uh, isn't around anymore, so Jon…he adopted me. We aren't…we aren't *actually* related." Oliver cut in, hoping to drive the conversation elsewhere. "I thought you wanted to talk about trans stuff—"

"It's cool," Markus interrupted, "your place is cool. Can I see your room?"

"I thought—I thought questions? I mean, interview, sorry." He fumbled, trying to get up the stairs before Markus did. *What if my room is too girly? Would that make me look bad? Would he leave? Get mad? Why am I so nervous?!*

"Yeah, I figured your room would be the best place to start.

That's like the most—" Markus gestured vaguely at him. "You."

"I just, I don't really like people in my room." Oliver countered. Dindet went in whether he liked it or not, and Douglass was basically always welcome. *What difference does it make, really? Stop being weird about it.*

"I mean, I haven't really cleaned it, so there are clothes and stuff on the floor." Oliver pulled back a bit, moving up a step or two to guide Markus toward his bedroom and not the attic. *It would be a nightmare if he saw what a mess that place was.*

He creaked the door open slightly, very ready to slam it back shut before the older kid could get a decent look, but before he had time to, Markus casually pushed into the space to look around.

"Okay—don't judge me," Oliver let out a reluctant sigh, trying particularly hard not to let his nerves override his sensibility. Never more than now had he felt the urge to spontaneously start cleaning. His bed hadn't been made, and both his bathroom and closet doors were wide open, showing off the mess of clothes on the floor and hair in the trash can from the last time he cut it. *Note to self: take out hair trash.*

Markus moved toward his desk, though, and tinkered with the light and all his sketchbook papers littered around it. "You do these?"

"Uh," Oliver craned his neck, coming up behind the much taller boy to see what exactly he was looking at. A ton of half-finished renditions of Dindet in her least human form, a couple of crinkled watercolors of his cats, and his unfinished attempt at whittling the clown into a block of wood.

"Yeah, I mean, I did, but those aren't really done." Total lie. He gave up on them halfway through. "I'm not as good at drawing as I am sculpting."

"You *sculpt?*" There was a tone to Markus's response that Oliver couldn't exactly guess was positive. So he simply gestured at his shelf full of wooden and stone figurines he'd made.

"Soapstone mostly, 'cause it's really easy."

"Badass."

Really?

Oliver's face burned at the compliment, and he moved to look at his collection of little accomplishments. Most of them were animals, some busts, and others were attempts at replicating the ornate patterns and Hindu scripture that decorated his home. "I mean, they aren't, like, *that* good."

"Dude," Markus picked up a flat, circular mandala made out of just regular soap, holding it up for Oliver to see. "This is better than anything I could do. And I thought I was cool for winning state on the swim team. You sell them?"

What? Oliver promptly took the suddenly very precious thing he had made out of the boy's hand.

"No." He didn't mean for it to come out as harsh as it did, but Markus didn't seem to care. He was too busy toying with the rewards Dindet had won in the Peace Zone.

"Those are just some things Dindet and I got at a…carnival." Oliver watched closely as Markus moved from the crystalline medal to the dry wreath of flowers on the shelf. He plucked one off to inspect it closer, and Oliver promptly tried to remove it from his grasp. "Careful, those are kind of weird—"

"Oh, yeah?" The senior eyed him, twirling a solid bulb in his fingers. "Is it like weed? Don't tell me you're a druggie."

"I'm *not*. They just make you feel weird, is all." Oliver grabbed the rest of the wreath and slid it into a trashcan before attempting to take the flower Markus had plucked. "I don't know if they still have the dust that does that—"

"I bet it's edible," a wide grin slipped across Markus's face. He opened his mouth, but before he could chomp down on what was most definitely an alien plant that he had no knowledge of—let alone if it were even safe to eat—Oliver stole it from his grasp.

Markus's smile fell, and he took a step back. "Dude, I was

joking. They just look like the ones my brother got from Amelis, is all."

"Well, how was I supposed to know that? You literally had it in your mouth." Oliver retorted, "You...weren't recording yet, right?"

He pointed dumbly at the camera, and Markus shook his head.

"Well...to be honest, I kind of just wanted an excuse to get to know you. So there's not really, uh, any kind of interview?"

Oliver's finger drooped, and he turned incredibly flush, suddenly at a loss for words. *It's just a distraction. A good distraction. At least he's being honest? That's good, right? He hasn't even really done anything. It's not like he's Matthew.* "I, uh, I appreciate the honesty?"

Markus blinked, some flicker of realization crossing his face before he mouthed a little 'oh' and dug in his pocket for a grubby folded-up piece of paper. "I'm sorry, that probably sounded really creepy. Me just sort of tricking you into thinking we were doing one thing, but doing something else. Definitely asshole move on my part."

"I—It, it's not really that bad." Oliver stammered, still staying a solid two steps away from the boy. "I kind of was using you, too. I don't really want to do some dumb interview."

Markus gave a nonplussed shrug and plopped down on the bed, panning around as Oliver awkwardly, and with increasing nervousness, began picking up clothes from the ground and tossing them into his closet.

"So, what did you *want* to do?"

Oliver wrung his hands in a moment of abject and wordless anxiety. "I don't know?? I didn't really think this far ahead, and I *definitely* wasn't planning on *outing* myself. I just wanted some dumb distraction 'cause my mom—"

Oliver stopped himself, and he quickly ducked into the closet to avoid being seen altogether.

Markus sat on his bed, his gaze rolling up and around as he whistled over the boy's clear panic.

"So…when did you get adopted?"

"Few weeks ago," Oliver answered from inside. "There was this whole custody case with—with…my father and my step-dad."

"Ah," Markus tilted back until he dropped flat on the mattress and stared at the stars stuck to Oliver's ceiling. "You're the kid whose mom died in that explosion earlier this year, aren't you?"

"It was an accident." Oliver felt his breath hitch at the mention of it. "I'd rather—rather everyone knows me as the kid whose mom died than the school—nevermind."

"Is that why you, you know?" Markus stood up, prompting Oliver to escape his closet and close the door before he could get a peek in. "Lost your shit?"

"Do you honestly think I'd tell you?" Oliver didn't mean for it to come out as rudely as it did, so he attempted to save face with a nervous little laugh and started occupying his hands with something else. "I'm sure you've probably heard plenty about me from literally everyone else at school."

"Well, we aren't really in the same grade. I didn't want to assume. Do people say you're like—like a hermaphrodite?" The senior watched idly as Oliver nearly slammed his fingers into the drawer of his nightstand at the question.

"No," Oliver muttered, dropping his gaze off and away. "Some stupid girl spread stupid rumors and called me a t—a slur. *That's* why I was freaking out."

The senior made a noise of partial understanding and nodded.

"Ahh…" Markus tapped his fingers on his camera in a soft moment of thought. "Do you maybe…wanna get out of here?"

Oliver blinked, utterly confounded by the prospect. "You just got here."

"So? You seem stressed, holed up in this tiny house," Markus argued lightly. "I know this place that's perfect. It's like fifteen minutes out."

Oliver moved back toward his door, gaining distance from the boy in an effort to collect his thoughts around the idea. The whole reason he let him come over in the first place was for a distraction. *Dindet isn't here, and Dad is at work, so he probably won't even come back 'til late tonight...* "Is it walking distance?"

The senior shrugged his shoulders with a shake of his head and looped his camera strap back around his neck. "It's fifteen driving, but like, I get if you're not down—stranger danger or whatever...though you *did* already invite me to your house."

That's true. I did do that. Besides, it's not like I can't call Dad to tell him we went out. Dindet or Douglass might freak out a bit.

But it's really only this once. It's fine.

"Let me shoot my dad a message so he knows I won't be home for a bit," Oliver answered finally. He pulled his phone out and sent out a little text to his father, followed up by one to Douglass. Unfortunately, aliens didn't have phones, so Dindet would simply have to get word from somewhere else.

Fearless

Markus drove a stick, and Oliver sat uncomfortably in the front seat with his legs hiked up to keep from stepping on old energy drink cans and sandwich boxes. It made him feel better about his room because the car was significantly messier. Or maybe that was just because it was a confined space. At least the drive wasn't super far.

Most of it was spent with idle chatting and Oliver frequently checking his phone for a reply from his dad. He had successfully gotten a thumbs-up about fifteen minutes in. Douglass, on the other hand, had a few choice words about him hanging out with Markus at all.

"So, where are we going?" Oliver kept his focus on the mess of double texts Douglass shot off in succession instead of the winding mountain road they drove down.

"It's this vacation house my dad owns. It's sort of by the ski lodge," the senior answered, taking a turn and causing every can of soda in the floorboard to roll into Oliver's ankles.

Apparently, Markus lived on the northeast side of town too, further south than the cabin, but in that suburb of fancy rich people's houses nearest to the ski lodge up the mountain. He had a stick-built house and everything. The kind with big stone basements that dug into the ground in case a landslide occurred, and a wrap-around porch about three times bigger than Oliver's.

His residence was a far cry from a dingy, crappy apartment or a prefabricated cabin carted in on a big rig.

Markus led Oliver through the gate and up the stone steps to his back porch, unlocking the back door of the covered area to allow the two of them onto the deck.

"My step-mom is out on vacation down in Galveston right now, so I've got the whole place to myself. Well, Mulligan will be here, but he won't come home 'til after his shift," he explained, letting Oliver look around the pristine home. It looked like the kind you saw at an open house. That pretend lived-in look where all the furniture matched the architecture, matched the interior design.

"Mulligan?" Oliver echoed the name, ambling behind Markus like a lost little puppy in a very big, very dark house.

"My step-brother." Markus pulled his head out of the refrigerator, along with two bottles of what very clearly looked to be alcohol. "He's a real asshole."

"I don't drink," Oliver added softly, feeling those nerves come back full blast. "I—I'm underage."

"LOL, so am I" Markus chuckled, shooting a sparkly smile back at the boy.

Oliver averted his gaze uncomfortably. *Matthew drank...a lot.*

"Suit yourself," the senior shrugged, changing out one bottle for a canned soda instead. Oliver took a small step back as the senior rounded the bar.

This doesn't feel right. I probably shouldn't have come. I'm probably being a bummer or a loser. He probably already hates me.

Markus pressed the can into the side of his arm, and the kid shifted slightly, causing him to drop his casual demeanor for a second.

"Hey, you're good," the senior said, pressing into Oliver

gently and making him shudder at the touch. "It's no big deal. I still think you're cool, and I still like you."

He meant that, right? It was fine, right? I'm just being insecure, silly. Immature. I could be better. I can be mature. Lots of kids drink when their parents aren't around. It doesn't mean anything. It isn't like they're all a bunch of Matthews that get angry and loud and violent.

"I mean, I guess it wouldn't hurt. I can't drive or anything," Oliver deliberated softly, "and I can't go back to school until Wednesday…my dad wouldn't know."

Would Dindet?

Markus nodded and once again exchanged the soda for a beer, "You brought a change of clothes, right?"

"Oh," Oliver hesitated, wrapping his arms around himself at the prospect. *Markus wouldn't do anything. He likes me. He hasn't been like Matthew, and this is just a distraction. Stop being dumb. I'm just like any other guy to him.* "Uh…for what?"

"Hot tub, duh." Markus gestured vaguely toward him. "I guess you could just wear your underwear and borrow a shirt or something? I don't mind."

It's fine. Really. Why are you scared? What can he do that hasn't already been done? Stop being so ridiculously paranoid!

"I don't—it's cool if I just stay in my clothes, right?" Oliver glanced back out the deck door at the slow crawl of the sun over the clouds. "I don't want to change."

***

"How come you didn't wanna say your mom was the lady that died in the accident?" Markus asked, sinking down into the lounge section of the hot tub. Oliver forced down a gulp of his second beer and fumbled to get it back on its coaster.

The water and the jets and his fuzzy head made it particularly hard for him to stay rooted to the seat. On top of that, he was short, and the seats were made for much larger people. And every time he moved, the jets blew up the bottom of his shirt, causing it to balloon out in likely the most embarrassing way possible.

"Actually, I don't even know if she's dead," Oliver answered. "They work on a bunch of different stuff there, and my dad is pretty sure she got like...sucked into a different dimension."

"Wild," the senior hummed, taking another sip from his bottle.

"Yeah..." Oliver sighed, his thoughts sinking back into the dark at the mention of it. "I think, maybe, she just didn't wanna be around me anymore."

"That's bunk," Markus attempted to sit up but just as quickly slid back into the same position. "Why?"

Oliver murmured some small, sad noise to himself. *Why did she ever leave me alone? With Matthew? She was always in school or working, never around to stop him from—*

"Probably because I came out?" He guessed, taking a much bigger sip of his drink. Still tasted awful, but at least the weird heat of it curbed his thoughts. *Maybe that was why he drank so much.*

"Bullshit," Markus retorted.

"Well, I mean, it makes sense, right?" Oliver argued, sitting up and simultaneously trying to balance himself on the lip of his seat so he could keep his head above the water. "The accident happened right after. I'd just started blockers and everything. She wanted me to wait until I was eighteen to do anything. But Jon helped me convince her...."

Oliver paused, his mind settling on the idea. It made too much sense. He was the reason they moved. He was probably the reason she was gone. *Maybe she just...didn't want me anymore.*

"I wish," he mumbled, finishing off the last of his drink. "I wish people wanted me..."

It would be nice. For a change. Jon wants me, but how long would that even last? If Mom came back, would he change his mind? Would he give me up?

He didn't even know how Dindet felt. *Probably bad.*

Considering he had a habit of making her feel bad. He made everyone feel bad. It made him feel bad. And all Oliver ever wanted was to just…feel good.

"I wanna feel good," Oliver sighed, setting his empty bottle down and sinking until the whole bottom half of his face was submerged in bubbles. The water made it harder for Markus to see that he was hiding his tears with it.

The senior sat up. *You're ruining it again. He's gonna not ever want to be around you if you keep ruining things. It's why no one ever wants to be around you.*

"We're a lot alike." Markus's voice made him pull his head out of the water, and Oliver let out a disgruntled noise of objection.

"Yeah, *right.*"

Markus rolled his eyes and reached out, "I mean it, though."

Oliver grabbed the edge of the tub to keep from being so easily pushed by the jets. It was a nice thought, a really nice one.

"I do," the older boy grabbed the sides of the hot tub and pulled himself into the center of it. "Can I tell you something? Like, personal?"

His voice sounded sincere, though it gurgled and cut out when the jets grew in their intensity, and Oliver slowly drew his focus to the senior's face.

"Uh-huh." Oliver sucked in a breath and lifted his chin. His answer prompted Markus to move his hands to his shoulders, pressing him lower into the seat and the jets that battered right up his back, bubbling his shirt like a wet, lopsided balloon.

"I know you weren't freaking out because of some dumb rumors."

No.

Oliver jerked up, some inkling of leftover sobriety hitting him with the words that drifted over the steam.

"I don't know what you—what do you mean?" He rephrased,

casting a look back at the deck doors.

Markus leaned closer, moving his hands from Oliver's shoulders to his wrists, and his voice lowered even further.

"My dad…used to hit me."

Oliver blinked and shifted, losing his grip on the seat as he backed up with silent shock. Markus's eyes dropped down to the bubbling water, and he felt the senior's grip tighten to keep him from falling under the surface.

"It was really bad, with my mom and I. She got the worse end of it," he continued, "she managed to divorce the bastard, but when she remarried, I got paired up with Cody, and he's…he's just as bad."

So you… "You're like me?" Oliver breathed, leaning back into the corner of his seat to gain room for air. "I…I'm sorry."

He dropped his gaze, hesitant to give that same pitying look he so dearly despised.

Markus drew closer.

"That's why I wanted to talk to you," he said. "I know that kind of fear, you know? It's scary, and I thought that—"

Markus laughed and pulled away, drawing Oliver's gaze back up as his interest piqued. *Thought what?*

"I thought, maybe having someone else who understands, who *really* understands what it's like would be…"

"Nice?" Oliver finished, hanging on to the sentiment like it were some magical epithet to his life. *If only.*

Markus blew out a soft laugh. "Yeah…can I—can I kiss you?"

Oliver drew back, his swirling head reeling from his thoughts on top of Markus's words and the heat of the water and the alcohol in his blood. "I—but I've only ever—"

"It would just be this once." The senior turned to face him, some sorry and sad frown pulling at his lips. "And if—if you're not into it, that's fine. I don't know how, uh, boy girl—girl boys work, lol."

Oliver's mouth clamped shut, and his head snapped toward the doors once more. It was dark out now. And he couldn't tell just how many hours he'd been sitting in the water, sipping on beer. His nerves had dulled to a small buzz in the back of his brain, and Markus was *so* nice. *So, really, it would be fine. For just this once. It's not like it's anything more. Nothing will happen. Matthew isn't gonna just jump out of the bushes to beat me up.*

"O—okay…" the permission fell out of his mouth with little regard, and before Oliver could truly comprehend it, Markus had his thumb to his chin, turning him away from the doors to face him.

It happened in a way that made it feel like time had slowed down, hands tracing down and knees that pressed into their now shared seat. Oliver tilted up and back to make as much room as he could, but Markus pressed closer.

He was warm, and it was nice, the softness of it all. That tactile tenderness that Oliver had absolutely no idea he craved so deeply. It was also slobbery.

Those kinds of kisses you see in movies where the people involved are so in the heat of the moment that they aren't paying attention. Oliver wasn't paying attention.

Especially not until the senior's tongue shoved itself down his throat.

"St-stop—" Oliver cut himself off, that shuddered constriction of his muscles screwing him up with an involuntary jerk, an exhale, and he promptly shoved the senior off of him.

"I-I think I might be overheating," he mumbled, evading Markus's hands as he moved from one end of the tiny pool to the other. The moment he stood, though, it felt like a steam driver was shoved into his skull.

The air was significantly colder than a few hours earlier, and with all the water clinging his shirt and shorts to him, Oliver shivered and struggled to get himself standing.

"Dude, you'll fall—you drink both those beers?" Markus reached up from behind him and pulled Oliver back down into the warm water. He'd forgotten that the thing he'd been drinking was beer. That must have been why he was so dizzy.

"I'm all right. I just…you didn't do that on purpose—" Oliver hissed out and stifled a wince as the deck light flipped on, blinding him with too many layers of hazy lights.

"Markus," a wholly different voice interrupted from the brightly lit deck doors. Oliver lifted his chin, and the boy behind him removed his hands the moment he registered the other person.

"Mulligan." Markus dropped his voice in a way where it sounded much more like a low growl than any sort of greeting. Oliver sat upright, rubbing the sting from his eyes so he could gather what was going on.

Markus's brother stepped out into the light, donning what was most definitely a housekeeper's apron, still sticky with dried splatters from a dirty mop, and his hair laid over his forehead like a chestnut wicker hat underneath his beanie. He looked to be about the same age, though Oliver could only focus on one part of him at a time as he wobbled in the water.

"What are you doing?" Cody Mulligan asked, moving closer. Markus sloshed to the other side of the tub, leaving Oliver stunned and confused on the front steps.

"We're just hanging—we were just hanging out," Oliver hummed in reply, trying to figure out if he was ready to stand or not. The world was fuzzy, and he couldn't quite tell if it was because he was way too hot or because he was drunk. He wasn't even certain he wanted to leave just yet. The water was warm, and outside was cold.

He threw his head up in an effort to get the hair out of his eyes so he could see exactly where his hands and feet were. *If I put my hands out first…*

Oliver leaned forward, if not a little overbalanced and

attempted to catch himself on the hot tub cover. Markus moved behind to support him, but his brother promptly cut in, grabbing Oliver before he toppled face-first into a hard plastic jacuzzi cover.

"Is—is she *drunk*?!" Cody shot a glare at Markus and gently nudged Oliver's dehydrated and inebriated self toward a small outdoor island while he tore a towel out from under it.

"It was only one bottle—"

"I thought it was two?" Oliver stumbled around, being met in the face with a very soft and fluffy towel. Cody patted him down, sort of like he were much smaller and younger than he was, but it was nice, and he hummed and struggled to keep in one spot. At least until a very cold bottle of water pressed into his idle hands.

"Here, drink." Cody stood in front of him, gesturing at the bottle of water with a flicker of his gaze. Markus was quiet and dripping by the railing. "Come on. You'll pass out if you don't cool down—sober up."

Oliver deftly screwed the cap off, gulping down all its contents in one sitting before attempting to breathe again. He shivered. "S-sorry…I ruined it."

His cold little mumble caused the brothers to exchange a look. Though Cody's face looked far more like a scowl than Markus's soft shock. Oliver dropped his embarrassed gaze away from the two of them and pulled the towel further around himself in quiet shame.

"You didn't ruin anything," Cody corrected, escorting him toward the much-better-heated home. "My brother did."

"But I don't feel dizzy anymore? And I didn't vomit or anything," Oliver argued meekly, despite his lack of physical objection to being pushed toward a very warm home. "I feel fine."

That's when Cody's gentle direction pulled away, and Oliver stumbled.

"See that carpet?" The brother pointed at the edge seam of the deck rug, though his eyes stayed firmly trained on Markus, still standing quietly in the corner. "You can stay if you can walk *right* on top of that line. Without stumbling."

Oliver blinked, and his whole head dipped when he looked down at the carpet edge. *That's easy.*

It wasn't.

"All right." Cody slid the deck door open and gestured for Oliver to enter. "I'm taking you home since *Markus* is too drunk to drive you."

Bajra Khichdi

liver sat in the passenger seat of Cody Mulligan's beat-up SUV. It creaked when it rolled down the curves of the mountain and the power steering was going out because every turn was accompanied by the most brain-splitting squeal.

"How much further?" The older boy kept his eyes on the road, flipping on his brights once they reached the dense trees. Oliver's face screwed up with a scowl, and he begrudgingly stared out the window in search of the service lot that led to the power transformers.

"About five miles," he answered, keen on keeping conversation to a minimum. He may have been intoxicated, and not very good at standing, but Oliver kept Markus's words over his brother in his mind the entire drive to his home. *Don't trust him.*

Some idle silence fell between them, though it was intermittently interrupted by the car's squeaks and creaks every time it hit a pothole.

Cody's eyes flitted down to Oliver, and the boy quietly pressed his plastic bag of soaked clothes into his lap, returning a glare in kind.

"So what sort of sob story did he give you?" His voice was quiet, cold, and jaded. Like this wasn't the first time he'd asked the question. Oliver deliberately ignored him and ignored the heat of shame burning his face.

Cody shifted and blew out a sigh. "You a freshman? The girl from the orchestra pit?"

"I'm not a girl."

"And you think Markus believes that? You sure don't look like a boy." Cody stifled a laugh. "Did he hurt you? Touch you—"

"*No.*" Oliver shot daggers back at him and pulled the hem of his oversized and borrowed shirt to his knees to close off as much of himself as possible. "We just talked and…that's all."

Cody bit his lip and pulled his attention back to the road, prompting Oliver to raise his gaze. He stared at him, trying to gauge the same level of violence he could so easily see in Matthew. But the senior just sat there, looking more frustrated and worried than he did angry.

"We…kissed…sort of," Oliver admitted, much softer this time.

The older boy cursed under his breath and covered his mouth, taking a turn Oliver had directed him to, but he didn't reply and didn't speak until he rolled up the dirt road and into the driveway of the cabin.

The SUV pulled to a stop in front of the orange and soft glow of the front porch, and Oliver glanced around in search of his father's car.

"Your parents' home?" Cody asked, popping the locks on the doors and getting out. Oliver watched as he circled around the car and opened the passenger door, a strangely gentlemanly display for someone assumed to be so cruel. *Matthew used tricks like that too, though.*

Oliver kept his hands to himself, staring down the boy until he took a step back, allowing him to get out of the car himself. When he did, Cody followed him to the porch, his own personal tentative housekeeping nurse, making sure he wasn't still stumbling on his way up the stairs.

He stopped at the edge like a vampire that knew it wasn't allowed inside. It made Oliver turn and give him one last once over.

"You said he kissed you?" Cody asked. Oliver dropped his gaze off and to the side. "That was all he did, right?"

"I...well..." The boy kept his eyes on the floor, his insides turning at the physicality of his memory. He picked at the hem of his shirt.

"You should stay away from him." The senior cautioned, and Oliver looked up. He looked so sincere, believably sincere, at least.

"I mean it," Cody added in lieu of the boy's silence. "You seem like a good kid, don't be a *stupid* one."

Oliver narrowed his eyes and took a noticeable step backward. "I'm *not*."

***

The home was quiet, uncomfortably so. Cody had left, and Oliver moved from room to room, flipping the lights on, expecting to find the clown or his father. Mostly, he expected to smell that warm, savory scent of freshly cooked dinner when he opened the front door. But the whole house was empty.

Where is everyone?

He peered through the sliding glass doors to the back porch, hoping to see Dindet caked in her thin layer of frost, surrounded by his breakfast club of cats, but even her regular spot was devoid of life. *Cat's probably hid under the house again.*

Oliver dug through his bag of wet clothes and pulled out his phone. Normally, if there was some sort of change in plans, Jon was the type to send him a message, especially if his cooking was on the line.

He dialed him and paced around the house for a moment in search of clothespins he could use to string up his soaked garments, even though he knew that by morning, they'd likely be frozen.

"You've reached Dr. Jon Ruhn Jariwala. Please leave a

117

message, and I will get back to you as soon as I'm available. Thank you."

Oliver waited for the beep.

"Dad, I'm back from my friend's. I thought you said you were gonna come home and make dinner, but I can make it if you're gonna be late…also…is—is Dindet with you?" He glanced up the stairs to the slightly ajar attic door and opted to check if she was toying around with the machine. He peeked through the door. Nothing but mice and metal and lots of blue paper. "I can't find her, and I figured she'd be back from Cassidy's, so if you—"

"The message you are trying to record has reached its limit. If you would like to record another message, please press three."

Oliver pulled the phone away from his face with a small pout and promptly ended the call. *It's fine. She probably got sent on an errand while I was out. And Dad'll be back later tonight anyways. It's only nine p.m.*

Oliver glanced around the house. It was so big when he was the only one here. Late at night, no noise. It reminded him of before he'd moved here. *I should do the dishes.*

Oliver turned heel and pointedly made his way to the kitchen and began on the task, like a little robot that grabbed a stool so he could reach the sink before he realized he didn't need one anymore because he wasn't small. And this wasn't the apartment.

Oliver blinked, rubbed his eyes, shook his head, and kicked the stool to the side, far too unaware of how tightly he gripped the sponge in his hand. *It's fine. I'm good. At least the dishes are done.*

He moved onto a new task, something that took more focus, hopefully. And checked the time again. It was common for his father to work nights because his sleep schedule was a constant train wreck, but it wasn't common for him to spend over twelve hours in the lab. And it *definitely* wasn't common for Dindet to just not be here.

Did I do something? To make them go? Is it because of what I did with Markus?? Do they know?

Oliver drew in a soft breath and checked the porch once more, then called his father. And then added a small text to Douglass just to see if he was awake, then one to Cassidy asking about Dindet.

It's fine. I'm good! I'm not—

"You're not in trouble. It's okay," he whispered to himself, rubbing his face to make his brain stop buzzing with anxiety. He needed to move. Distract himself from it. *They'll come home. And they don't know.*

"How could they? I didn't say anything, and I don't think she was even there. It's *fine.*" He laughed off his thoughts, the absurdity of them. *What if they do, though? She can read minds. What if—what if she was in the In-Between the whole time?*

Oliver glanced over his shoulder, swiveling on his feet to rid himself of that terrible feeling like he was being watched. "Dindet?"

The house was silent.

See? It's nothing. Oliver blew out some soft relief and wandered aimlessly in his house for a moment, trying to find something else to occupy his time, his thoughts. Something nice.

Oh. That's perfect.

He stopped at the small lip of a threshold where the corner of the home was blocked off for the mandir. It hadn't been cleaned since Jon last used it before the accident. A small pile of ashes had accumulated and spread over the surface of the wood and murtis, making Vishnu and Lakshmi's paintings look a little less than perfect.

Oliver picked off the dried flowers and set them on the coffee table so he could dust off the altar and prepare it for prayer.

When Jon had done puja early in the morning before school, he never really *disallowed* Oliver from partaking and even got him a little notebook he could write his prayers in. He'd shown him all the steps and special things to do. What they meant and how important it was to keep the holy place tidy. But those efforts had fallen by the wayside for half the year, and Oliver wasn't entirely sure if he was even allowed to do it on his own.

The boy left the Mandir for some cleaning supplies and a fresh batch of ghee for the lamp. And once that little corner of the room was spotless and prepped, he plopped down and dug into the bottom drawer for his notebook.

It wasn't anything ornate or special looking; it had scuffs and scratches, and his handwriting at eleven was horrendous. But it was one of the small and very important things that Jon had given him. An unorthodox but astoundingly kind way of including him when he didn't need to, but wanted to.

Oliver read his younger self's words, their lamentation over being stuck in a tiny, half-built cabin with mom's new boyfriend and how they wanted Matthew to stop trying to take him and how going to school sucked because being around so many people all the time was weird and scary.

It's so annoying that everyone thinks I'm some stupid little baby when all I do is just stay quiet. Momma says I shouldn't have to talk if I don't want to, but her new boyfriend keeps taking me to see this therapist lady who keeps trying to make me talk. It's dumb. I can write, can't I? What's the big deal about using words out loud?? Is it because I have to go to public school now?

What if I've got nothing to say? I know how to keep secrets. It's easier if you just don't talk.

Is it true you can get rid of problems? Can you get rid of my dad? And, like, make me a boy? You probably can't do that. Also, I think Mom would be SOOO mad if you did.

She said if Dad wasn't around anymore, I'd stop wanting that. But it's not, and I think it's getting worse. I like Jon, though. He doesn't make me dress up all girly (even though momma hates it)

Can you make her change her mind? Also, I'm sorry I broke you. Jon showed me how to make stuff, so I hope the new version is okay.

Even though you're a little ugly now.

Oliver couldn't help but snort at the frank letter. He glanced up at the murtis, deeply contemplating whether or not he could be bold enough to do the whole routine without Jon as a safety net. *It's been a while…what if I do it wrong? Would he get mad at me?*

Am I allowed?

Instead of entertaining the idea, he quietly closed his prayer book and finished cleaning up the area so he could move onto some other task that involved not sleeping and not thinking about his deeper insecurities.

Tuesday

Dindet phased directly through the side of the cabin, through the back of the refrigerator and into the kitchen, only to slip on a plate Oliver left on the floor and faceplanted the moment she formed into a solid.

"I'M UP!" Oliver shouted, startled awake by the clatter of aluminum, glass, and gelatinous alien goo. He shot up from the table and swiveled his head around at the utter mess he made of the kitchen while cooking in his sleep-deprived and definitely not *completely* sober state.

"That's good!" Dindet replied, offering a weak and wiggly thumbs up from the floor as she picked herself back up.

Oliver rounded the table, dusting off the turmeric from his shirt and began kicking her slime into smaller, more contained piles on the floor. "Where were you?"

"Huh?" The alien pulled herself back together, clearly pretending she didn't hear him as she vanished for a second and returned with a weird, blinking and beeping cube thing.

"You didn't come home last night," he explained, watching her act like that was a very common and totally normal thing she did often when they both knew it wasn't. "Normally, you're on the porch all frozen, and I know my dad was at the lab. Where were *you?*"

"Cassidy's, remember?"

Oliver's brow furrowed, and he plucked whatever Dindet was messing with out of her hands. "No, you weren't. I asked her, and she said you left *yesterday.*"

"What were *you* doing all night?" She turned the same incredulity back on him, gesturing at the mess he made attempting bajra khichdi. "I thought *all* human people had to shut down when the sky circle stopped being there?"

"I couldn't sleep." Oliver rolled his eyes and began cleaning up his kitchen mess and packing away the uneaten bowl he'd reserved for his father along with all his leftovers into the fridge. "And Dad said he was gonna be home to make dinner but he wasn't, so I made it...but I guess he's still not back yet.."

"Oh...is he busy?" There was a slight shift in the clown's tone, like she was somewhat glad he wasn't here. It garnered an incredulous look from Oliver as he wiped down the counters.

"Probably?" He shrugged, ignoring that soft pang of sadness at the thought of him having to work again. "He said the lab called him in for a meeting, but normally they don't make him stay overnight...unless he's gotta start some new project."

Dindet hummed in soft thought at his answer and bounced from his right to his left and back, tossing the cube thing in the air like it was a juggling baton and not a probably priceless piece of electronic equipment. "You wanna come with me to a spaceport?"

"For what?" Oliver moved to the sink to wring out his towel, only to have that same cube shoved right in front of him.

"For this," Dindet answered, pulling back to inspect for marks or scuffs. "It's a MacGuffin, and I stole it from some giant bug space pirates, but we don't really need it, so I have to give it back."

Oliver stopped what he was doing, slowly registering the words that the alien had just rattled off and tried to picture that string of events. "Am I gonna have to wear another costume?"

"No," Dindet tugged the towel from his hands, leading him further into the more open living room. "Humans exist there, so you don't gotta worry about that. You probably need to put pants on, though."

Oliver blinked and let go of the towel, watching the alien shift into bright yellows and pinks as his whole face lit up with happy shock. "You said *pants*."

Cassidy managed to teach her that clothes are not connected to your body?! I owe her big time.

"Lemme get changed."

***

"You said no costumes." Oliver tugged at the absurd harness and leash strapped around his chest, ready to press the latch before Dindet swatted at his hand away and wagged her finger.

"It's *not* a costume. Human people here are, uh…rare?" She explained, guiding him through the enormous and oscillating spaceport. "Here they exist but they aren't super popular, and most other species…specieses? Most other uh…*things* like to keep them as pets—"

"So, slaves." Oliver scanned the catwalk, offering plenty of returned scowls at the aliens and creatures that turned their noses—or what could have possibly been the equivalent thereof—down at him. "That's, like, really messed up. You know that, right?"

"I know." Dindet tugged him forward lightly, gesturing toward a giant boulder that sat quite conspicuously on the edge of the catwalk with a merchant booth haphazardly hammered onto it. "But I really don't want you to get eaten either."

"What is it with aliens and *eating* people??" Oliver rolled his eyes, following her to the boulder booth. "What have humans ever done to you guys?"

"A lot."

"Like what??" Oliver cast the clown a short glare, though his attention drifted directly past her and her dissertation on the history of the Peace Zone to a strikingly familiar door that stood on its own among the crowd.

Oleander Blume

Is that…?

He paused, ignoring the gentle pull of his harness until Dindet's voice pulled him from his dead stare. Her face drifted into view, and he leaned back, breaking his gaze to look at her.

"We're here," she stated, her eyes flickering back to the direction he was looking, though she seemed not to see the door at all. The clown wrapped her arm around his shoulder, directing him into the makeshift booth run by what looked like a regular human guy, though his skin was just barely tinted blue.

The pirate leaned forward over the counter, looking Oliver over for a solid couple of seconds before his attention turned to Dindet, and a smile pulled at his lips.

"Our colorful caper returns," he drawled, "I'll let you keep our MacGuffin if you trade me your pet."

Oliver shot him a glare. "I'm not a *pet.*"

The guy chuckled, and two massive, metallic spider limbs reached over the booth counter, lifting him up as the beaming red robotic eyes poked out from under the pirate's scrawny legs. "Best not to go around saying that, kid. Real humans fetch a pretty penny…I hear the spleen is a delicacy in quadrant four."

Oliver instinctively stepped behind Dindet before his eye caught the straps that held the pirate in place. *Spider…wheelchair?*

"Is your bug here?" Dindet offered a placid smile, despite the fact that she ran through colors faster than a spinning wheel when Oliver brushed against her. "We just came to give back the thing I took. I'm really sorry, but it sort of turned out I didn't really need it."

The spider pirate's smirk faltered, and he dropped back down behind the booth and knocked on the boulder behind him. "Khet'di, the beanie baby is back with our MacGuffin, and she brought a real-life *human.*"

The boulder had a surprisingly metallic noise to it, which made a lot more sense when a whole panel cracked with light and

125

slid away to reveal another pirate. This one was an actual bug, an enormous green and hairy praying mantis that ducked her head under the doorway and stepped into the booth.

"Khhlowwnn…khhumann." The alien regarded the two of them with a dip of her head, and Dindet pulled the object she'd stolen out of herself and set it down on the counter.

"She says they don't really need it," the spider guy mocked, picking up the equipment and skittering back into the boulder that was actually a spaceship. "Steals our engine support, leaves us stranded in the freaking Peace Zone wastelands to get picked up by the nearest *Randy's* cargo hauler, and *she doesn't need it.*"

Oliver rolled his eyes at the pirate's griping and turned his attention back to Dindet and the mantis she was having a slow telepathic conversation with. At least until he saw it again.

The door.

It sat in a different place now. Deliberately closer, it seemed. And directly across the catwalk from where he stood. Normally, any random door standing free in the middle of a transdimensional space station revolving around a self-contained black hole would just naturally draw attention, one would imagine.

But this one drew Oliver's and Oliver's specifically because it was an apartment door. Apartment 809.

And it stood there like it *wanted* his attention. Craved for him to open it. And, just as naturally as a random apartment door in a oscillating space station could be, it made *him* crave to open it.

Deftly, Oliver clicked the little latch that held his for-show harness on and wandered into the crowd, taking that soft and short, straight line to the old and scuffed door with a broken peephole and a faded bloodstain in its center. He didn't even think about Dindet or the fact that she was still conversing with the alien bug.

"Yhour khhumann iss running ahhwayy," the mantis said aloud, pulling Dindet out of her law-evading negotiations. She snapped her head back in search of the boy, catching him just on the other side of the catwalk.

"Oliver?" she called, though it was more of a confused mumble. Then, in the split second before that false entity revealed itself, she saw him open a door. And all of her stiffened with terror.

"OLIVER, DON'T!" Dindet screeched, flitting and shoving aside bystanders to get to him in that quickly closing window. He couldn't see the disguise such a beast of a creature had and couldn't see its deadly maw closing down over him as he stepped through its blinding threshold.

Dindet slammed hard into the door, splattering and remaking herself so she could fling it open and drag him out of the monster's invisible stomach.

But he wasn't there.

***

Oliver's eyes clenched tight for uncountable seconds in the silence, the bright light and warmth, like a hot breath that blew out from the door when he cracked it open. And when they opened again, he sat on a couch.

It was an old couch, green and grimy, and he could remember the feeling of nail polish caked into the fabric when he made the mistake of spilling it. He stared at the television, and the static that played on it, trying to make pictures from broken pieces of lines as garbled voices grew from the speakers.

Oliver moved to his feet, meandering around the kitchen in search of the place-less noise. He was taller than he was when he remembered living here.

Before, he had trouble getting to the sink and could distinctly remember requiring a small stool to wash the dishes that piled up over the course of the week. The awful smell of them mixed with pungent lavender soaps. He hated the feeling of the water on his skin.

Now he stared at it from above, keenly aware of how small it was.

Oliver moved from the kitchen toward the tiny dining table in the corner. Little notches in the wood where knives had cut out pieces and printer paper drawings that looked absolutely horrendous compared to his skill now.

It was like a time capsule—of days he mushed together and forced out of his mind. Even the old upright piano had the stain of blood on the leg when he glanced back at it.

"You won't hit her, right?" A small voice drifted over the static of the television. Oliver turned to face it, squinting in an effort to see what pictures could be made in the mess of black and white. Nothing easily perceptible.

"It's just a talk, baby girl. You know I love you," another voice replied. "You didn't mean it, and you *are* sorry."

At that, Oliver shifted, stilted and uncomfortable steps as he shuffled back to the couch and sat down.

I know this.

"I'm home," right on cue, the woman's voice followed.

"—told me something today."

"What'd she say?"

I didn't mean it. I didn't mean to make this happen. I'm sorry. Please—please don't make her say it.

"Well?"

"Don't..." Oliver breathed, begging for the girl's soft voice to stay silent, though he knew if she had, the same thing likely would have happened.

"I said..." *Don't. Don't say it. You know what will happen.* "I was tired...of being a girl."

"You know she doesn't mean anything!"

Oliver squirmed unconsciously at the rise in the volume of the television, like the words reverberated around that crusty apartment he sat in. It was fine.

"It's not the first time."

"I—I didn't mean it! I can change my mind. Daddy made sure—he showed me!"

"It's—her!" His mother's voice was raw, vile with hatred and anger. It made him jump.

"God-dammit, Marie!" Matthew's voice crackled over the television, "Don't tell me how to raise my daughter when you're—yourself out to anyone interested!"

"DON'T HURT HER!" The sound of Oliver's own voice nearly crippled him, and he shot up from the couch in an effort to turn the television off.

"You."

"You said you wouldn't—you promised!"

He pressed the buttons with increasing zeal as the screams grew louder, cracking with squeezing electricity as the volume grew. None of them worked, though.

The awful sound of glass shattering against wood made him swivel his head back toward the untouched piano by the wall.

It was disjointed, unfamiliar to him because he had cut up every moment and scattered them into a disgusting collage that made no sense. It needed to not make sense.

"MOMMA!"

Oliver ripped the old tube television away from the wall, tearing out the plug in an effort to make the noise stop.

"DON'T FUCKING RUN FROM ME!" It screeched, loud and buzzing as the static jolted in conjunction with the movement just under its surface.

"MOMMA—MOM, PLEASE!!"

Oliver scrambled back from it, the plug wrapped tightly in his fingers as he tried to process how he got here, and what happened. What nightmare this was. It wasn't like the ones he had before.

It's never this one.

"I'LL FUCKING KILL YOU!"

"Stop!" Oliver kicked the screen, causing another burst of noise to erupt from the monstrous memory. "Stop it!!"

He remembered being trapped, banging and screaming and

begging for help. Oliver gasped at the wretched sound of skin tearing, the thud of one body hitting another, the softest exhale of breath after.

The boy pulled in on himself, curling up and pressing his palms so hard into his ears to drown out the noise. God, how it filled the room. Like it came from his own head.

"What are—what are you doing?" Like a match to flame, the words caught fire in his mouth. He wasn't the one who uttered them, though.

"Teaching you a lesson."

No...please, I have to—

"STOP!! Stop it!! Please, PLEASE—"

It was loud and violent, with every tear and rip of flesh and fabric, blood and tears and sweat. And the room was empty.

The little girl screamed, a horrific, ear-piercing shriek that made his head ache as though he were doing it himself.

"Please—I can't! I can't do this—"

"MOMMA!!" Her voice cut through his whispers. "MOMMA, PLEASE!! HE'S GONNA KILL ME. HELP ME!!"

Oliver pulled back, lost and stupid and trying so hard not to hear it. It wasn't happening. *It isn't real.*

She was screaming and crying, begging so loudly, so desperately, and all he could do was to move away, slowly, before he felt himself hit the soft cushions of that ugly green couch.

"IT HURTS!! IT HURTS—MOMMA, PLEASE, HELP ME!"

"MAKE IT STOP!!" Oliver shrieked through the static, folding in on himself as though he felt that tearing, ugly pain in that very moment.

And in that moment, the room filled with silence. Cut out by his cry.

"I can't—I can't do it...I can't do it anymore, please...I wanna go home...please...Dindet—"

Gently, a small hand glided across his back, and two slender arms pulled him into a soft embrace.

"Hey..." the familiar voice broke through his quiet, shuddering tears. "It's okay..."

Oliver shifted in the familiar stranger's arms and eased his irritated eyes open to look up at their face.

"It hurts, a lot..." she said softly, glancing down at the gaping nothingness that bled from the center of him. He hadn't even noticed it there. "I imagine."

He stared at her, some soft memory returning to his bleeding, terribly lost mind. She was like a ball of colors, foaming up and floating away in little recollections.

"It's all a big jumbly mess, and you feel everything, all at once, and very hard...I know," for a moment, those colorful memories turned a shadowy grey, and the fuzziness of her began to solidify, growing edges and lines that made her look like a painting on a canvas. She stood up, crouching only a bit to take his hands in hers.

Dindet offered a warm smile, "You don't have to do it alone."

Cornered Animal

O liver wrenched himself awake with an ugly gasp, kicking and screaming and choking on the noxious air as he tried to pull his wits about him.

He glanced around the area. It was a flat, white expanse of nothingness. If he were sitting on a floor, there was no indication of it. But something about the place was wrong; the air burned every part of him through his clothes and left his skin red and blotchy. It had a foul stench to it, and it stung his nostrils, tongue, and lungs, regardless of if he covered his face with his shirt.

He swiveled his head around, finding Dindet in what he assumed to be the same strange dream state he was in a few seconds prior. He crawled over to her, looking her up and down in an effort to figure out what was going on. *How did we get here?*

Oliver searched the emptiness for something, anything to indicate what exactly was going on, but there was nothing. Just the two of them, and he had no idea how long they had been here. Or even what 'here' was.

***

"What's it like to be scattered?" Oliver asked, kneeling down to set a small bouquet of roses and pink lilies at the foot of his mother's gravestone. Dindet stood behind him, a humble observer to this human ritual.

There was some sort of solace she felt in the sinking sunlight as the last bit of snow melted into the grass, there in the cemetery. The softness of the area flickered. ~~hurting and breaking~~ just long enough that the alien only half noticed it.

"You see everything, all at once. And then it's gone forever," she answered.

"Does it hurt?"

"I don't know." Dindet hesitated, raising a hand in an attempt to comfort him, but she stopped and instead wrapped her fingers tight around her arms. *This was familiar. She recognized it. But they had not been here before. Not yet—*

"I don't want you here anymore."

Dindet blinked, caught off guard by the sudden chill of his words. Her eyes drifted down to the wide and empty hole in the ground.

"Wh—what?"

Oliver straightened himself and turned, drawing her attention as he stared her dead in the eyes. He ~~clipped and fractured.~~ ~~Screaming static in the layers of him that molded and joined with the rest of the world.~~

Then he was normal again.

"It's all right. I don't have to know." Oliver nodded and reached for her, donning a smile that made it seem so easy that nothing was out of the ordinary. But it still collapsed with another version of him that ~~shrieked and screamed~~ just under the surface.

"Oliver? Something's wrong." Dindet took a hesitant step back, prompting the Not Oliver to furrow his brow in confusion and concern. But that version of him was only ~~half real.~~ Suffocated by the growing, awful static in the clown's head as he drew increasingly close. And became increasingly less of himself.

"What's wrong?" he asked, seemingly entirely unaware of the way his skin ~~glitched and folded,~~ sparkling and cracking and breaking away. Then reappearing as if it hadn't changed at all.

"I—I don't know, something isn't right," Dindet's head swiveled around, and she searched the cemetery for something, anything that could indicate how they got there, when—if this had already happened or not.

"WE WERE SO CLOSE WHAT WERE YOU THINKIN G!" Oliver's vile rage built through the growing static.

Dindet snapped her head back to the boy, and he was green and broken, lashing at her with such visceral hatred in his eyes.

Why was he mad? What had she done?

None of this made sense. This wasn't real, right? It never got this bad. It never layered this much.

"You were supposed to HELP!!" He shrieked, advancing toward her as he clawed for her bean. "You said you came here for ME! To help ME! Right?!"

"ALL YOU DO IS HURT PEOPLE!" he screamed and shattered, the words falling distorted and ugly out of his mouth. "All you do is hurt me! And my Dad! And EVERYTHING! YOU'RE A MONSTER!"

"You failed."

The clown drew in a ragged mock gasp, the soft voice creeping up and into her like some gentle and breathless death. It burned all of her as the shimmering and glistening woman rested her hand over Dindet's shoulder and leaned forward.

Her hair was long, spilling out around her and shadowing the hundreds and hundreds of layers of her screaming friend from view. Marie's voice was unmistakable.

"You have to try again."

***

"Dindet." Oliver half coughed, waving his hand in front of her to try to get her attention. She was entirely still, aside from the ever-changing kaleidoscope of colors she shifted into as she stared blankly ahead.

Suddenly, her face twisted up in terror, and her rainbow of colors plummeted into a nearly black purple. Oliver sucked in a painful breath with the quick realization that whatever dream she was having had just turned into a nightmare.

"It's a dream! It's okay. You have to wake up!" He leaned in, reaching toward her, only to have the alien kick and flail with a terrified howl as he hassled to get a grip on her.

"It—it's okay—" Oliver dodged her claws, trying to keep some kind of hold, but she jerked and yanked so quickly that his burning hands couldn't maintain any grip. Whatever nightmare she witnessed was so awful that it made her bubble and split as she cried and screamed.

Oliver dropped down on his knees, pinning her flailing legs to the ground, and grappled with her for her arms, finally clenching his fist around her wrists until his knuckles turned white with the force, and yet she still persisted.

***

"It's okay." Marie's voice was sweet and kind, tinged with a kind of flavor of anger that burned Dindet's insides. Marie glided around her, reaching out to press her semi-corporeal fingers into the jagged and split conjunction of Oliver. And finally easing the scattered leftovers of the memory.

"You can try again," Marie said, turning her gaze back to Dindet. The alien shuddered, and parts of her splintered at the thought.

"No, no. This isn't right. This isn't real." She sputtered, desperately trying to collect the mismatched pieces of her thoughts. "I didn't mess anything up yet—right? He hasn't died—"

"But he will." Like thousands of voices on top of one another, it drew the clown's attention. Dindet whipped back only to be clamped and trapped in the long black claws of something far bigger than she could ever be. The jester loomed, black as a shadow, with narrowed empty eyes and a smile that split its face.

"No, I promised!" Dindet retorted, more confused than ever at what she couldn't yet grasp. *There was something here. There was a reason, a desire. She swore.*

"And you will fail." The jester removed its grasp and bent forward, pressing its long fingers into the earth around her. Large cracks jutted from beneath it, slicing through reality and all its infinitesimal replicates. "Like you always do."

Dindet stumbled and scrambled in a desperate attempt to escape, but some awful thing held her there, surrounded by the inevitable destruction of the present, the past, and the future. It struck lightning to her core, and she let out a horrendous, awful cry of agony.

***

"It hurts! It hurts—make it stop, MAKE IT STOP!!" The alien let out a horrified, pained, and concussive shriek that nearly knocked Oliver out.

Whatever static she'd put up as a barrier between them had completely dropped, and he was forced to smack his hands over his ears to quell some of the pain.

Oliver felt blood trickling down the sides of his cheeks and struggled to regain the hold he had on her, grabbing her face and holding it as still as he possibly could while her internal cries rang out in his head and made his nose bleed.

"Dindet—Ah!" He grimaced and gasped in the foul air, losing his grip for a moment when her talon-like fingers dug into his skin, piercing his sleeves and staining his shirt with fresh blood.

Her face had gone still, but he could still hear her shrieking and wailing in his head, crying out desperately for someone to make the pain stop.

Oliver winced through it, fighting against her mortifying strength to keep her still enough that he could yell back. He clapped his hands around her head, feeling his fingers plunge through whatever could have been considered skin as it ate away from her face and whipped out like floating slime.

"I know you can hear me," he said, struggling to keep his voice calm while his adrenaline kept him able to overpower the alien. "Dindet, I'm right here. You need to wake up."

For a moment, her eyes flickered up at him, and he thought she would snap out of it, but instead, another terrible, ear-piercing, and mind-numbing shriek poured out of her head and rattled his brain.

"Okay, maybe you can't wake up—that's fine! It's fine. You just, you just…" he winced, resisting the urge to pull away to protect himself. "You just need to move us."

His fingers began to sink into her head, and her vice grip on his arms only made it harder for him to maintain consciousness.

"You can do that!" He yelled, beginning to lose himself to the agony she implanted in him. "I know you can, please!…*Please*."

Oliver felt himself falling, and for a moment, everything turned black, and then he was sitting on his living room floor, and the clown was still tearing her claws into him and screaming in his head.

Oliver wrenched his arms away from her and scrambled to his feet, spinning around to make sure this was the place they were supposed to be before sprinting up the stairs into his bathroom and plunging his bloody forearms into the sink to run water over them.

Every part of him ached, and he numbly watched the cold water wash away the blood from four deep puncture wounds that tore into his muscles.

After all the blood had been washed away, or most of it, he grabbed some gauze and wrapped as much as he possibly could over each arm, keeping it tight enough that it helped stop some of the bleeding. Then, he stripped off his shirt in exchange for a different one and quickly ran back downstairs to check on Dindet.

She sat on the floor, still holding her arms up in a daze. Half of her was floating black ooze, and the other half still had a look of sheer horror on her face, and big, bubbling black tears streamed down her cheeks into a pool in her lap.

Oliver stopped at the edge of the stairs and thrust his arms behind him before slowly making his way toward her.

It would have been a lie if he weren't even a little curious at what she saw. A twinge of shame and guilt panged in him for the thought. He had never seen someone look so completely and utterly fearful. He drew near, hesitantly stepping in front of her and dropping into a crisscross.

Oliver gently rested his hands over hers and lowered them down to her side, watching her face for some moment of recognition in her eyes.

She blinked rapidly, growing more relaxed as she left the nightmare trance and re-entered reality, staring back at him with worry and regret.

"Oliver, I'm—"

"It's *okay*." He cut in, pulling his hands away from his lap. "It was an accident. Nobody got hurt."

***

Oliver kept his distance from the clown and opted to retreat to his room instead of trying to ask about what she'd seen. She didn't seem keen to tell him anyway, and he convinced most of himself it wasn't important.

He lay up on his pillows, lifting and lowering his left arm in a makeshift pain gauge. They ached, but so did the rest of him. Still, though, he could feel the sting of each individual puncture wound and knew it was more like a dog bite than sharp nails.

Oliver held his hand up in front of himself and attempted to close his fingers into a fist. Only getting about a quarter of the way there before pain shot up through his arm into his wrist, leaving that tingly numb feeling in his fingers.

They were both bad, but his left was worse, and he only had nominal movement in his right—enough that he could close and fan out his fingers and force his hand into a fist if he tried hard enough.

He imagined he should be mad about it. It would probably leave a lasting impact on his motor skills, and the scars would be pretty gnarly too.

He wasn't mad, though; it was the same sort of feeling he felt when a dog chased Bacon into a corner and the terrified cat bit him when he yanked him out of the dog's jaws.

You don't think about how much it hurts or how much blood you lost, or even worry about yourself. All you're thinking about is getting a terrified animal to safety. They don't know you were trying to help, so they hurt you out of fear and confusion.

He couldn't blame Dindet for something like that, and he definitely couldn't with the echoes of her terror rattling around in his head.

That was the only other thing he couldn't get rid of, and his terrible curiosity only made the remnant screams louder.

What is she so afraid of? What sort of secrets does she have?

Oliver's eyes drooped, and he struggled to stay awake long enough to think about it further. The comfort of his bed, in contrast to the ache of his body, was enough to lull him into slumber.

Until he accidentally rolled over on his arm and shot up with a gasp, jerked fully awake by the sudden reminder of his injury.

***

Dindet sat on the couch with the quilt wrapped around her the same way she saw Oliver had it when he gave her cocoa. Of course, it made so little difference that she didn't feel it at all. Besides, her mind was entirely occupied by constant repetitive images in her head and the gentle memory of sheer agony.

She felt split almost, ~~like half of her existed in an entirely different dimension and the other half was here.~~

and both were screaming at each other

until the world around her was so

tired she was almost certain everything

about this was

Wrong

"Hey."

Oliver's voice pulled her out of her trance, and she turned to see the sleepy boy wobbling next to the couch. The clown shrank into the blanket, covering most of herself to hide away the overwhelming guilt that twisted up painful knots in her stomach.

Oliver sat down and took a few large gulps from the water he'd initially come down to get. He waited, not expecting her to say anything, and simply just watched her, trying to figure out what was going on in her head.

"It's okay if you got scared." He broke the silence and sat down, pulling his legs up onto the couch. "It was sort of like a bad dream, and I have those all the time."

"I don't." Her words were incredibly small, and she turtled back into the blanket so only half of her face was visible.

"Manpreet always says nightmares are just your heart trying to tell you something your head doesn't want to hear." Oliver reached toward the quilt, tugging at it to try to get her to come out. "If you want to talk about it—"

"I don't..." she croaked quietly, poking out her hands only so she could pull the blanket up and cocoon herself even further. Oliver averted his eyes and pulled back, feeling at a loss for how he could comfort her.

"Would you feel better if I told you about mine?" he offered.

The cocoon shifted, and a nose and mouth peeked out from inside.

"No," she answered before closing it back up. Oliver nodded and glanced out the back porch door for a moment while he contemplated what to do next.

"When I woke up, you were also asleep—I think? I kept trying to wake you up, too." He shifted, tenderly grazing his fingers along the cuts she'd made and seeing if she had reacted at all.

The blanket moved, her head pushed out, and she pulled the rest of it around her. As if to protect herself from something before she sunk back and nestled her chin into the quilt funnel she'd made.

"I was dying."

Oliver drew in a very soft breath at the alien's answer. The hollow way in which the words left her made him shudder uncomfortably at the notion, and he tried, and failed, to hide his unease.

"I—I'm sorry—"

"Why do you wanna bring her back so much?" Dindet changed the subject.

Oliver leaned forward to get a better look at her hidden eyes. But she only stared at the floor, the pasty whiteness of her face illuminated in the soft glow of the moonlight.

"You want her back so much," she murmured after Oliver's silence lasted too long. "Why?"

It was a good question. One he didn't think about often because he thought he already had the answer. He wanted her back because she was his mother, the person who saved him, who could protect him. She was safe. *But she also—*

"I don't know," Oliver answered, forcing down the darker part of his thoughts. The pile of quilt shifted, and Dindet turned to stare at him, her eyes flitting up and down in an effort to read what the answer meant.

"I don't know...because—" Oliver bit his lip, dropping his

gaze. "Because she's my mom? If she came back before...Before Matthew, none of that would have happened. I wouldn't have gotten taken and—"

"Hurt?" Dindet finished for him, prompting an uneasy little nod from the boy.

"But you were hurt before then, too," she added softly. She began picking at the quilt, pulling up the loosened seams of the patchwork as she spoke, "It doesn't seem fair..."

Dindet's gaze flickered up from the blanket to the television, finally resting directly on Oliver. "It doesn't seem fair for the people who make you to also ask you to hurt."

He stared at her, and she at him, until her eyes boring into him made his skin crawl and his chest ache, and he looked away.

"I want her back...because maybe if she's back, she can fix things." He said finally, keeping his gaze on his twiddling thumbs as Dindet nodded.

"What's broken?"

"Me."

Bad at Lying

"**A**re you ready?!" Dindet's chipper voice rang out in the dark as she jumped through Oliver's shut door and bounced around the room, acting as his new personal alarm clock.

Regardless of what he preferred, she seemed particularly keen on being around him at nearly all hours of the day. Or none at all. There wasn't really an in between. Especially after Tuesday.

The sleep-deprived boy rolled over with a loud, reluctant groan and bopped her lightly on the head to get her to stop for a moment. After a couple of seconds of silence, she leaned in close. "Are you ready now?"

Oliver peeled his eyes open and let them adjust to the darkness of the morning, making out Dindet's pale face and silly, excited grin, and nodded slightly. He sat up, flailing his arms a little to maintain balance, and very slowly blinking away the little sleep he'd gotten.

"Okay, I'm up." Not really, but it's not like she knew better. He was pretty sure she was up all night doing god only knows what. Or watching him to make sure he didn't die.

Oliver lolled his head back to look at the clown, who eagerly sat on her knees, waiting for him to start getting ready for school.

So he obliged and threw off his covers, stood up, and shuffled, still half asleep, to his closet.

Dindet followed him, waiting patiently outside of the closet as he decided which outfit to wear and came back out in a sort of frumpy green sweater that made him look a lot smaller and stick-like than he actually was.

He rubbed his face, murmuring something about a haircut, and swiveled around, flipping on the bathroom light and bracing for the brightness. Dindet followed him inside, completely bypassing him to look around at the tiny room she hadn't been in since she first came here.

"Dindet."

"Okay." She nodded with a smile, dropping the toilet brush she was undoubtedly trying to understand the purpose of and popping back outside the bathroom door.

Oliver shut the door, hearing her immediately fall against it and slide down to the ground. She apparently had the same level of patience as a needy cat.

In reality, he understood the clown's upbeat exterior was a poor attempt at not looking nearly as worried and guilt-ridden as she no doubt felt for his health. The past couple of days, he had maintained that Tuesday wasn't her fault and that he wasn't mad, but words did nothing to sate her.

The bathroom door opened up from behind her, and Dindet promptly fell backward on the ground with a startled little giggle. Oliver stared down at her, more awake than before but still in the process of becoming a person.

"Enjoying yourself?" he mumbled sardonically, pressing his foot gently into her face and making her break into further laughter. He lifted his leg to step over her and out the door, only to get caught and tripped up by her hand as it wrapped around his ankle, preventing him from moving very far.

"What are you doing?" He kicked the air awkwardly, trying

to keep his balance and also get her to let go, but she was lost in a fit of snorts and wheezes. Even the static in her head was drowned out by her giggling.

Oliver let out a small huff, resigning himself to the grinning ball and chain, and began dragging her step by step. He was halfway to his door when she finally quieted down, hummed her last bit of chuckles and stood up.

"You have way too much fun," he remarked with a small smile as she nodded and circled him to get out the door.

"Only 'cause you never have enough," she playfully retorted, already halfway down the stairs and flipping on lights to get out his routine breakfast. Oliver followed, taking the bowl of cereal she had poured and grabbing a spoon from the drawer.

"I'm not mad," he said, casually taking a bite. Dindet paused, almost dropping the box in her hand.

"What?"

"I'm not mad at you. I never was." Oliver took another, smaller bite. "It wasn't your fault, and you're not my mom, so please stop acting like I'm so fragile." He paused, slowly setting his spoon down. "The hospital too…You didn't make me sick, none of that was your fault."

"Oh." Her moment of soft hesitation quickly dissipated, and she slowed until she was almost completely still. "Okay."

Oliver finished up his cereal and quickly headed for the door. Until he realized she wasn't bouncing behind him, ready to devour the feelings of every kid on campus.

"Are you coming?" He stopped, holding the door open for her. But the alien just stood there in the kitchen, staring at him like he was asking the impossible.

"Actually, I—I have an Aaron to run?" She lied. It was a very obvious lie because Oliver could see the chartreuse and ugly green colors blotching like patches of bruises on her when she spoke. "It's for the machine. And, uhm. Super *super* important."

Oliver's brow furrowed, and he narrowed his eyes at such a terrible excuse. "You mean an *errand*? Where are you going? You know if you keep missing school, people will start getting suspicious, right?" *I'm getting suspicious.*

"I know!" Dindet gave a very big and very fake-looking smile, popping from where she stood to directly in front of Oliver so she could gently force him out the door. "I promise I'll come back tomorrow. I, uh, I promised Cassidy I'd give her some of my matter to study."

"*Right.*" He retorted sarcastically, leaning back to force all his weight on the alien so it was harder to make him leave. It wasn't, and she very easily shoved him out the door and shut it behind him.

"Hey!" Oliver spun around, swinging the door open to catch her, but she was already gone.

"Uhm. Morning?" Douglass's tired voice drifted over the snow, drawing Oliver's attention away from his Houdini of a houseguest. Oliver grumbled and closed the door, thoroughly uninterested in any more conversation as he kicked snow off the porch and trudged down to join Douglass.

"Morning."

***

"Dude, are you all right?" Douglass pulled Oliver's attention away from the checkered linoleum school tiles that he purposefully stepped around in an erratic zigzag maneuver.

Oliver glanced up and promptly stumbled over his own feet, forcing his friend to catch him by the arm to keep him from hitting the ground. Oliver turned beet red and shot a baffled yet flustered glare at him for distracting him from his distraction.

"S-sorry," Douglass quickly let go, "you just look off today."

Oliver shrugged but kept his still hot face turned away from him until he could gather the conviction to answer.

"I don't know what I'm supposed to do," he replied, not

clueing Douglass in on what he was referring to.

"About what?"

"Something is wrong with her, and she won't say anything about it," Oliver replied, offering a frustrated gesture to the air at Dindet's overt avoidance of him. "This is like the sixth time she's skipped school with the *worst* excuse ever."

Douglass offered a pensive look and turned down the hall toward the gym, forcing Oliver to follow as he continued.

"It's just—Dad had to go back to work earlier than we expected, and now Dindet basically wants nothing to do with me half the time. And that's *weird* because she still acts like she always wants to hang around and take me to—take me out around town. But then the other half of the time she's like a rock or something."

"Well, I know she and Cas get along. Maybe she's just spending more time with her 'cause they're both from other countries?" Douglass countered pragmatically. "Also, no offense dude, but you aren't exactly the 'going out' type."

Oliver rolled his eyes with a huff. *If you only knew.*

Douglass turned another corner, heading down the hall to where the courtesy drivers' ed courses took place in the since-defunct home-ec classroom.

"You're gonna miss the bus home if you keep following me," he said, glancing up at the clock on the wall above the lockers. Oliver slowed his pace slightly, hoping to pull the boy back from his determined trek to his after-school class.

"I can take the activity bus; I was..." he hesitated, dropping his gaze to try to hide how hot his face got at being called out. "Sort of hoping I could just hang out in the back of class until you're done."

Douglass stopped and turned on his heel, some sly little smile creeping across his face at his friend's embarrassment. "You *lonely?*"

Oliver's head shot up, and he sputtered stupidly for a second or two before words actually formed in his mouth. "No! I'm *not.*

I'm *bored*. And I don't want to go home 'cause I know she's not going to be there—or if she *is*, she's gonna play busy."

"*Riight*." Douglass took a step back and placed his hand on a classroom door. "And you'd rather sit in an empty classroom while the rest of us are doing circles at five miles an hour in the parking lot? You'll be just as bored, dude."

"Well, it's either you or I go hang out with Markus again," he retorted.

"Oh," Douglass tried to sound much less vile than he did. He rubbed the back of his neck in guilt. "I didn't know you were actually talking to him. I thought you blocked him."

No. Not exactly.

"I mean—I meant to," Oliver hesitated, hating the idea of telling Douglass he not only *hadn't* blocked him but also spent nearly an entire day with the guy. "I just forgot, and while I was stuck at home…we, uh…we hung out. It was—it was sort of nice?"

He winced unconsciously, unable to look in his direction while Douglass formed the inevitable connection.

"Oh."

There it was, the softest breath of understanding that Oliver dearly dreaded. It made sense, though, for him to come to that conclusion.

"I'm sorry—"

"Did you guys do stuff?" Douglass interrupted, slightly louder, enough to break Oliver's apprehension like a swift slap in the face. He blinked, unprepared for the kid to even ask the question.

"Like—like *stuff*? Or just, just like you know, stuff?" Oliver very well knew what the correct answer to his question was but avoided answering it nonetheless. "I mean—h-he…we, *I* didn't do anything."

That deplorable response made Douglass stare at him, his face twisting up in what was most assuredly worry mixed with jealous rage. He pulled away from the door.

"He—he's nice!" Oliver interjected before the boy had a chance to respond. "He likes me, he said so, and he—he thinks I'm cool even though I'm trans, which is hard to come by. And—and it's not like I did anything. We just drank! He said I was good—"

"You drank? *Alcohol?* Oliver, he's using you," Douglass stated matter-of-factly, prompting Oliver to roll his eyes in defiance.

"No, see, it's the other way around," he argued, albeit very poorly and with only the motivation to convince himself of it. *It wasn't bad. He didn't hit me. He didn't do anything.* "I only wanted to hang out with him because I was bored. I made him drive all the way to my house to pick me up. I just wanted a distraction—I was *bored.*"

"You told me you were just doing an interview. Not getting drunk!" Douglass shook his head and pressed his fingers to the bridge of his nose in frustration. "Ols, what if he does something?"

"Like what?" Oliver's tone shifted. *Why is he mad? I didn't do anything wrong! This was normal! It's totally normal for kids to get together in high school, totally normal to experiment and do things. He's being a jealous prick about it.* "He didn't hit me. All he did was kiss—"

"You *kissed?!*" Douglass raised his hands to his head, shaking them in frustration at how naive Oliver sounded. "You're *fourteen!* He's a creep! And you got drunk with him?"

"He didn't hit me or anything," Oliver retorted angrily, "and he—he's not a creep! He's like me! We just hung out. It was totally normal."

"How would you even *know?!*" Douglass saw right through Oliver's dismissal of his worries and frustratedly readjusted his bag over his shoulder. "You've only been around other people for *three years.* You don't even know what normal is like—"

"I know what's normal." Oliver cut in.

"*How?*"

"Because—because he treated me just the same as—as any other *guy*."

"Yeah, but you're not—" Douglass stopped himself, immediately biting his tongue and dropping his gaze well and away from Oliver.

"Not. *What?*" The boy's face hardened at the unspoken message. It had been delivered loud and clear.

"Nothing, I didn't mean it like that." Douglass backtracked, picking up his pace in an effort to avoid the inevitable confrontation. Oliver just as quickly stepped in front of him, barring his way with the ugliest scowl he had ever seen.

"Say it," he ordered, causing the boy to curl in on himself in obvious regret.

"Oliver, I'm sorry, you know—"

"Just say it! Douglass." Oliver glared at him, stepping in front of the boy at every attempt he made to break free from his anger. He knew what Douglass was going to say. What he meant and worse. That *that* was what he thought of him.

"Please—"

"No, I wanna hear it," Oliver cut in, forcing out an anxious laugh. It hurt. *Why does it hurt?* "I don't count, do I? 'Cause I'm not really a boy. Right?"

"Oliver, I'm sorry—"

"No, I get it." Oliver stopped him from trying to leave again, this time forcing him back down the hall a few steps as he continued. "I *can't* count. He can't actually like me for what I am because I don't have the parts. Right?! I'm just some dumb, weird girl *pretending* to get attention. That's what everyone else says, so it has to be true!"

"That's not—not everyone says that, I just—" Douglass struggled to come up with a response. He could see so clearly the way all the cogs clicked in Oliver's brain, locking in and making him sputter and laugh because he didn't know what else to do.

"You're not pretending, and I don't think of you like that."

"Don't *lie*." Oliver stopped laughing. "You think I don't pay attention? Or have any idea what people say about me? They don't care. *You* don't care. It's all courtesy 'cause Jon made them."

"I *do* care," Douglass argued, once again trying and failing to get past Oliver. "I just don't wanna see you get hurt—"

"You only say that because you still think I'm a girl!!" Oliver shoved him back, taking a moment to collect whatever control he had over his stupid feelings. It bubbled up, everywhere around him and made his chest ache and the breath in his lungs stop existing.

"You—you only say that 'cause you don't see it, you don't know," he stammered, brushing his fingers through his hair and grazing the cut Matthew made on his forehead. He winced. *It hurts so much. Everything hurts all of a sudden.* Oliver could feel every ounce of his skin like pin-pricks all over. He hated that feeling. The ugly reminder that what he was *wasn't* what he was.

"You say that—but he told me, he told me it was fine. That I still count, and he's not like Da—like Matthew, he's not. He believes me, okay? He *wants* me," Oliver mumbled. Most of what he said, Douglass could barely even hear through his stupid and frantic breaths. *It was fine. Markus was fine. He likes me. That means I was good, was being good. Markus isn't like Matthew. He likes me. And it's normal.*

The feeling didn't go away, though. It just got worse, like his skin had caught on fire and the smoke was choking him. Reminding him of what he was and how it ruined everything. How *he* ruined everything.

Douglass tried to come closer, his gaze flickering over for a second or two to see the home-ec door open. Oliver jolted in front of him, trying once more to bar the boy from retreating.

"Oliver, I'm sorry, you're right—I don't know. And I was a total dick for jumping to conclusions, okay?" he admitted softly, though his gut screamed that he was dead on, and Oliver was just too in denial to see it. "I—class is starting. I have to go."

He pressed a hand into the boy's shoulder, and Oliver promptly stepped away, keeping his focus on the ground. "So you're just going to leave? That's it?"

The bite in his voice caught Douglass off guard, and he struggled not to take it to heart. "Yes, but we...we can talk about this later, all right? I'm not mad; I'm just worried—"

"No. You're *cruel*." Oliver interjected, steeling himself in his own rage as Douglass stepped past him. *Just go. You clearly don't care. You're busy. Everyone is busy. And I'm too much.*

If he had some strength of patience left over, Douglass would have corrected him. Because both of them knew Oliver was lying. Oliver *wanted* him to correct him. To stand there for just a little bit longer and tell him he was sorry and that he wasn't actually too busy for a stupid conversation. He wanted him to say that what he did with Markus was okay. That it was normal. *Not...bad.*

But he didn't. Instead, Douglass's lips curled in a half-hidden snarl, and he grabbed the classroom door before it shut after another student.

"You know what? You're *right*," he said, lifting his chin with indignance. "Markus *does* want you. But it's not because you're trans. Or in spite of. It's because, to him, you're just a *dumb girl*."

Oliver stared at him, mouth agape like some dumbstruck child, astonished that he would say such a thing. Until his face crinkled and twisted with rage and he raised a hand in objection.

"You take that ba—"

"Go *home*, Oliver," Douglass cut him off, briskly shutting the door in his face before he could even get a foot in, leaving him standing there in the middle of the hall, seething.

Oliver stared at the door handle, the deep desire to throw it open and drag Douglass out of the room before he could take his seat, driving him mad. His whole body shook and flashed hot like his bones were cracking from the fire inside them.

He wanted to tear his skin off completely and throw it at that stupid boy's feet so Douglass could dance all over it again. *You jealous, awful—evil PRICK!"*

"I *HATE* YOU!!" The words rose up out of him before he could even think to stop them, and Oliver promptly smacked himself hard in the head for not controlling them. *It doesn't matter! He doesn't matter! I don't care about your stupid opinion. I never asked for it! I never cared!! I don't need you to tell me what's normal and not! I don't need you at all!!*

Figure it Out

"**H**e makes me so *freaking angry* sometimes!" Oliver spat, gesturing up at the locker room ceiling as he ranted about Douglass. Markus was on the floor below him, pulling his gym bag out from under the bench Oliver lay on.

"It's like he just *knows* how to piss me off, like he wants me to care about his opinion! I don't. *Obviously.* I can do whatever I want. He can't make me change my mind, and he doesn't even know you! It's so—so *stupid!*"

"Yeah, he definitely has a crush, my dude." Markus sat back on his knees, and Oliver rolled his eyes at the statement.

"No, *duh.* I already knew that. He's liked me for as long as I've known him, even *after* I told him I wasn't a girl," he answered. "It just—he just—he's not *like* me, so he'll never really get it, you know? Not like you get it, at least."

"You mean your dad?" The senior sifted through his bag to find his swim shorts, only briefly glancing up at Oliver while he vented. "What was his name—"

"Well, yeah, sort of. Like he knows, but he doesn't know everything." Oliver cut him off. "I mean—nobody knows *everything* except for Jon and Dindet. Douglass *definitely* doesn't. And—and I don't *want* him to, you know? He's just gonna treat me like everyone else does. Like a poor little broken toy."

"Why are you even friends with him if you don't actually like him anyways?"

That made Oliver stop and drop his hands back to his sides.

"Well...I don't *not* like him," he backtracked quietly. "He just...I know he cares a lot, and he's a good person. He isn't, like, obligated to hang around me or anything. He just *does*. And I...don't have very many friends..."

"Am I not your friend?" Markus leaned forward, prompting Oliver to scoot a little closer to the wall.

"I don't think friends kiss."

The senior let out a dejected sigh. "So I'm not your friend 'cause I kissed you?"

Oliver's eyes rolled up to catch the look on the older boy's face, and he sat up to gather a better form of phrasing. "I mean—I don't think they're supposed to. But that was—that was just one time, and honestly, I don't even know why I let you do that in the first place."

"So...you wouldn't want me to do it again?" Markus stared at him. That way that made Oliver's skin crawl with anxiety as he fumbled for words.

"I...uh...well—"

"I only ask because I wasn't lying, you know..." the senior cut in, looking positively downtrodden by the boy's poor attempts at saving face. "I do *really* like you. And I *would* like to do it again..."

"I mean—it was nice I-I it's hot. Are you hot?" Oliver scooted along the bench toward the door, keeping his eyes firmly on Markus as he pulled his shirt off. "I really—*honestly*, shouldn't be in here. If I get caught, I'm pretty sure the school will—"

"They don't have cameras or anything, plus I can vouch for you. You said you missed the bus, right? I can even take you home after I do my laps." Markus interjected, stripping even further down as Oliver corralled himself in the corner of the bench and lockers.

"Yeah, but I was just gonna take the activity bus with Douglass once he got out of class. We live on the same road, so it's just easier." He laughed, albeit way too nervously for his words to be any semblance of convincing.

"Right." Markus nodded. "After he slammed the door in your face, I'm sure he'll be *all ears* about how you chilled out with me, *the big scary senior.*"

He probably would be mad. More mad than he already is...if he knew I was here, yeah. Oliver grew quiet, the thought sinking in and under his skin. *He'd call me a dumb girl...*

"You don't—you don't think of me as a girl, right? I know you said you didn't. Or I *think* you did. But..." Oliver paused, dropping his gaze when Markus turned to face him in nothing but his school swimwear. "I worry that...maybe that's the only reason you want to talk to me?"

The senior's eyes drifted over him, and despite the fact that he was the only one fully clothed, it felt far more like he wasn't.

"I don't really know," he answered, which took Oliver completely by surprise.

"You don't really *look* like either. Especially when you have that—what's it called?"

"Binder?"

"Yeah." Markus sat down on the bench, spreading his arms so he leaned toward the boy and kept his gaze in a deadlock with Oliver's. "You're very pretty, though. With blond hair like that. And I like your dark eyes."

Oliver leaned back, his breath laying locked in his lungs when he dropped his gaze and realized just how close Markus's hands were to his hips. It made his insides rot and his legs hot, and he couldn't tell if it was because he was afraid or if it was because no one had ever been so generous with their compliments.

"You are...very close," he stated, as if it weren't an obvious fact. It did nothing to deter the boy, though.

"Is that okay?"

No...yes?? I don't know?

In lieu of an answer, Oliver just made some pitiful noise of confusion and pressed his back against the cold metal of the lockers.

Markus leaned in further, pushing his knee up and in between the opening of Oliver's legs until it pressed into his inner thigh, and he jerked.

"Am I making you nervous?" Markus's eyes turned down, prompting Oliver to follow his gaze directly to where his fingers inched uncomfortably close to him.

Stop.

As if the senior read his mind, they pulled away, or Oliver thought they had. In reality, Markus's hand moved to his face, tilting him back until he stared right at him.

Oliver made another noise, this one much more a soft and shaky breath than anything else.

"Is this okay?" The senior asked, his eyes half-lidded like some freckly, cinematic love interest.

All Oliver could hear, though, was his own heart beating in his chest, rapid and loud, and it pounded up and down his body, making him tremble.

Oliver's eyes flickered down at movement, at pressure, and he grew very still and very quiet.

For some flash of a moment, his mind whirred with graphic images. Possibilities in the minutiae of the second before Markus asked his last question.

"Is *this?*"

The words drew his attention back to the senior's eyes, just before they closed, and he pressed his lips into Oliver's and pressed his thumb between his legs. It made him move, that familiar sensation, and instead of jerking back or pushing him away as he expected himself to, Oliver instead sank back. It was fine. Really.

It felt nice. It was normal.

But he couldn't quite grasp why it felt like something had carved a hole in his chest that made it so impossible to say no. To speak at all.

***

Something is wrong.

Wrong.

You know something is wrong.

Do something about it.

Everything is layered.

layered

layered

Layered on top of everything else.

Do something.

Before it's

TOO LATE.

Figure it out

Figure it out

Figure it out

Figure it out

They are going to find you.

And they are going to kill you.

Leave! Find a way out!

They are going to kill him!

Smite is coming.   *Do something.*

DO SOMETHING.

FIGURE IT OUT...

FIGURE IT OUT.

What's missing. You know something.

Is missing.

What is it?

Find out.

NOW.

What is it?

It's too late

Too late

TOO LATE

"Dindet?"

What.

She blinked, pulled from the ever-raging static in her head as the *layers,*

layers

layers folded away, slowly melding into *one another* as this dimension seemed to bend, and buckle, and sandwich itself on top of so many others that looked and *tasted,* and felt exactly the same.

***

"Are...you okay?" Oliver asked hesitantly. Dindet had been staring at the wall for hours, and at first, he thought it better not to disturb her, but now it was well past dark and she hadn't so much as even noticed him.

He waved his hand in front of her face and she jerked back, glancing up at him as though he appeared out of nowhere.

"Have you been sitting here all day?"

Dindet glanced around as if trying to recall whether or not she had. And then shrugged. "I got distracted, sorry."

You've been distracted.

Oliver let out a small sigh and nodded. It was late, and he wasn't expecting to get any information out of her, what with the dazed and empty expression she gave him. It was like only half of her existed here, and the other half was still in space, and both were trying to figure out what the hell was going on.

"It's all right," he muttered, "I just came down to tell you that

I'm going to bed and...if you need anything, you can wake me up."

Those were not the exact words he wanted to say in the moment. Really he wanted to shake and yell at her for being so inconsiderate—that would be really stupid to do, though, and it wouldn't accomplish anything. *If she doesn't want to share, she doesn't have to...and I won't make her.*

"Oh, okay." Dindet offered a smile but stayed sitting on the couch, not making any effort to move from the place she had cemented herself.

"...okay." *No. NO! It's not okay! How can you just sit there and pretend that nothing is wrong when I know you're lying?! You've been a stupid rock for weeks, and I'm supposed to just accept that? No! I don't!*

Oliver clenched his jaw, biting back his thoughts in an effort to control how angry he was, and promptly headed back to his room.

This is unacceptable. It's unfair! Whatever vague notion of concern she has in keeping the truth from me, pretending everything is fine when it so clearly is not, if it's some misguided, stupid attempt to protect me, it sure is a crap one! I don't need protection, least of all from her! It's just a stupid show of her stupid idea of keeping things under a control that clearly stopped existing!

Oliver flopped down on his bed and let out a more than disgruntled groan. It took so much effort worrying about her, how she was doing, if she was safe, if she was hungry—that so little else consumed his mind. He wanted to just forget about her. Stop caring altogether because it really seemed like she was trying to do that for him.

For a while, he lay there, staring out the window, expecting her to sneak in and look at the picture he kept on his nightstand. He contemplated asking her about it. Why she was so interested in it, and furthermore...if she knew his mom.

By now, it would have been a rhetorical question. Of course she recognized her. The real question was how. And why.

Oliver sat up and stared at his door for a bit, still deliberating on going downstairs to ask her. He pushed his covers off and snuck out of his room, hanging by the loft walkway as he stared down at the alien that sat on the couch, inhumanly still.

"Dindet."

Her head swiveled around, and he felt her eyes bore into him, prompting the boy to shuffle down the stairs to meet her.

Oliver paused at the edge of the couch, suddenly far more anxious than need be over a dumb question. Still, he sat down next to her as casually as he could manage.

"I have a question," he muttered, making an effort not to look at her.

"Yes?"

His eyes flickered back just a moment, and he could see tiny bubbles around her float up in the air, a show of her own discomfort at this sudden conversation.

"I wanted to ask..." at that moment, anything but what he really wanted to ask, honestly. "H-how do you know...my mom?"

There was a silence between them, or nearly so, all but the deafening sound of Dindet's hands brushing over the blanket as she pulled it close to herself. He half expected her to disappear.

Her nigh refusal to answer—or reluctance to speak at all was far more discomforting than he expected it to be.

"She pulled me out of the dark."

Oliver leaned back into the couch, very slowly processing whatever that meant.

"The dark?" he asked, pressing his palms into his thighs in an effort to get rid of his clammy hands.

"The place before you exist," she clarified. "It's at the center of the Cornucopia."

"So...she's alive?" he questioned softly, finally turning to look

162

at her. The alien looked more like a kaleidoscope than a person, and her eyes stared off at nothing as her face shifted into some amalgamation resembling a Rorschach rather than clown paint.

"...I can't remember…"

Beanie Baby

Some Saturday morning and after a restless hail storm of a night, a very lost and confused Dindet crawled through Oliver's window, fumbling around in the dark until she just lightly grazed a foot half-fallen off the corner and realized she was, in fact, in the right place this time.

The clown felt around the bed and crawled up on top, situating herself just so that she could sort of hear whatever he was dreaming about to make sure it was really, and very specifically, Oliver. And not some poor witless person she would soon terrify.

His dreams were odd, mostly having to do with spaceships, and, for some reason, she was also in them, but she didn't look how she imagined she was meant to. It was definitely him, though.

"Oliver," she whispered, shaking him lightly. The boy groaned and swatted at the air, just barely clawing through her face. Dindet shook him again, this time a little harder, and he made a frown in his slumber. "Oliver, wake up. I need your help."

"Mrrrrgggghhh." She was fairly certain that wasn't a word and folded her arms with a small huff.

"Oliver, if you don't wake up I'm gonna become a solid," she threatened, condensing herself just enough that she began to weigh him down at the waist until he let out a little squeal and his eyes popped open.

His hands shot up, and he quickly shoved her off the side of the bed, sending her tumbling into his desk with an unceremonious splat.

"What was that for?!" He gasped, sitting up and staring out into the dark room at the half-puddle of alien. It took a moment for her to become whole again, so he flipped on his bedside lamp and rubbed his eyes, quickly heading into the bathroom to take care of stray bloodstains on his clothes.

"I lost my bean," Dindet said through the door.

Oliver rolled his eyes, changing out his bandages again to see how much the cuts healed. *Not much.*

"What bean?" he questioned after shoving the bloody tapes under the counter. He opened the door, and she was facing his bed, pulling off her hands and wringing them anxiously before switching where they were supposed to go.

"Hello? What bean?" Oliver grabbed her shoulder to try to get her attention. The clown swiveled around with a startle and blindly reached out in front of herself, touching and patting his face for a solid ten seconds before actually responding.

"My bean, you know? The little roundy thing at the center of me? I lost it."

Oliver's brow furrowed, and he grabbed her wrists, tugging her hands away from his face.

"You mean your nose?"

"It's not a nose," she corrected, "it's a *bean*. Every clown has a bean. How else would I be able to see and eat and hear?"

She wiggled her fingers above Oliver while his sleepy head slowly processed what she was trying to say. "But you're looking right at me?"

Dindet's cheeks puffed up as she held back a burst of laughter, wiggling her arms as she nearly dropped to the ground from the sheer hilarity of his statement.

"You thought those were *real*?!" She cackled, "You know how hard it is to make real, *functioning* human eyeballs?"

Oliver frowned and dropped her hands, deciding not to deal with her making fun of his ignorance. It's not like he would know about alien clown anatomy. And when she explained it, she wasn't particularly thorough.

"Oliver? Oliver, where'd you go?" He turned back for a second, watching her stumble around in his room. The kid grimaced, and a bit of sympathy prickled his spine at her inane attempts to find him. He went back to grab her hand so he could lead her away from where she was headed, which was out the window and halfway down the side of the house.

"Can you only hear me 'cause I'm touching you?" he asked, taking her by the shoulders to have her sit down on the bed. She nodded dumbly, not facing him but still trying to look mostly like she was. Oliver rubbed his face with discontentment and a tired sigh, then took her hand.

"All right, what happened?"

Dindet perked up and shifted herself so she could actually face him now. "Well, I was outside and walking around, and then it started raining rocks and—"

"It doesn't rain rocks. You mean hail?" Oliver interrupted. "Also, what were you doing out last night?"

"It's not important—anyways, I was minding my own business, and it started raining rocks—"

"Hail."

"Hail, and one shot right through me and knocked me out, and now I don't know where I am, so I spent all night trying to find *you*, so you could help me find my bean." Dindet finished her little ramble and made what Oliver assumed was a pouty face, except what were probably imitations of pupils were steadily heading off in different directions.

"All right...where were you last?" He groaned.

"You know those big tower things with wires everywhere?"

"The power transformer?" *Seriously? She was five miles away from the house*?! "All right, we'll start there."

Oliver led the bumbling alien down the stairs and outside. "It's too early in the morning for this."

It was too early in the morning for everything. The only person he knew would probably be out was Douglass, because he was one of those weird kids who got up really early in the morning to go on walks.

"I thought all of you was that black sparkly stuff," Oliver remarked, tugging her forward while she haplessly tried to veer off in directions she didn't need to go. The middle of the road, for instance.

"Nope, well, it is, but it's not *all* of me," Dindet answered, "It's just a part of me, like, a really big part, but the most important part of me is my bean."

She pointed at her face, where her orange nose was supposed to be. "Without it, the rest of me is kind of useless—Oh, OH!! I see something!"

She stopped and started bouncing with excitement, jostling him in the process.

"I thought you couldn't—"

"I can't see *you*, but I can see where I am. And there are human people!" She grinned, trying to go off in some direction without more than a second thought until she very quickly and not purposefully splashed onto the ground as a watery black puddle.

Oliver fell down on his knees and frantically tried to pull back the slowly widening mess to prevent her from bleeding out on the sidewalk. As he scrambled to keep the majority of the clown in one place, the liquid was already beginning to congeal in his fingers until it gradually came back into shape on its own.

First, a hand, and then a couple more extremities, and Dindet practically crawled out of herself, shaking her head in confusion for a second before she reached out to steady most of herself on his shoulder.

"Ow," she muttered. Oliver helped her upright, glancing around to make sure no one out and about noticed any of what had just happened.

"Are you all right?" He watched her ripple a little, like she was still in the process of becoming whole. The clown shook her head vigorously and offered a smile to the air.

"Yeah, I'm okay." She wobbled a little but was still remarkably chipper.

"You said you saw people?" He stopped her from heading into the woods. Dindet circled around for a second, almost like she was looking for something.

"Yeah, two people, one was pinkish green, and the other one was sort of blue and orangey-yellow?"

That isn't how people are supposed to look.

"Like the clothes they were wearing?" Oliver questioned, trying to understand what she meant.

"No, more like kind of happy and jealous, and the other one was sad and worried?" That helped even less.

"What do they look like?" Oliver quickly yanked Dindet out of a near-miss with a utility truck and decidedly moved the both of them a good ten feet from the road *and* the sidewalk so he didn't have to deal with her ending up as a glorified windshield splat.

They probably went around in twenty different circles before Oliver finally got some kind of lead out of the clown.

And that was after she went from solid to liquid and then gas. By now, she was giggly as a drunk and dumb fool, slinging herself blindly around him while a third of her sagged like hot putty.

"Ooooliv…er!" Dindet mused, swinging an arm over his shoulder and melting into him with a content hum. "I know whateerrrrhhh where I am."

The boy let out an exhausted sigh. "Where are you?"

I swear to god, if you say you're with me again, I'm going to drop you on the ground and leave you here.

"Do...dou...doug...glasssssssss...essshouse."

The clown pointed at nothing and nuzzled her chin into his neck, staining his shirt with the black, sparkling goo that seeped out of her. The feeling of it made his skin crawl, like he was covered in a partially rotted creamer that would probably never wash out.

Oliver dragged her halfway up the walkway to Douglass's house and promptly shoved her off into a bush to ring the doorbell.

"O—Oliver?" Douglass peaked out from behind the door, then opened it a little wider when he realized who it was. "What's up? Are—is...is everything—"

"Dindet lost something really important to her, and I was wondering if you saw it?" Oliver interrupted, glancing back at the bush he pushed the clown into in order to avert his gaze from Douglass. However, he was unaware that she had already sat up and was blindly, deafly, and dumbly wandering her way around the backside of the house.

"Oh...what did she lose?" Douglass tilted his head back inside his house, hearing his dad shouting excitedly.

"You know, the..." Oliver awkwardly pointed to his face, trying not to look as stupid as he felt. "Her, uh..."

Douglass's eyes widened with small realization, and he mouthed a little 'oh' before opening the door wide and beckoning him inside.

"I saw this weird orange thing on my walk this morning. I didn't know it was hers." Douglass led him back toward his room and began sifting through his clothes-covered bed and rummaging through his desk. "I swear I put it here somewhere. Oh!"

He shot up and filed past him toward his garage door, leaving the boy to awkwardly stand in his room, trying to get past that unpleasant anxiety you get when you're a guest in someone's house and they leave you alone.

Oliver looked around the room, sizing it up a little and comparing it to his own. It was a lot messier. Granted, most of *his* mess stayed in the closet.

Douglass had a case full of rom-coms and a box set of pride and prejudice—extended cuts—on the first couple of shelves, and the rest had nothing but manga and poorly written romance novels. One of which was provided by Oliver's own shelf.

Whatever interests you, right?

"Is this it?" Douglass came back into the room, holding up a small, oval-looking thing in his fingers. "My dad was messing with it in his lab. I probably left it there by accident when I got back."

Douglass reluctantly handed over the bean, dropping it into his hand with a little sigh.

"I hope she's not upset," he muttered. Oliver shoved the bean into his pocket and shook his head.

"Trust me, if she were, you'd know," he offered briskly, stepping past him and into the hall. "She has a colorful temper."

"I just feel bad." Douglass followed him. "'Cause I've done so much wrong to her."

"Douglass, she doesn't hate you," Oliver retorted, getting a little fed up with being his unwilling therapist. "She probably cares more about how you feel anyways."

"Do you? Hate me, I mean, for what I said about...about Markus...and you." *There it is.* He dreaded the words the moment Douglass said them. Oliver curled in on himself in an effort to hide his discomfort. But it was clear as day.

"I don't..." he answered softly, "I just, I needed—it was really my fault for being such a dick...I think—"

"It's all right." Douglass cut in, offering that gentle little smile that slowly grew a whole habitat of butterflies in Oliver's stomach. "You don't have to explain it. I get it."

"Th-thanks..." Oliver glanced back before leaving, hoping his words weren't completely meaningless to Douglass. "I should—I should probably find Dindet."

Outside and away from prying eyes, he went off into the bushes around Douglass's house in search of the clown, who, almost as he expected, was not there. Luckily, there was a trail of her heading around the back of the house toward the garage, where he found her shoving her head into the wall.

"Found your bean." He pulled the little thing out of his pocket and rolled it around in his palm. Dindet spun around and stumbled toward him with a silly little laugh, reaching out to grab it and promptly falling flat on her face. She let out a quiet, tired groan, and Oliver's eyes nearly rolled to the back of his head.

Great.

He put the orange thing back in his pocket and began to drag the clown the good quarter-mile home while she murmured some delirious nothings in his head.

"Yoooooouuu…should smile…morhh," Dindet hummed, poking him in the face with her finger. "H… hav I dold you? Ahhbout smilll…smi…smihh-ile."

"Please stop poking me." Oliver shifted his weight so he could open the front door without dropping the ever-sagging alien.

"Caahnn I hav muh beannow?" She reached over his shoulder for his pocket, inadvertently putting all her weight on him and pulling him down along with her as she toppled over onto the floor.

"You're so gross." Oliver held back a gag as he sat up, throwing her gunk off of him and immediately stripping down to his underwear so he didn't have to deal with trying to wash her out of it, knowing eventually it would come out when she woke up.

She would get up again at some point. He figured this was the equivalent of taking a nap for her. A really gross, gooey nap.

So, he just sat on the couch and turned on the T.V. to drown out her nonsense talk and messed around on his phone.

After a couple of hours, she was still mostly a puddle on the floor, and the boy let his attention wander off to the bean she apparently needed so badly. *It probably isn't best to mess with it.* It didn't look like anything other than a kind of squishy oval tomato that wasn't quite ripe yet.

You don't need to mess with it.

Oliver reached over to the end table and plucked the bean up to inspect it for himself. It was small and soft and ridiculously hot. It didn't even look like something important. And he couldn't really figure out how she used it to see or hear. *Unless it's just...her.*

He held it up in the light to see if it was like a sort of shell and a much tinier version of her would be silhouetted against it, like those pictures of embryos in textbooks.

It wasn't, but there was something dark and round inside it, and he was absolutely certain he saw it beat like a heart.

He closed his fingers around the little object and felt his stomach curdle at a memory that rose up to the front of his head. He'd hit her right on the nose with a rock. And felt good about it.

He hadn't realized he hit her so hard or that she was actually so small. *No wonder she made herself so terrifying, I could have probably, accidentally, killed her.*

Two black fingers gently reached down from over his head and pulled the bean out of his hand. Oliver looked up at where a still-a-little goopy and amorphous Dindet stood behind him, slowly beginning to regain color.

"Sorry." Was the first thing out of her mouth, but he was more inclined to ignore the useless apology.

"That little orange thing is just *you*, isn't it?" he asked instead. She shrugged, still looking rather tired and maybe even a little uncomfortable at the notion.

"Yeah..."

"Like, your heart, and brain and everything? It's so...small." He held up his hand. "Smaller than the palm of my hand."

"Yeah..."

Nightmare Fuel

Oliver turned around and held up a polaroid picture of a beach ball he had taken a few summers back.

"What colors do you see?" he asked, pushing it a little closer to the clown so that she might see better. She cocked her head and furrowed her brow.

"Mostly yellow? Some browns and blues and a little bit of purple-pink. Oh, and black." She nodded with affirmation, and Oliver shook his head.

"I mean in the picture," he clarified, handing her the photo so she'd be at least somewhat less confused, and headed to change into pajamas.

"It's just a bunch of lines on white." She turned around and raised an eyebrow. "Why are we doing this?"

"Because." Oliver popped his head out of the closet. "I think you might be colorblind…or your *species* might be?"

The clown frowned and looked back at the photo, quizzically holding it up to inspect it harder. "I can see colors just fine, though."

"All right"—Oliver came back out of the closet and pulled up a tuft of his hair—"what color is my hair?"

The clown stared at him, and her frown grew in her almost spiteful silence.

"Blue."

"No." Oliver brushed the tuft back down and made his way over toward her. "It's blond."

She rolled her eyes and let out a disgruntled little huff. "I don't see why this is so important."

"It just explains a lot, is all." He took the photo out of her hands and went to pin it back onto his corkboard next to other photos he had taken. "If you can't see stuff, that's okay. It just means you need to be more careful."

When he glanced back at her, she looked baffled by the idea, like she was offended almost. Oliver let out a tired sigh and gestured at his nightstand lamp. "Can you see this?"

He pulled the string and turned the lamp on, creating an orangey hue that filled up half the wall. Dindet's silence spoke volumes, so he flipped it back off and sat down on the bed next to her.

"See? If you can't see the difference between light and dark, how are you supposed to know if a car is coming at night? Or if it's lightning outside? And that's probably why you don't sleep either."

Dindet averted her eyes and turned away from him in quiet shame. "It's not like I was supposed to know that. It doesn't make any difference to me."

"Except it does," Oliver argued gently. "That place we got trapped in was nothing but white, empty space. You would have been completely blind if you were alone."

He tugged at his sleeve a little to hide the edge of his bandage. "That doesn't scare you?"

She didn't answer and instead kept looking away from him, lightly pulling at her fingers and letting the floaty bits circle around before they reconnected.

She was small and fragile, and Oliver caught on fairly quickly that she really didn't like to look at herself as such. He couldn't help but feel concerned, though, and he caught himself staring at her real self in their shared silence.

"There are tons of people out there who can't do things the same way as most." He tried his best to comfort her. "You shouldn't feel bad about it."

He half-bit his tongue at the last bit of his words. *She probably wouldn't feel bad about it if I hadn't brought it up in the first place.*

Dindet nodded and smiled half-heartedly. "It's okay."

Her voice almost cracked as she spoke, but her smile didn't fade, and she hopped up off the bed with a little twirl and rippled in an effort to conceal her colors. "I don't feel bad at all!"

She was a terrible liar, but he let it slide. He had a feeling she was intentionally avoiding him now, and he wasn't particularly in the mood to pry about it.

Oliver was certain she was purposefully derailing topics concerning herself, growing more and more estranged when he asked where she went at night.

Dindet never actually budged on the subject and remained adamant that whatever it was she was up to wasn't important.

Except it was, otherwise she wouldn't have been out, and she wouldn't have lost her bean, and he wouldn't be lying in his bed, racking his brain trying to figure out what she was doing in the middle of the night—why she knew things that she shouldn't possibly know.

He sat up and turned his lamp on, deciding to go check on her to make sure she wasn't doing something dumb. It was around two in the morning, so if she were helping his dad, they would have been done now.

Oliver snuck down the stairs and peered over the back of the couch to see if she might have cocooned herself up in the quilt like the last time. He pulled back the blanket, and she wasn't there.

He felt his heart almost skip a beat, and he hesitantly turned to see if she maybe was sitting outside on the back porch. She wasn't.

It must have been twenty degrees out with the windchill that whipped through him when he stepped outside and did a brief barefoot perimeter check around the house to look for the clown.

If she were anywhere close, though, he didn't expect to see her in the dark. The only light nearby was the streetlamp at the end of the road, and, considering the alien couldn't perceive light, it wouldn't serve much help to draw her in.

A few minutes in, he felt his toes start to go numb in the frosty grass, so Oliver ran back inside to grab a jacket, flashlight, and some warm shoes before sneaking out the front door. First, he started down the road, waving around the flashlight at the tree line to see if she went over toward the suburbs past the woods. He'd check that way second if she didn't show up anywhere nearby.

"Dindet!" He called, and as expected, there wasn't an answer. He flashed his light over Douglass's house, shining it into blackened windows before moving it down to the bushes around and searching the shadows for movement. Nothing.

Oliver stopped and turned back toward his house. None of the lights were on, which meant his dad was definitely sacked out.

He glanced back toward the streetlamp that flooded the junction between the main road and his with an eerily soft blue glow that flickered on occasion.

Most of the time, he didn't think about where he lived and how dark it got just a few miles away from town. How isolated it was, off down a backroad and halfway into a forest of eighty-foot pine trees and even taller mountains that blocked out the light from the cookie-cutter neighborhood just forty acres away.

Only now did he really think about it.

Oliver shivered and headed back toward his house, veering off the side of the road and down a well-enough-tread dirt path he and Douglass used to use to get to the cliffside on the other side of the woods. He steadily kept the light trained on the ground, only occasionally swinging it out into the dense treeline when he thought he heard something.

Owls. Probably.

He wasn't scared, of course. There wasn't a reason to be. There weren't any monsters out to get him. No ghosts or creatures that kidnapped you and drove you insane, like Douglass mentioned once. There wasn't anything dangerous out here. *Except for Dindet.*

Oliver ignored his growing tension at the silence of the night, focusing only on the dirt in front of him until he reached the open field that ran down a steep hill; it broke the woods for a few acres before trees came back.

From the top of the hill, he could see the suburbs, illuminated by strings of way too early Christmas lights and street lamps.

The stars were miraculously bright for the night, and a large, orangey-red full moon hung in the sky, only blotched out when stringy clouds rolled by. It was peaceful and empty, far less claustrophobic than the forest ahead.

"DINDET, ARE YOU OUT HERE?!" His voice carried across the plain, and he heard a few birds flutter out of their nests at the sudden break in silence.

She probably isn't, but yesterday night she made it all the way to the power transformer, so it isn't out of the question. He was determined to figure out what she was hiding. What she was doing when she left.

Oliver scanned his light over the treeline at the edge of the field. The trail broke off here. He would need to find the old creek that ran behind the other neighborhood on his own. Hopefully, it wasn't flooded after the hailstorm.

He made his way down, picking up speed until he was nearly sprinting out of control down the hill. He braced himself for impact, smacking into a tree with his arms out to buffer the impact. It hurt, a lot, to put that much pressure on his still-healing wounds, but if he was bleeding, he couldn't tell.

Oliver made his way into the second half of the woods, back

into the dark shadows of the trees, in blind search of the creek bed that led to the houses.

This part may have been closer to people, but it was larger and far less familiar than the woods outside his own house, and Oliver quickly found himself turned around in a little empty patch of dirt surrounded by tall, spindly trees. He couldn't help but focus on the noises around him. The sound of crickets, the chirping of frogs, and occasionally the scrambling of something jumping around in the branches of trees.

And then it stopped.

Oliver drew in a faint gasp, feeling the hair on the back of his neck rise up in dread at whatever made the noise of the night halt. He didn't want to move, let alone shine his light anywhere around him, for fear of what it might illuminate.

Whatever it was, he knew it was watching him, biding its time.

It could be a mountain lion. Those are native around here. Or a bear, which is significantly worse.

A quiet, guttural clicking noise rose around him, and he felt his heart drop to his feet and every single muscle in his body clench. *Run. You need to RUN.*

The noise was behind him. Materializing closer to him and in his terror, Oliver turned the light off. Some terribly small and probably stupid part of him hoped that it would make it lose sight of him in the darkness.

It didn't.

He held his breath and clutched the light close to his chest, coming up with a plan to distract and probably hit the creature with the light and bolt while it was down. It was an awful plan, and he was 100% sure he was going to be eaten, but it was better than just letting yourself get eaten.

The soft growling stopped for a bit, almost long enough that Oliver might have thought the creature passed him entirely, until it dripped down from above him, louder than ever.

It was dark, incredibly dark, and if it weren't for the moonlight, he wouldn't have been subjected to seeing its long, sharp fingers and claws that spidered down from the trees and waved around his head, popping and cracking as they bent in front of his face.

That's not a mountain lion.

Or a bear.

He trembled, taking in short, shallow breaths that didn't serve any purpose other than worsening the horror.

The thing splayed out its fingers and began wrapping long, gangly arms around him that weaved around themselves, contorting in ways not humanly possible as it pressed its hands into the dirt and lowered itself even closer, to the point that he could hear its voracious salivating next to his ear.

In less than a second, and what felt like twelve minutes, Oliver flipped on the flashlight and spun around, chunking it hard into the monster's face and catching a glimpse of its pale, wide, and wild eyes.

He bolted out from under its reach and ran as fast as he could manage, tears streaming down his face until he slammed into his back door and forced it open.

He didn't even bother to take off his jacket or dwell at all, for that matter. He sprinted upstairs instead, tossing himself into bed and pulling his blanket over in a frantic effort to be as unseeable as possible.

The house was quiet, and for a bit, he felt safe, until he heard the soft and horrible creak of his bedroom door open. He clamped his eyes shut and kept his entire body taut and covered in blankets, silently praying for the night to be over as he heard footsteps coming closer and felt a weight pull on the blanket and impress into the mattress near his leg.

"Oliver?"

He opened his eyes and nervously peeked over the blanket to

see Dindet staring at him with worried eyes. She was almost black against the darkness of his room, but he could make out her pasty face.

Slowly, he lowered his blanket and stared at her before fumbling in the dark to turn on the lamp and flooding the room in a soft orange glow.

"Oliver, I'm so sorry I didn't realize—"

"That was *you*?" He interrupted, exhaling just about all the air in his lungs. She lowered her head and looked away from him in regret, and he noticed her clench talon-like claws into a ball in her lap.

"I...I'm so sorry.."

Girlfriend
Boyfriend

Six in the morning, still dark out, but Oliver's eyes popped open regardless, almost expecting to see the clown somewhere invading his personal space, especially after her third near-consumption of him. She wasn't, though. In fact, she was nowhere to be seen.

Groggily, he sat up and rubbed the sting from his eyes and blinked away leftover sleep. He still ached.

Considerably, and sometime in the night, he rolled over on one of his sides and accidentally bled through his shirt and into his bedsheets.

Oliver threw off his covers and began unbuttoning his nightshirt, tossing it onto his bed before fumbling in the dark toward the bathroom and temporarily blinding himself with the light when he flipped it on.

It didn't look as bad as he expected. A stain on his tank top, and his right arm was crusty with dried blood, the left was less so, but his gauze had unraveled a decent amount.

He pushed the door closed with his back and began gingerly

taking off his badly kept bandages, throwing them in the trash in exchange for new ones.

After another run under water and gentle scrubbing, followed by a quality slathering of antibiotic cream, he wrapped them up again and tested with a few incredibly painful flexes.

Then, he moved on to clothes, quickly realizing a grave repercussion that, up until this very moment, he hadn't even thought of.

There's no way. He wouldn't be able to get it on, let alone take it off without accidentally tearing either it, or himself.

The boy grimaced, staring at the binder he held up, knowing exactly how aggravating it was to put on *without* being in pain. He didn't want to imagine trying *with* it. And he'd already gone through every last one of his more easily removable ones.

Today is going to be a really bad day.

Reluctantly, he threw on the baggiest sweater that fit the weather, which went over at least two other shirts before he frumped downstairs for breakfast, catching Dindet just as she tried to discreetly slide the back door shut.

"What are you doing?" His frank tone made her jump, and she swiveled around with a small startle.

"Feeding…the, uhm, cats." She was an awful liar, but he didn't have the patience to chastise her when he already knew she had been out hunting. He just didn't know *what*.

Just about as immediately as she saw him, Dindet tasted something weird. She couldn't exactly put a name to it, but it was something she recognized as entirely unpleasant.

She followed him to the kitchen, resting her elbows on the island while she watched him meagerly pull out his cinnamon toasts and grow increasingly more uncomfortable with whatever strange feeling he had.

"Oliver, you taste really weird. Are you okay?" She asked, leaning a bit over the counter. The boy turned around and almost slammed his bowl onto the island when he set it down.

"I want you to think really long and hard about what just came out of your mouth, and *never* say it to me ever again."

Dindet clamped her mouth shut and nodded, still a little shocked at his mean attitude. He wasn't mad, though, and she could see the hole in him wasn't fluctuating as violently as it could.

After an extraordinarily quiet breakfast, the two of them began the trek to the bus stop where Douglass was already standing, looking particularly drowsy.

"Hey-aahhh…guys." he yawned, waving as they walked toward him. He dropped his hand, already starting his morning monologue. "Sorry I didn't wait up, I've been up all night helping my dadOliveryou'renotwearing—"

Oliver smacked his hand over Douglass's mouth, briefly ignoring the ache of his arm, and quickly spun him around and away from the clown.

"I swear to god Douglass, if you say a single word about it, I am going to sneak into your room tonight and personally burn every last copy of Jane Austen you own," he threatened softly before pulling his hand away and retreating back to an even more confused looking Dindet.

If Douglass wasn't already a well-meaning thorn in his side, and Dindet wasn't bobbing around him trying to figure out what his deal was in the most annoying ways possible, the day may have been slightly more manageable. But alas, Murphy's law struck Oliver and struck him hard.

***

"Class, my name is Mrs. Schreuder." A short, old, and angry-looking woman stood at the front of the classroom, with her hair tied up in a bun so tight she was showing signs of tension alopecia. It didn't matter what her name was, even as she harshly wrote it out on the whiteboard. She was infamous. She was The Bun Lady.

"I will be your substitute teacher for Mrs. Hardgreeves today."

She practically yelled every word she said, probably because she hadn't turned on her hearing aids, or she just liked to be loud—as well as mean. "We will begin with roll call."

Immediately, Oliver slouched down and crammed his face into his desk, dreading the very thought, and that dread just about doubled each time she called a student's name as she went down the list, knowing he would be one of the very last ones called.

"Denise, Dindi...Din—"

"Dindet." Cassidy corrected, causing the woman to snap her head in her direction with a scowl.

"I know how to pronounce it, thank you, Miss Trombone," she retorted roughly, and Cassidy's whole face screwed up with anger. The substitute flagrantly ignored her second correction, repeating the clown's name once more and marking her here when Dindet finally replied after a decent moment of trying to figure out what was going on.

She was far more distracted by Oliver and his ever-increasing anxiety until it seemed to come to a head with one utterance.

"Olivia," The Bun Lady called, and in less than a second, every single student had their eyes trained on Oliver while he was not so very discreetly banging his head on his desk. "Olivia?"

The boy let out an incredibly soft whimper and sat upright to call a meager 'here' before just as quickly sinking back into the depths of his dysphoria and returning to his rhythmic and gentle head banging.

This was something he had thought at some point he would become accustomed to. Of course, he usually had something else to distract him. Most of the time, it was Dindet being ludicrous but right now, he wanted nothing more than to rip his skin off and crawl out of the shell like an eldritch beast.

On the bright side, the class was just going to watch a movie, and as soon as English was over, every other teacher would address him correctly.

So, Oliver relegated all his attention toward his sketchbook and kept his head low as best he could. At least until a ruler smacked down hard in front of him. He jerked up and met eyes with The Bun Lady as she scoured him with not-so-discreet judgement. "Young lady, you need to pay attention. No doodling in class."

Oliver stared up at the substitute teacher, still reeling from the slight startle, and gulped dryly. His skin crawled under her glare, and he slowly closed his sketchbook and set it aside, at which point she lifted up her ruler and went on to hopefully torment anyone other than him.

Dindet sat quietly behind him, still in the process of trying to figure out why his flavor was so distinctly unpalatable, until Douglass interrupted her struggle with an elbow to the side that was almost hard enough to pierce her completely.

"He's gonna be like this all day," he whispered, briefly pulling her attention away. "It was a lot worse when he first came out."

Of course, she had no idea what he was talking about.

As soon as the bell rang, Oliver bolted out of his desk and went straight for the hall pass before making a beeline down the hall to get as far away from everyone as possible.

He veered left, then right, walking at a slowly increasing pace until he finally whipped around to give a dagger glare at whoever he felt following him

"What do you want?!" he snapped, though just as quickly, all the breath fell out of his lungs at Douglass's startled face.

"Hey—"

"S-sorry," Oliver dropped his gaze immediately, folding his arms gingerly over his chest to hide it. "Thought you were someone else."

"It's all right. Bun Lady sucks…" Douglass gave a soft smile, rounding Oliver's side to walk with him wherever he intended to go. "You skipping again?"

185

"Probably," he muttered, allowing the boy to follow him down the mostly empty halls. "I just got stressed out in class and needed some air. You don't have to follow me around."

"What if I want to?" Douglass butted into his side softly, garnering a reluctant smile from Oliver as he thought about it.

"Don't really have anywhere to go," he argued, albeit very unenthusiastically. "There's the Make-Out Closet, I guess?"

"Or the bathroom again?"

"I can't," Oliver huffed, taking a left down the hall that led to one of the furthest wings of the school. "I've been caught like three times already, and I'm pretty sure Bradshaw will start chaining me to that stupid unisex one if she catches me again."

"It's *literally* on the other side of the school. It takes less than half the time just to go to the ones right down B Hall." Douglass gave a sarcastic roll of his eyes at the rule. "It's stupid that they make you do that."

Oliver responded with nothing more than an ambivalent sigh and turned down the hall that would eventually lead to that dumb bathroom. "It is what it is...I don't mind hanging out there for a while, though."

He made it to the door and stuck his personal key in, swinging it wide and gesturing for Douglass to go in before he followed suit and promptly plopped down on the floor. Perks of being the only one with access meant it was always significantly cleaner, so Oliver lay back and splayed out on the tiles, staring up at the buzzing fluorescent lights.

"Look at you being a *bad kid*, skipping class with a delinquent," he said, his gaze flickering back to Douglass as he slid down against the wall opposite of him. "Pretty soon, your grades'll start slipping, and *you'll* be the one walking around with an emotional support clown."

Douglass chuckled. "I dunno. I think I like the influence."

Oliver felt a smile creep across his face at the idea, but it fell as his thoughts moved toward the notion. He *was* a bad influence. For both of them. *That's probably why she keeps leaving.*

"I wanna rip my skin off." He decided to change the subject, hoping it would hurt less than the slow realization that everyone was just...going away.

Douglass leaned forward, blocking out Oliver's view of the light with his concerned face.

Oliver watched as his look softened and he leaned back, prompting him to worm his way toward Douglass until he rested his head on his stomach and dumbly fiddled with his thumbs. "Like...full body circumcision."

"That sounds *awful*," his friend answered softly, adjusting his position so Oliver sat more comfortably against him. He still laughed a bit at the word choice, though. "Weird question—if you had uh...*you know*, would it even be circumcised? Like—like if it grew overnight or something?"

Oliver snorted and tilted his head back to look at him. "Douglass, if I grew a penis overnight, I'm pretty sure the *first* thing I would do is jack off. I don't think I'd even stop to see if it came with a foreskin. Also, *gross*. Why would you want to know?"

"I—I mean, like, I just wanted to know, not for any, like, weird reason." The boy's whole face turned red at Oliver's response, and Douglass stumbled over his words. "Plus, don't they have surgery for that sort of thing also? I figured you'd want that too."

"I—" Oliver stopped himself and sank back down into his friend's stomach. "I haven't decided on that yet. I just know...I...I don't ever wanna...have a baby."

There was something solemn in his voice that gave Douglass pause. He clearly hadn't even thought about that. That Oliver had even thought about it. *That I have to think about it and he just...doesn't.*

"I...I'm sorry I asked," Douglass murmured. Oliver rolled over to face him and stared at him for a couple of seconds before his gaze drifted down, and he focused on Douglass's hand on the tile.

"It's all right," he said, taking his hand and picking the dirt out of his fingers methodically. "I can be okay…with what I have for now."

"I think you'd be a good dad, though," Douglass mumbled softly, only paying attention to the way Oliver stared intently at his fingers.

"You *say* that," he retorted, not looking up. "I'd probably be worse than Matthew."

"Or better than Jon." Douglass countered gently, "You *do* adopt every stray you see."

"That doesn't mean I'm good."

"Doesn't mean you're bad either." Douglass pulled his hand out of Oliver's grasp and gestured for him to sit up so he could lie down on his back.

Oliver dropped back on top of him with an indignant little exhale and took his hand back. He was quiet for a while, playing with Douglass's fingers as he thought about how he wanted to broach the subject. How much he didn't want to hurt him in the process.

"I wouldn't *actually* burn all your books…by the way," Oliver said in lieu of what he wanted to.

"I know."

"I…" Oliver pressed his friend's palm into his face, hesitating and trying very hard to swallow down the rocks in his throat. *It's going to hurt him. You're going to hurt him…* "I think I like him…Markus…"

Douglass drew in a long, deep breath, the kind that lifted Oliver's head and lowered it back down with the exhale. But he didn't respond. Instead, the only thing Oliver heard from him was the slow pace-up in the rhythmic beat of his heart.

"I'm sorry…" he continued, much softer, "I know…you

wanted me to be your girlfriend before...but you're—"

"It's all right," Douglass's voice was choked up, but there was still something so kind in it. He lifted his hand from Oliver's face and brushed his fingers through the boy's hair. "I like—I like being your friend still."

Oliver nodded slightly, and his eyes drifted up to him. Douglass stared at the wall with the softest smile on his face that was so clearly meant to hide how much he hurt. *How much I hurt him.*

He is a good kid. A good person. Too good. And I'm...not.

"Douglass—"

"The lunch bell's gonna ring soon," Douglass interrupted, finally turning his gaze back to Oliver. It made him feel so unbelievably small, the way he looked at him. Like beneath that constant warmth and kindness sat so much rage. Instinctively, Oliver shrank back and moved to sit on his knees.

"Right...yeah, I—I should go..." He stood up and backed toward the door. "I—I'm sorry."

Pain of Progress

Douglass waited so very patiently for Oliver to leave, despite wanting nothing more than for him to stay there, lying on top of him and letting him play with his hair. No matter how much it utterly devastated him.

He numbly pressed his palms into his face after the door had closed, dragging them down his cheeks in order to stop himself from choking on that ugly and painful ache in his throat. It wasn't fair. It wasn't fair, and he was so *unbelievably* mad that Oliver couldn't see that he was *right here*. That *he* liked him. That *he* wanted him. Wanted to be around him. *All the time!*

And Oliver was so stupid and naive and such an *idiot* to pine after some boy he'd only just met. It wasn't fair.

Stop it. Stop being jealous. Douglass drew in a breath to calm himself down, but even that made his whole chest ache and cave in like he had had his ribs torn open and his heart ripped out.

It didn't matter, though…how much it hurt. Whether Oliver could even comprehend how *hard* just being around him was. None of it mattered because he didn't like him back. Not in the way Douglass did.

And the thing that made it so much worse was that Douglass tried so incredibly hard NOT to feel the way he did. To stand back and let him do whatever he wanted, to not get hurt when Oliver lied and hid things and pretended.

It hurt so much more watching him run around in circles trying to find something that was always right next to him, but he just *could not see*.

***

"Oh, look at this, Douglass!" His father cut through Douglass's thoughts and spun around, handing him a piece of paper he had torn off from the test results. He'd been messing around with whatever goop they found around the house after Oliver came by to pick up Dindet's weird orange thing. "There are tons of electrodes bouncing around in this stuff! I wonder if it's conductive."

The scientist quickly moved to another machine that somewhat resembled a coffeemaker and dropped a dose of the matter into the glass casing, setting it to fifteen amps.

The machine whirred up with a high-pitched squealing noise, and a small arc of electricity shot down into the substance, causing it to spike out like an urchin and redirect the current out toward the glass.

Chris promptly shut it off and shot a wide, happy grin at his son.

"I think I found what I need for my machine!" He remarked, pouring out the now liquified matter into another test tube as he licked a label and taped it across the glass. "I don't know what Jon made, but I'll have to stop by to ask him if he has more of it."

Douglass passively tinkered with the tubes of matter, only half listening to what his father was raving on about.

"You really think he'd give it to you?" he asked absent-mindedly. He picked up the test tube his dad had just set down and inspected it closely. "He might need it for his project, too."

"I doubt it—if he synthesized it for his molecular transporter, he wouldn't have let me take the sample in the first place. I think it's a side project the lab had him start on, or he just wanted to play around with his chemistry set. You know how he is."

"I don't, Dad," Douglass replied hollowly. His father had a habit of forgetting that he wasn't actually his lab assistant, and never knew what his coworker did in his free time, and on top of that, Oliver rarely mentioned any of it to him. Come to think of it, he seemed to avoid the topic altogether.

"Right, right, Kistle and Abadi would have a hoot hearing about all the help you've done," his father mused as he left the garage to grab something from the kitchen to snack on. "Oh, by the way, they're headed over to have a few drinks tonight if you want to join us?"

"I'm good…" Douglass heaved a tired sigh and began idly reorganizing his father's tools, at least until he felt a hand over his shoulder followed by a gentle embrace.

"What's going on? You're never this spacey." Chris pulled his son away from his busy work, and almost immediately, the boy's fragile facade crumbled, and his face twisted up in torment.

"I like Oliver! I like him so, *so* much but he doesn't—he doesn't *like* me like that! He likes this—this other guy and I—I don't know what to do, Dad!" Douglass practically fell into his father, clinging to him and leaving the man in a baffled stupor as he rambled on about all his pent-up feelings. "I know it's bad. I know how Gary talks about him and—and how Mom—"

"Douglass," Chris stopped him and filed his hands between the two of them, pulling his son away so he could look him in the eyes. "It's *okay*."

"But—he's not a girl anymore…"

"And that's *okay*, son." Chris offered a kind smile and wrapped his boy in the tightest embrace he possibly could. "It's okay that you like him. It's okay to like boys, or girls, or both, or *whatever you like*, Douglass."

"You're not mad?" he questioned feebly, his voice muffled in his father's chest. Chris dropped down and planted a kiss on the top of his son's head, prompting him to break up with another little sob. "I tried—I tried really hard to stop…I'm sorry."

"Don't be sorry, Douglass. I'm not mad." his dad pulled his fingers through the boy's curls, easing his trembling ever so slightly. "I know you. I'd never be mad about that, and you have no reason to be sorry, son."

"What—" Douglass shifted in his arms to look at him. "What do I do? He doesn't like me. He likes someone else."

His father's face softened with a look of pure understanding, but he offered a gentle smile, regardless. "Do what you've been doing."

Douglass stared at him for a few moments, trying to process all his messy and confused thoughts at once. "But I'm so *mad* at him. I'm so mad that—that he doesn't even care. He doesn't even know how stupid he's being. *He's gonna get hurt.*"

"And you can't stop him," his father added, prompting Douglass to pause and think about the words coming out of his mouth for a second. "You can't control him or make him do what you want. Oliver is a whole separate person from you. I get that it makes you mad, and it hurts a lot...It hurt a lot when Missy left me for Gary…but it wasn't my place to make her stay if she didn't want to…and we both understood that."

"So I should just…let him?"

"You should *be there* for him," his dad corrected. "If he gets hurt, you can still be there for him. Even if he doesn't like you like that, you can still be his friend."

"I don't want to *just* be his friend, though," Douglass whined softly, "I want to be more. I *like* him. I like being around him and I—today—today we hung out. Like we used to, you know? I got to hold him, and I *like* that. I *like* getting to play with his hair and—and talk and when he holds my hand…"

Douglass paused, his thoughts collecting on his feelings in a little pile in his mind. The things he liked the most about Oliver were so small and silly, and most of them were just…gone. "I asked him out before already…right before the accident."

His father made a noise, and Douglass continued. "He's so…different now. And I don't know what to do or—or how to fix it. It's like he stopped existing after what happened, and he *won't* talk to me anymore. I can't tell if it's because of me or because of his mom or Matthew, or something else. It's not like Jojo."

"Douglass," Chris's voice drew his attention, and his dad pet his head softly, pressing into him just a bit before he spoke again. "Losing Jojo was very different from the kind of loss Oliver feels right now. You can't expect him to deal with it the same way we did. It's…harder…when it's so sudden."

"I know, it's just—it's like he's pretending it never happened. Like she'll just come back or something, and the way he talks about it—" Douglass hesitated slightly. "He talks about these *awful* things like they're normal. Like it doesn't even matter. It's like he doesn't even hear what comes out of his mouth sometimes."

"He's had a very different—difficult life, son. How often do you talk to him about Jojo?"

Almost never. Douglass dipped his head in shame at the thought. Maybe he was asking too much. Expecting more than what Oliver was willing to give. Expecting him to work and function and deal with things the same way he did without even thinking about all the differences that divided them.

Oliver *wasn't* him. Plain and simple. He was a lot of things: angry and bitter, sad and lonely. Afraid. But he dealt with that in a vastly different way than Douglass did. Oliver coped with his existence in a way that—to Douglass—didn't make any sense.

"I think…" Douglass pulled away from his father, taking an extra step to gather his thoughts and wipe away stray tears. "I think I need to think about some stuff…"

***

Oliver sat at his desk, numb beyond belief and trying desperately to figure out a way to fix it.

He tugged at a few pieces of sketch paper until they fell out in a pile on his desk and then rummaged through them for one that was hopefully mostly empty. Most of them were animals and cartoons he had doodled before the accident.

He thumbed through them until his eye caught something he didn't recall drawing at all. It was a picture of a jester, uncolored, and it was kind of creepy, with a wide black smile and slitted eyes. He crumpled it up and threw it in the trash along with other unfinished works so he could start on something new.

Time melted away when he drew, and he had a habit of putting his face so close to the paper that he was practically touching the desk with his nose. It wasn't until the sun started setting and his own shadow kept him from being able to see that he stopped to turn on a light and see the finished result.

It was a pretty simple picture of Dindet sitting out on the back porch with all the cats gathered around. Just a dumb thing he thought of, but he liked the calm of it. It was the only thing he could think to draw at the moment.

He leaned back in his chair for a stretch and turned to look at the door, taking a small moment of hesitation before making the decision to check on the two of them toiling in the attic.

Oliver stood up and quietly made his way up to the attic door, listening to the murmurs from behind it.

"After this, after my wife comes back. You have to go. It's not saf—"

Oliver pushed the door open, cutting off anything else from being said as he walked in and ignored their staring.

"How close are you?" he asked, looking at the machine in the center of the room as opposed to either of them.

"By the end of the month," his father replied, not looking up from the control panel he was rewiring. Dindet was busying herself, taking pieces out of her and making components that had been drawn up on blueprints, but it was easy to see her rippling and struggling to stay together.

Oliver nodded and swiftly turned heel, flashing a glare at his father before he slammed the door shut behind him.

He grit his teeth, expecting quick retaliation, and when it didn't happen, he returned to his room to sulk for the night.

He tried to go to sleep but only really tossed and turned until he flipped his lamp on and just sat there, staring at the wall, thinking about how stupid his dad was being.

It wasn't his fault or Dindet's that he was so obsessed with that stupid machine. But to Jon, it was like none of that mattered. Nothing mattered except getting Marie back, and everything else got in the way of that. *Including me. I want her back, too. I miss her too.*

Oliver grabbed his phone, flipping through windows to get to his messages, when he stopped and hovered over the two most recent conversations. One pathetic apology he'd sent to Douglass after ripping his heart out and ditching him in the bathroom. It sat with a little gray box that said 'read' in the bottom corner. And no response.

The other conversation was with Markus. A long and meandering one that they shared in the middle of the night a few days prior.

The boy drew in a soft breath, quietly deliberating on which of them he could use as a temporary source of dopamine. A little distraction.

Lightning Storm

"There is a severe lightning storm about ten kilometers out, heading north toward the greater Henison area. It should disperse by three this morning. But in the meantime, prepare for heavy showers."

Jon leaned forward, filing his fingers together as he watched the meteorologist sway about in front of their green screen, gesturing vaguely toward a large color-coded blob that represented cloud cover.

"It comes from the sky?" Dindet didn't sound particularly uncomfortable, but bits of her spiked up at the thought of it. She already couldn't see it, and now it came from essentially nowhere.

"It's not that bad," Oliver remarked, flipping the television over to some cartoons to distract her. It would have worked, too, if his dad hadn't taken the remote and changed it right back.

"She has every right to be worried, son." Jon retorted, "and it looks like it's headed right to us. We might have to trip the breakers so we don't blow the fuse box."

Oliver rolled his eyes and let out a small grunt.

"I was just trying to help," he muttered under his breath, trudging over to the door to grab a raincoat. He gestured for the clown to stay put and headed out into the wind and rain to turn off half the power to the house.

It was a bad one. The wind shot right through him, and sleet blasted his face the second he stepped out into the rain. Oliver hurried to the breaker box and flipped off all the least important ones, then quickly ran back into the now-dark house.

Jon was already making rounds, lighting candles along the walls and handing out flashlights, while the severe storm warning rolled across the television screen, saying something about wind and rain, and a hail warning.

"She won't need that," Oliver said, interrupting his dad before he handed another flashlight to the clown. "She can't see light."

Jon nodded and set the light back down on the coffee table, heading off toward the kitchen for some leftover kindling for the fireplace.

"When it storms really bad, we have to turn the power off. Since it's not part of the city, it'll get fried if there's too much lightning," Oliver explained, though it didn't really seem to calm her nerves.

Dindet nodded, glancing out the window in a futile attempt to see the lightning that crashed into the dirt a few miles away. Thunder rolled over their heads, making her jump and draw in a false breath.

Oliver shook his light a bit, aiming it up at the ceiling to check for any potential leaks. The last time it was this bad, he and his mom had to pull out the pots and pans, but the whole roof of the cabin was replaced a couple of years ago when they built the room extensions.

"There's nothing to be afraid of. Lightning probably won't hit the house," he comforted, shining the light back at the clown so he could see her better. He didn't think she believed him— because she was all spiky and changing color every time the thunder cracked.

He moved to close the back door curtains so the thunder

would be slightly more muffled and directed her over to the couch to sit while his dad started up a fire.

Dindet kept to herself, scrunched up on the other side of the couch, twiddling her thumbs and trying very hard to not spike out every time the humming started and the thunder clapped. She didn't like it, not a single bit, and she could only hear it getting louder as the storm came closer.

"Hey." Oliver tapped her foot lightly, drawing her attention away from small terrors that picked at her mind. "If you count between the thunder, that tells you how many miles away it is."

He waited for another sound of thunder and began counting up to five before another racket sounded over them.

"See? It's still five miles away." He smiled, hoping that if she knew that, she would stop being so worried about it. Though, he knew she wasn't afraid of the thunder at all.

Dindet nodded a bit stiffly, counting quietly on her fingers between the next clap of thunder and holding up a three for him to see until she stopped and a terrible look of fear flitted across her face.

"Do you hear that?" she asked, swiveling her head around to find where the much closer hum was coming from, concern growing in her eyes.

Oliver cocked his head, "Hear what—"

Before he could even finish, a strike of lightning landed down just a few hundred feet from the house, and before the thunder followed, the clown had completely vanished.

"Dad?!" Oliver called, leaning over the back of the couch to see him coming downstairs with a bunch of old blueprints as fire fodder.

"Where's Dindet?" Jon asked, briefly glancing around in the semi-lit living room for the alien. Oliver stood up, already shining his flashlight into the darker corners.

"The lightning scared her. I think she went to hide somewhere." It was the only thing that made much sense. If she hid from the microwave, she would probably hide from lightning too.

Jon set his papers down on the hearth and shined his flashlight up toward the attic, in case she was somewhere along the loft walkway. "You don't think she went to that, what is it—In-Between place?"

"No," Oliver shook his head, creeping over toward his parents' room. "Time is really slow there, so it would take longer for the storm to pass."

She wasn't in his parent's room, or bathroom, or the closet. So, he shined his light into the kitchen to see if she might be there. Jon began up the stairs, only to stop halfway to answer a phone call with a small curse under his breath.

"It's the lab. Chris is up there and says it's urgent." He hollered downstairs for his kid to hear, "I have to go. Hold down the fort while I'm out?"

"You sure?" Oliver shined his light up to see him nod, already scrambling back down the stairs to grab his keys and coat.

"It could be about the accident," he answered, halfway out the door. Oliver let out a small grumble of disagreement and started up where his dad had left off.

The storm was right on top of them now, and he could hear the wind howling through the cracks in the walls. It shook the windows. He headed up to the attic and briefly shined the light in, long enough to startle some of the mice still in their cages, but short enough that he didn't have to linger in the doorway.

"Dindet?" he called, moving back toward his room and rolling a spotlight over the corners. If she were here, he couldn't hear her.

Oliver crouched down, checking his bed just in case she squeezed herself under it. "It's okay if you're scared. You don't have to hide!"

No answer. And she wasn't under the bed.

"Did you go In-Between?" he asked, kind of hoping she had,

either way, he shined his light into his bathroom and pushed the shower curtain aside to see if she found a hidey-hole there.

Disappointed, he went back into his room, at a loss as to where she was until another crack of lightning hit a nearby tree, and he heard a stifled whimper from his closet.

Oliver whipped around and shined his light under the door. A shadow moved behind it.

"Are you in here?" he asked softly, more to himself than her as he pulled the door open, only to freeze in quiet astonishment at the state of the clown.

Dindet sat huddled back, half under his clothes, curled up as best as she could be, while trying to contain the parts of her that jutted out in dangerous spikes over her whole body. She made small noises, whimpers that turned into gagged-up half screams, and he knew with visceral familiarity what was happening.

"Hey, hey, *hey*..." Oliver spoke softly and lowered himself slowly, setting his flashlight down so that it bathed her in a gentle blue hue. He dropped down on his knees, keeping his voice as calm as he could, despite her obvious terror and inability to recognize that he was even there at all. "It's all right."

For less than a second, her tiny pupils flitted up to meet his gaze before another rack of invisible pain pulled the alien back. With a silent wail, she tried to constrict herself even further.

Oliver leaned more forward, enough that she flinched away when he attempted to take a hand that was taught up to her chest in a jagged, catatonic claw.

"What do you see?" he asked, and she screwed her face up, almost like she wanted to talk but couldn't. He didn't need her to, not in a sense that he wanted to know what she saw.

He just needed her to look at him, and not that.

"It's not real." Oliver placed his other hand over hers, gently prying it away from her in order to get more of her attention. "It's a bad picture, that's all."

"I can't!" she sputtered, raising her head up and away from him as she half-fought against his efforts.

"I can't, I can't, I can't, I ca—" Dindet repeated herself, clenching her eyes shut in some small, defiant effort to make whatever this awful, terrible thing was stop. "It's broken—the world's broken...I can't, I can't—"

For a bit, she relaxed, only long enough that he could situate himself close enough to grab her face and make her look at him.

"Look at me...Dindet, *please*." Oliver struggled to keep his grip through the parts of her that had lost control and stabbed and pricked at his palms like several thousand tiny needles. "What do you feel?"

"S-scared!" she answered in her panic. "It hurts! It hhh—make it stop..."

She wrestled a bit, raising her hands to grab his arms, but they only trembled in the air. She let out another anguished, empty cry and wrenched forward, nearly hitting him in the head and forcing Oliver to dig his fingers into the sides of her face to keep her still.

He butted his forehead into hers, pressing as hard as he could against the continuous poking and prodding, and forced her to look directly at him.

"What do *I* feel?" he asked now, making sure that if she saw anything at all, it would be him and all his colors. Dindet's eyes flickered down and up, and her mouth opened and closed in a small, failed attempt to answer.

"C-calm," she stuttered, and he felt the jagged parts of her begin to slow and recede. Still, he kept his grip just in case.

"Think about that then," he said. "Think about only that. What does it look like?"

"P-pink, it's pink," Dindet answered, attempting to lift her head, though he didn't let her.

"What does it taste like?"

"Sweet..." the alien began to relax, shifting awkwardly in his grip as her focus turned more toward his compassion rather than the shattering memory of death repeating in between the consciousness of her being and the cosmos.

"You're okay." Oliver smiled, pressing his nose up against hers for a brief moment before pulling away entirely. She clung to him, though, and only hesitantly released her vice grip on his shirt. "It's over now, and you're *okay*."

Almost immediately, she averted her eyes and folded back in on herself, full of a terrible shame and exhaustion that made her ripple with the effort of keeping together.

"See?" Oliver sat back on his knees and pulled a spare blanket from the shelf over her head, letting it drop on top of her. He crawled underneath it, flipping on his flashlight so he could see her in the dark. "You're safe. Nothing's gonna hurt you, and I'm right here."

She stared at the light for a bit, cupping her fingers over it and turning the blue light a gentle, starry purple when it shone through her fingers.

"It's really pretty." Oliver described, "It looks like stars, purple and blue with little white spots all over."

He wished she could see things as he did, little wonders of the world to him that were nothing but white and lines to her.

Dindet's gaze moved up from the light to him, and she pressed her head into his shoulder. She was tired and had never been so tired as she was right now. And all she could think about was that sweet taste that she never once realized Oliver possessed. She just didn't want to hurt him.

She didn't want to fail. Again.

Losing Control

Jon threw the door open, searching the dark room for his son and the alien until he caught the two of them sitting on the couch, murmuring to each other under a blanket with the flashlight on.

First, Oliver's head popped up, swiveling around to look for the intruder, then Dindet followed, mimicking him almost to a tee.

"Is everything all right?"

"No."

Jon ran outside to turn the power back on, and by the time he returned, his son was standing dumbly in the living room, trying to catch up on whatever was going on.

"Dad?" he asked, attempting to follow the man as he paced from room to room, checking each fixture as though it held a tiny microphone in it.

"Dindet, I need you to unmake everything in this house and remake it—anything that looks or feels off, leave out," he ordered, tossing aside books and old dishes in order to climb up onto a chair and check the ceiling fan light.

The clown shared a confused glance with Oliver, and for a moment, her eye marks swirled out from the flavor of Jon's fear, and she promptly began doing as instructed.

"Dad! What's going on?!" Oliver grabbed the clown's hand, pulling her away from a speaker before she'd begun taking it apart and dragging her along with him to his father. "Did something happen at the lab?"

"Yes! Oliver—I, It's complicated. If you're not going to help, just—" he was cut off by a loud knock on the door.

Jon dropped down from his chair, holding out a hand to gesture for the two of them to remain still and silent until he directed Oliver to take the alien out of sight.

He crept over toward the door, peering through the glass on the side to see Chris standing outside, twisting around anxiously as though he were being watched. He opened the door just before Oliver managed to push Dindet into his parents' room. In a heartbeat, she caught a glimpse of the scientist and froze up, inadvertently stabbing the boy in her quick terror and forcing his attention away from whatever dire conversation the two adults would have.

"It's okay! It's okay," he said, peeking back before shutting the door to the room so she didn't see him anymore. "He isn't gonna hurt you, I promise…"

Oliver trailed off, distracted by the conversation with Mr. Furkin. He wrapped an arm around the clown and deftly pet her head to try to calm her down.

"Jon, what were you thinking?! We both know exactly what that thing is—if they find out, we—we're going to prison, Jon! I can't do that! I can't leave my son!"

"It's not going to end up that way. We just have to be careful, play nice. Do what they say, and I will figure something out."

"I don't know how to build that contraption, though—I can't even read half of these blueprints! I—"

"O-Oliver." Dindet's trembling voice brought him back to the present, and he suddenly noticed that she was beginning to stab him in a quiet and desperate effort to remain under control.

"It's okay." He cooed, shaking his hands in the air before placing them back on her shoulders. He turned her around to face him. "Remember what I said, right?"

"F-focus on-n…other things."

"What do you see?" He asked, only half listening to her as she whispered off colors and tastes and things she noticed.

"How are we gonna cover this up?!"

"We're not!" He heard his father's voice raise, then lower again. "All we're gonna do is ride it out until it's over. I will talk to Dindet, make sure she leaves."

Leaves?

She can't go. Not yet.

Oliver's grip tightened around the alien, and she unintentionally drank in his anxieties, creating even more of a panic within her as she squirmed in his arms.

"It's okay, Dindet, you—"

She let out a muffled little scream of disagreement and tore out of his hands, tumbling into the bed frame with an ugly splatter. Oliver hurried forward, losing his concentration on the conversation between his father and Chris, and drew all his attention back to the alien that was desperately trying to stop existing in this world.

"I can't, I can't, I can't be found! I have to go, I have to—" She shook her head vigorously, tearing herself almost in half and looking as though she glitched out with the concerted effort it took to try and escape.

"You won't be found. You won't get—"

"They'll kill me. Smile—I can't leave! I can't—" Oliver cut her off, grabbing her hands and pinning her back up against the bottom of the bed frame so she would stop moving so much.

"No one is going to hurt you. I won't let them, okay? So, please, *please* calm down." He stared at her, patiently waiting for her to relax enough to actually listen to him.

"I can't move," she whimpered, beginning to dissolve in her desperation. "I can't move."

"I don't know what you mean." Oliver loosened his grip as she began to melt in his hands. "I need you to explain."

She tensed and wrenched her arms up close to her, forcing him to fight back again. "I CAN'T GO ANYWHERE!!"

Oliver instinctively slammed his hand over her mouth, forgetting for a moment that it would do absolutely nothing to quiet her. "Shh!"

Chris's head shot up and swiveled back toward the bedroom, but Jon kept him from inspecting it with a firm hand on his shoulder.

"You mean you can't go In-Between?" Oliver said softly, releasing his hand and letting her nod frantically.

"Like at the Peace Zone?" he affirmed, and she nodded once more, tilting her head back as another little wail came bubbling up. "Please, Dindet, it's okay. I'm right here. Focus on that, focus on me or…"

He paused as a small and possibly stupid idea popped up in his head. Quickly, before she even noticed it, he shoved his hand straight into her forehead.

Immediately, she turned into a starry abyss, and her eyes glowed white. It burned, a lot, but it worked. She stopped freaking out, and he dizzily pulled back, sucking in the breath that whatever he did had just knocked out of him.

"Better?" he asked, still heaving a bit. She nodded dumbly, and he slumped back on his knees, dropping his now aching head into his hands in effort to quell the light-headedness. "Good…you're not gonna freak out now, right?"

She nodded again, still trying to wrap her mind around what just happened. For a moment, maybe longer, she was entirely sated. And it baffled her.

"It's gonna be okay, *okay*?"

"Okay.."

***

Chris left well after midnight, allowing the two to sneak out of his parents' room and find safety in Oliver's, away from whatever stress hovered in the air like a fog around Jon.

Oliver flopped down on his bed and rolled over with a weak sigh, staring up at Dindet, wondering if she were paying enough attention to see how confused he was by her.

She wasn't, probably. She looked more concerned with the air around her and twitched every now and again at little innocuous noises until he finally broke the silence.

"Who is Smile?"

She practically spazzed out at the question, prompting him to sit up and stare at her ten times more intently.

"Dindet." Oliver kept his voice low and tried to look a little less worried by her obvious discomfort.

The alien averted her eyes completely from him, though, and tinkered with the things on his nightstand, making soft little whines like a frightened kitten while bits of her began to float away in the air.

"No one." It was an abysmal response, a half-choked word that came out more like a pathetic wheeze than any semblance of English.

Oliver leaned forward and eventually gave up on waiting for her to answer him. He stood up and casually pulled her hand away from the unfinished wood sculpture she was rolling around in her palm.

"Look," he said. "I'm not good at this—I don't know how to make you not afraid, but...I've seen this kind of thing before."

He didn't look her in the eye and knew that if she were listening to his head, she would easily tell he was so terribly close to saying he had been here before. Instead, she was quiet, almost remorseful looking.

"If they're bad...if you're *this* afraid of them, then something is wrong, and you need to say it." He held up her palm to face him, squeezing it just tight enough that it squished out little droplets of stars, causing her to pull back slightly.

"I'm going to hurt you, Oliver," she avoided, taking another step back from him. "I don't want to hurt you."

"You're not," he corrected softly, though she only took another step backward, flitting her eyes to the side and back to him.

"I *will,* though," she argued, forcing him to come up with another way to get her to talk.

"Dindet, I need to know what's going on, why you came here, 'cause if you're running—" he hesitated, unable to shake the unsettling feeling that twisted up his guts and told him that she *was* running. "If you're running from someone who's gonna hurt you, I have to know."

So I can protect you.

She didn't answer him and only wrapped her arms around herself, closing off from him as some small self-comfort.

"Is…is Smile like Matthew?" he asked instead. She glanced up at him, then quickly brought her gaze back to the floor, confirming all he really needed to know with the subtlest gesture of absolute distress.

"Is that why you came here?" he continued. "To get away from them?"

The clown shrugged but still didn't answer, prompting Oliver to question her further. There was something, *something* missing here, and he couldn't figure out what it was. *She knew my mom, and she's running from this Smile person..*

"Are…you the reason my mom is gone?" Oliver grit his teeth, clenching his fist in anticipation of an answer that he really, desperately hoped wasn't what he thought it was going to be.

"I'm…" Dindet started, causing him to look up at her and watch her squirm so uncomfortably under his gaze. "I'm not sure…anymore."

Not sure. Not sure?! How can you not be sure?! You're either responsible or not! There isn't an in between. There is no 'not sure'!

He forced himself to relax and shook his hands slightly in an effort to release some tensity.

"Okay," Oliver replied, taking in a deep, hopefully calming, breath and exhaling slowly, "okay...it's *okay*."

He turned around, unable to face her for the time being and began pulling the blankets off his bed.

"Oliver—"

"Don't," he interrupted, dipping his head slightly, "you don't need to explain anything, so please...let me go to bed now."

He felt her hesitate to leave but didn't move again until her presence had gone, at which point he dropped down on his knees and promptly screamed into his pillow in order to muffle all his confusion and frustration.

She was lying. She was a liar, and how dare she make me care about her! How stupid am I? How dumb and thoughtful and ignorant and trusting and—GOD, THIS IS ALL A HUGE MESS!

And I am so worried, so worried about her. If—if anything, I shouldn't care less! But now, oh now, I got invested! Some powerful god monster that is literally just a stupid kid, running from everything the same way I—a-and it's infuriating!

That he loved her...and couldn't let her get hurt.

Too Big Not to Notice

Thanks for letting me come over." Oliver twirled a ball on Markus's bed, trying to focus particularly hard on that and not all the unruly thoughts in his head. It felt like the world was falling apart, and no one was there to help fix it. *Dindet keeps hiding things. Douglass probably hates me. Even Dad is acting weird.*

"It's chill," Markus replied from his comfortable position in the corner of his mattress. "I was worried I'd scared you off after the locker room."

"You….actually like me, right?" Oliver asked, craving that validation. The proof that he wasn't here for nothing. That he wasn't doing this for nothing. He *wasn't* being used. "I'm sorry I ask, It's just—I get worried that maybe you're just tricking me."

"Your other boyfriend getting to you again?" Markus sat forward, drawing Oliver's attention away from the borderline pornographic poster on his wall.

"I—he's not my—But you like me as a boy, right? Not like a girl?"

"Course." The older boy gave him a kiss on the side of his neck, and Oliver's face screwed up at the familiarity of it. He quickly put small distance between them.

"And...not 'cause I let you"—Oliver choked on the word in his throat, dropping his chin at the shame of what he'd done—"do things."

"I thought you liked that?" Markus leaned into him again, threatening him with a very delicately placed hand. "You didn't stop me or anything?"

Oliver pulled himself off the bed and away from him further. "I do—I mean, I'm used to it, so I know what to do 'but...but I don't think...I think maybe we should stop."

"You want me to stop?" Markus scooted to the edge of the bed. "That's kind of funny because I *did* ask you, and *you* were the one who spread your legs, so I figured it was a go. Besides, it wasn't like we did a whole lot."

The way he said it so effortlessly like it was nothing. *It—it hurts.*

"Can—can you just take me home?" Oliver asked, "I think my dad's gonna make dinner tonight."

Markus made a noise, something like a mildly aggravated grunt that Oliver immediately recognized as what preluded an argument. *Violence. Pain.* He hadn't hit him yet. *How long will that last?*

"But we just got here," Markus whined. "No one's even home yet. We can use the hot tub...*naked.*"

No.

"I—I don't really want to. I'm sorry." Oliver took an idle step toward Markus's door, pulling his phone out of his pocket to check the time. It was late. Really late already. *Should have checked before giving that stupid dinner excuse.*

Markus stood up, wrapping his arms around Oliver in a gentle but terribly stifling embrace. He could feel the way the senior pressed into him, and he wanted so badly to leave. *Why couldn't I do that? It was so easy before. Did I break? Did something break inside me again?*

Oliver drew in a soft breath, that ugly realization dawning on him that he wasn't in control anymore. That was stolen the moment Matthew walked back into his life. He needed it back.

"Actually"—Oliver swallowed his breath, turning in Markus's arms as some ounce of confidence bled under his skin—"I don't want to be here anymore. Take me home."

The older boy blinked, visibly taken aback by his assertion.

"I want—" Oliver choked a bit, pulling away from him. "I *want* to go home."

"All right," Markus let out a soft exhale and gave a disconcertingly kind smile. He pulled away from him, alleviating all of Oliver's pent-up tension and allowing him to relax again.

"You—really?" He breathed, leaning up against the door with the weight of all his muscles finally loosening.

"I shouldn't make you do stuff you don't want to. So if you wanna go home, I'll take you home." Markus grabbed his keys and jacket along with his camera.

***

"How much longer?" Oliver watched his surroundings, sitting uncomfortably in Markus's car as he crept down the dark road. The defrost was on full blast, but it did almost nothing to fight the fresh snow that plastered up against the windshield.

"Not much."

Wherever they were was vaguely familiar, but in the night, he couldn't pinpoint how. Not until Markus took a hard turn and rolled into the motel parking lot and every muscle in Oliver's body tightened upon recognition.

Ehil Inn.

"I—I don't wanna be here. Why did you bring me here?" Oliver fumbled with his phone and the car door, struggling to keep oxygen in his lungs while his fingers failed him relentlessly. He'd forgotten it was locked. *Just like—*

"It's too dangerous to go up the mountain. What's wrong with here? It's just my dad's motel." Markus's calm voice drew the boy's attention away from his increasingly frantic attempts to unlatch the door. "You been here before?"

Oliver forced out an uncanny little laugh, trying very desperately to keep his nerves under control. *It's fine. He probably didn't see anything. He probably doesn't know. Stop freaking out.*

"You—you're sure we can't go a little further? It's not super bad yet," he countered, watching the senior grab his bag and keys.

"Dude, no." Markus offered a smile and unlatched his door, hopping out and circling around to open Oliver's. "It's way too dangerous, and I don't have the kind of tires for that. You don't have to worry. This place is basically a ghost town, and I've got an employee keycard."

"I'll have to call my dad, though. I don't think he'll want me staying here because the last—he won't want me staying here alone, I mean." Oliver rephrased, hesitant to accept Markus's outstretched hand. "He can pick me up if I—if I just stay in the lobby."

A gust of wind blasted up against the car door, splattering fresh snow into Oliver's face and sending a shiver down his spine. It must have been under sixteen degrees out, not including the wind that ripped straight through his bones. Markus leaned forward and grabbed his hand, tugging him out into the cold despite his excuses.

"Seriously, it's really not an issue. Come on." The senior gestured Oliver forward, leading him around a misshapen wooden fence toward the back pool entrance. "The rooms have heating. The lobby doesn't. And I'm not gonna just let you freeze to death."

Oliver winced in the cold, the snow smacking into his face and wind whipping his hair, forcing him to shuffle blindly in the solid two feet of powder behind Markus. He reached out, tangling his fingers up in the back of the older boy's jacket so he wouldn't lose footing.

He didn't want to be here. At all. But Markus was right. The weather was getting worse by the second, and he could already feel the snow seeping into his shoes and melting between his toes. It was freezing, so cold that it burnt, and there was no possible way he could walk home in it.

Markus stopped at one of the doors and sifted through his wallet for his keycard. However, before he slid it into the slot, the door opened, and Oliver peeled his eyes open far enough to recognize his step-brother, Cody, standing in the doorway in a housekeeper's apron.

"What are you—" Cody cut himself off, his gaze flickering over to Oliver before it settled back in an ugly scowl on Markus. "No. Markus. You're not doing this again!"

"Doing what?" Markus asked, taking a step back that forced Oliver back as well. "It's freezing, and it's not safe to drive right now. This was the closest place."

"Then what is *she* doing here?!" Cody sized his brother up, and the vile rage in his voice made Oliver jerk his head to face him.

"Can we please—"

"You said you would leave her alone! You are *not* keeping her here overnight," Cody interjected, shoving his brother back.

Markus stumbled and threw his hands out, loosing Oliver from his jacket as he was forced to edge further back into the untouched snow.

"Don't fight," Oliver called. He wanted to raise his hands but kept them firmly tucked beneath his arms so they wouldn't freeze. "It's cold. We just—I just want to be warm for a bit. It's fine!"

Cody's gaze flickered back to Oliver and how he shivered in the ever-deepening snow. "I'm calling the fucking cops—"

Oliver buckled, startled by the sudden and painful thrust of an elbow to his chest when Markus reeled back and he watched as his fist collided with Cody's cheek.

The jarring movement made him slip and scramble to regain his balance. Quickly, Oliver threw his arms out to grab the senior just as he felt the edge of something under his heel, and his whole body was subsumed by bone-piercing cold.

It forced his mouth and lungs open in an awful gasp that immediately drew in a breath of frigid chlorinated water as he flailed and choked under a collapsed tarp. It was like knives in his skin, burning and clinging to him with the weight of his clothes and dragging him further down despite every horrified and frantic effort to pull himself out.

And then, by some grace, his frozen hands smacked hard into a metal ring and net, and he wrapped around it, clinging to it as it jerked him forward to the edge of the pool.

Oliver threw his head up, searching for a platform and the strength to keep his body from shutting down. He dug his nails hard into the snow, still half holding on to the skimmer that Markus had used to pull him out of the tarp, and hoisted himself back onto solid ground.

"Olivia, are you all right?" Markus's voice sounded from above him, and a hand dropped into his view. Oliver simply coughed and hacked, nearly gagging himself to get rid of the water in his lungs and replace it with precious air.

As soon as he was able, he clasped his hand around the senior's and hoisted himself up, frozen so far to his core that he could barely comprehend what had happened other than that he fell and Cody was no longer with them.

"W-wh-where'd h-he g-g-go?" Oliver chattered, a painful ripple of cold rolling up his back and making him bowl over in an attempt to breathe. Markus's arm wrapped around him, gently guiding him toward the open suite door. "Y-y-you punch-ch-ched h-him."

216

"No, he freaked out when you slipped and went to go get help, but I got you. Come on." The senior pressed into him, his hands burning Oliver's face with the difference in temperature. "You're freezing. We gotta get you changed."

***

Dindet leapt from tree to tree, an ugly and galactic beast among the shadows that consumed everything in its path. Half of her flaked with the effort it took to hold herself together, and the other half was a ravenous creature that stalked the forest every night and nearly every day now.

More often, the alien prowled along the cliffs and mountains in search of big and heavy beasts that could keep her alive just a little longer. She had already come far too close to eating Oliver, and as much as she dearly hated hiding what an ugly and enormous thing she was, she needed to stay alive.

So she lumbered through the trees, clawing into the snow and dirt with more limbs than any natural creature possessed as she followed the faint scent of fear. It wafted around the forest, soft and billowing purples and blacks that grew in their potency as she picked up pace, a screeching and terrifying mass in the night.

Until she saw it. Forced to a scrambled halt by the source of all that terror, the gelatinous monstrosity of a beast broke like a wave around the human boy, splattering and swirling around his frozen spot to reform as her more approachable self a few meters in front of him.

Dindet swiveled around, stumbling and still trying to reconnect with the matter that floated nearby as she stared back at the human.

He wasn't familiar. And she couldn't gather what on earth he was doing outside in the cold, in the middle of a forest, standing still as a statue.

Hesitantly, she stepped toward him, expecting him to react, scream maybe? Or stumble back in horror at what he'd witnessed.

But he just stood there, trembling ever so slightly and staring straight past her.

Dindet moved closer and closer. Until she stood directly in front of him. He was older, taller than Oliver or Douglass. But not as tall as the scientist was, and not as old either. She circled around him, waving her hands in front of his face to see if he had any reaction at all.

Is he broken? Dindet tilted up, leaning uncomfortably close to his face. He was afraid, but he was also stiffened to the point that even the vessels of blood in his eyes were taut with the strain.

"Hello?" she asked, gingerly moving to poke him before she was stopped by the slightest part of his lips. Some ugly and terribly soft wheeze fell out of him, and his unblinking eyes began to water, prompting the clown to take a small step back. She had never seen anything like it, or rather, she had never seen another entity other than herself capable of immobilizing their prey in such a way.

The alien's gaze flickered down to the boy's hands. They were spread and arched like claws at his sides. *Something is wrong...*

Slowly, and with far more hesitancy, she grazed her fingers along his arm, drinking in his vile terror as she searched for what caused his suffering.

Instead, images flashed, quick and vivid—his memories. A room, it seemed, and the cold, she recognized the landscape as the winding road to a familiar building. *Is this—*

She wrenched back, stricken by some slice in her mind that screamed ice and water. Something very dangerous in a soft red pin of light and the throbbing ache of bones hitting bones. Then she saw him.

Oliver.

Undone

Oliver sat in front of the motel room's heater, holding the towel that was wrapped around his shaking and incredibly vulnerable body up at its edges so it caught all the heat and kept it trapped around his core. He shuddered, one of those uncontrollable ones that made his stomach ache and his face nearly break with tears.

Markus had brought him here and demanded his clothes from him. Every last article. 'I'll put them in the dryer,' he'd said.

Though Oliver knew better, sitting here in a musty room, naked.

Douglass was right. Cody was right... I'm so—so stupid. He drew in a breath through his nose, letting it take what little energy he had left with its exhale. He was cold and tired, and he wanted to go home. Wanted to lie in his bed, staring at the ceiling, wondering what Dindet was doing in the night.

If she were here, this wouldn't be happening.

He could almost imagine her telling him just how disgusting and distasteful his 'empty' was. He had a perfect image of it in his head, lashing and consuming him.

Part of him could feel it, that familiar ache in his chest like a hole was dug into it and left to fester and rot. It was the same softness as when Matthew had brought him here and obliterated any sense of safety he had left.

Sweet and conniving, effortless. And it was wrapping itself around his veins again now, bleeding under his skin and pooling in his center a most foul tar. *This is your fault.*

He breathed again, holding down and strangling the urge to crumble. *You got tricked. What were you expecting? For everything to be fine? Because it's always fine?*

You know what's going to happen.

You know what he wants.

"I'm back." Markus's voice severed his thoughts, and he heard the door shut and lock, though Oliver kept his gaze on the heater and the dust collected in its vents. The senior moved behind him, setting something on the television stand and playing with the wires. "You feeling better? I know the heating is shitty so—"

"Oliver," the boy corrected, so far delayed that Markus paused what he was doing and stared at him. Oliver shifted, dropping his arms to cover himself fully as he turned to look directly at him.

"You said Olivia," he added, watching the senior's face pale just slightly. "It's Oliver."

Markus laughed, the kind of laugh one makes when they just realized they slipped up. That Oliver had never once told him what his deadname was. That there was only *one* way that Markus could have known it.

"It was you, wasn't it?" Oliver asked, dropping his gaze back to the heater. "You spread that rumor about me…you saw me with him, didn't you?"

He already knew the answer, but some small and spiteful part of him wanted the older boy to say it. But Markus was extraordinarily quiet. Even as he continued to fiddle with the cables and pretend he wasn't caught in his treachery.

So Oliver continued.

"That's why you were interested in me." The words cut deep

and scathing wounds as he said them. *It was a lie. All of it. All the nice things, pretty words. You said them because you knew. And I was too stupid to catch it. Too scared of being wrong or being hurt…when…when it was right there in my face.* "You knew exactly what to say…to get me to…want it…"

Oliver grit his teeth, hissing those last words like poison from his tongue. He was a fool. A spiteful, naive, and *willing* fool. Because it was so wonderful, for a short while, to have the attention. Positive attention.

He shook, without his want or will, tremors that didn't quite stem from fear so much as they did rage.

"So you got me. I'm here. You *won.*"

Markus's silence was unbearable, infuriating even. Because it meant he was right and that all this, *all* of it. Was planned.

Oliver pressed his fingers into the heater, watching his knuckles turn white and begin to ache with the pressure before he stood, keeping his towel taut in his hand as he turned to face the senior.

"Just…get it over with."

Markus sat on the bed, staring at him like some dumb animal caught in a car's headlights. And when Oliver's towel dropped around his feet, he stood, slowly at first. Probably because he expected the boy to try to leave, escape him in some way. His eyes flitted off of him for a moment, and when they returned, Oliver saw the pull of a smile on his lips that Markus tried so very hard to hide.

It would have made his heart jump if he had more capacity to care. To be afraid like he figured he should be. But he was tired, and cold, and he wanted so badly to go home.

He'd been undone.

So he stood there, quietly, head hung as that all-forgiving deathless embrace of the empty wrapped around him, digging its claws into his back and burrowing into his aching chest.

Markus drew closer, enough that Oliver could see his shoes a few inches from his own bare feet, his hands and their slight hesitancy to lift. But when they did, and the hole in his heart constricted further, he didn't move. Didn't flinch or fight.

But simply allowed it.

The senior's hands moved over him, down from his shoulders to his arms, and for that soft recollection of Matthew, he winced, just a flicker of a moment where his anguish seeped out of his numb, protective shell. Then they moved to his hands, pulling him forward like a god stealing away a soul of the damned. To a place he didn't want to go, to do things he most definitely didn't want to do.

"I'll make sure you enjoy it," the god said. But it was lying. All it ever did was lie.

***

Dindet bled through the night, blending with the shadows and stars as she crashed into the dirt and flung herself toward whatever place she was going to. It was far, and she wasn't familiar with it. She didn't know why he wasn't at home. *He's always at home.*

The alien broke through the brush and trees, immediately compacting and twisting herself into the image he recognized before an agonizing jolt of electricity caught her entirely off guard and every particle in her form contracted inward. She collapsed.

"For something so massive, you are incredibly hard to find."

Dindet struggled to her feet, spinning on her heel to face the familiar voice. The moment she saw the woman's pale face and empty expression, her edges and pieces spiked and shuddered with a visceral understanding of what she was. Who she was.

Poppy.

"Though it doesn't help that every time, *I* have to start from scratch," the woman added.

"I don't want to fight," the clown said, her eyes flickering back at the motel she stood in front of. "He's hurt—"

Another horrific jolt of electricity shot up from the ground, and Dindet let out an ugly and metallic screech. "STOP!!"

"110 volts hurts, doesn't it?" Poppy cocked her head and pulled the stem of her cattle prod out of the ground, releasing Dindet from her torment. "Too much to knock you unconscious, but not quite enough to kill you...just disrupt your molecular control...you should get used to that soon."

Dindet sputtered and splattered parts of herself into the dirt. She melted, felt herself gushing and pouring and changing viscosity in an effort to stay whole. It consumed so much of the energy she'd just gained and left her weak and confused.

"Let me help him. I just have to help him," she mumbled. "Why—what do you want?"

The woman's neutral face turned down in a look of utter disgust, and she prodded the alien again, forcing out a mess of starry black bile from Dindet. "Have you not figured it out yet?! Are you really that divorced from yourself?"

Dindet lashed and clawed at her, each swipe crumbling upon impact before she realized escape was a much better option. She contorted into an abomination, smoking and billowing and slamming her claws into the ground to prepare for a launch before Poppy's hand cleaved through what little protection Dindet had left and wrapped her fingers tight around the core of her. Her bean.

Her touch was inhuman and artificial, and it burned so fiercely that the alien howled and fuzzed, bubbling and shrieking and spinning in a whirling and whipping mass that clawed to free itself from Poppy's grasp. But she simply squeezed tighter until Dindet was made to submit.

"Please—just let me HELP HIM!!" Dindet screeched. One last effort before the pressure placed on her heart was so strong she began to crack and crumble. Poppy yanked her bean from the rest of her, cupping it in her hand and rendering the alien blind.

"Now, why would I do that?" she said, chucking the orange

thing at the motel wall. Dindet crawled, melting further as she stumbled to her feet to find herself again. She returned her heart to the rest of her.

"I won't mess up again," she muttered, though the words were useless and obtuse, gurgled up with her failure to control all of her at once. Dindet felt her weight, all of it, closing in on the earth and crushing celestial bodies that dared to obstruct its path. And Poppy merely chuckled at her childish determination.

"Do you have any idea how many times you've said that?" She turned, her eyes dancing from Dindet to the sky and then to the locked motel door behind her. "Your pet is colorful…it'll make good bait."

Dindet responded with nothing more than an animalistic snarl before another piece of her splashed into the ground, and she hurtled toward the woman, losing what was left of her cognizance and control. She batted and cleaved through the air, slicing through the snow and sending flurries of herself along with it in her attempt to impede Poppy.

The woman dodged her easily, gliding through her matter and providing another agonizing jolt of electricity through Dindet in her feeble and exhausted attempt to turn and catch her with massive and almost frozen claws.

"Don't hurt him!" she howled, no longer able to maintain her human silhouette. She bubbled and grew, loosing herself of bile and sludge as more than three sets of claws and tails protruded from her Lovecraftian horror. She swiped at Poppy's weapon. The cattle prod twisted in the alien's gelatinous grasp, and she tossed it across the parking lot, dropping low in a vicious and predatory stance.

"It's not me you should worry about," Poppy retorted, and for some minuscule slice of a moment, the woman's neutral expression shuttered with a look of fear, and her eyes darted back to her weapon. "You haven't told him yet, have you?"

Dindet rumbled with a guttural growl, drawing closer as her excess limbs plowed into the snow and shifted it aside. It melted underneath her, turning to ice that cracked and split when her claws broke the fragile surface. Just like how she wanted to shatter that ugly human face. "I will eat you."

"Won't you?" Poppy snidely remarked, taking small, defensive steps back as she inched toward the cattle prod only a few feet away now. "I don't think I have enough fingers to count how many times you've already accomplished that."

The beast's white eyes narrowed at her, wavering with the concerted effort it took Dindet to see through the fractures in the universe. She watched the woman closely, every detail of her movement, waiting for her to attempt her break.

Poppy leaped for the TASER, and Dindet pounced, bringing her talons down and around the woman's neck and pressing her deep into the snow. The alien's mouth gaped wide, opening up a glow over Poppy's face as razor-sharp rows of teeth oscillated and bowed outward, threatening to close in and tear her filthy human form to shreds.

It would have been delicious. And deserved.

Dindet shrieked and leaned down until the horrific burning of her insides bubbled up and her body began to pop and melt and spike. It hurt and grew from deep inside her until all she could comprehend was that fiery burst of agony. The alien wretched and doubled back, twisting and flailing and clawing at itself in an effort to tear out the pain.

She melted and congealed, froze and liquidated over and over, until the thin particles threatened to collapse in on themselves and dissipate with every attempt she made to stay together.

Dindet collapsed into the fresh powder of snow, condensed and trying so hard to drag what was left capable toward the motel door that reeked of her friend's torment.

Her struggle ended, though, when the prongs of Poppy's cattle prod poked through the film of her head and gently pressed her broken face into the snow.

"I'd kill you now, but I need this constant," the woman said, dropping down into a crouch so Dindet could see her undisturbed face. "And I am *dying* to know what he tastes like."

"Don't—I can't..." The clown gingerly attempted to lift her head, to reach out for the woman as she stood. "I can't fail again, please—don't tell him. I can't let him get hurt. Smile will—"

Poppy kicked her prying hands away and stared down at her, her still face twisting up with visceral rage at the mention of the name. "*You* are not Smile's, you disgusting *amalgamate*. When you and that animal you call your *friend* die, all of this will end."

She paused briefly, her attention turning to the sound of a car door opening and closing before she knelt back down. "And I will *make sure* it is painful."

Dindet stared up at her, pleading silently for such a thing not to occur. But Poppy merely stood, providing one last awful zap that forced the poor clown to tense and spike and screech until she felt the slow shift of darkness envelop her.

***

The air was cold, so cold that Oliver could see his breath refracting the light from the street in little puffs. It was well past three in the morning, and he shakily pulled his phone out of his pocket, gathering the bundle of jacket and scarves and every loose fabric on him to keep warm in the increasing cold of winter. It was snowing still.

His options were limited. Dindet was out of the question. She'd know the second she touched him. And knowing her, she'd probably try to eat Markus as soon as she found out.

He could call his dad if he were even home. He would likely be awake. And awake enough to ask him why he was out without the clown at the same motel Matthew kept him in during the custody exchange. If he found out what he'd done, he would be livid.

The other option was only slightly less awful. *Douglass.* The only reason Oliver even contemplated it was because he knew the kid was learning how to drive. And Douglass *always* answered him. No matter how late it was.

He would ask questions, but Oliver wouldn't be obliged to answer any of them. And Douglass didn't *have* to take him home…necessarily.

Oliver bit the bullet and pressed the dial, trying very hard to curb his nerves before Douglass's groggy voice croaked across the line.

"Oliver, it's almost four a.m. Did you have sleep paralysis again?"

"No, I—I'm sorry, Douglass, can you…can you please come get me?" He failed to hide the anxiety in his words or the hoarseness of his breath. At least Douglass couldn't hear how much he ached inside through the phone.

There was a small shuffle and what Oliver knew to be the click of Douglass's light turning on, followed by a grumble about the electric bill shortly after.

"I can't drive yet. Why didn't you call your dad?"

"I know—I, I, I'm sorry, I can't call him and—and Dindet doesn't have a phone. Please—it's freezing, and I'm—" Oliver stopped himself, wincing when he moved just a little too fast and it felt like his insides would drop out of him. "It's not far. I'm at a motel? Ehil Inn."

"That's almost outside of town. What the hell are you doing there?"

"Douglass, *please*! I just—I was stupid, okay? I'm sorry. I need—I want your help…" He didn't expect there to be so much desperation in his voice. Oliver drew in a shuddered breath and wiped stupid and nearly frozen tears from his face.

There was a pause on the other side of the call, such a long one that it made Oliver's heart drop lower in his chest every second it went on.

"Okay…I'm on my way."

And the call ended.

Fool

Douglass arrived roughly an hour and five minutes later, creeping at an unbearably slow pace around the corner in his father's old pickup truck. He pulled to a bumpy stop in front of Oliver, struggling to put the car into the right gear and let him inside.

He looked dead tired, and the boy's glazed-over eyes scanned the snow-covered parking lot for a couple of seconds before they fell back on Oliver, who had moved into the front passenger seat. He sat tilted at an uncomfortable angle with his eyes planted firmly on the front dash and a twitchy false look of content.

"Were you with Markus?" Douglass asked, jiggling the gear to get it into one of the several different types of drive. When Oliver didn't answer, he glanced back at him, and the way he visibly prevented himself from looking like he was in pain.

It was a face Douglass recognized. The same one he had when he saw him in the bathroom cleaning that dress. It caused every ounce of sleepiness to drain away from him in a single instant.

He let out a forcefully calming breath and turned his attention to the road for a moment, trying to figure out how to address the silence.

"Ol—"

"Can you take me to see it?" Oliver cut in, only very briefly flickering his gaze away from the snow melting over the windshield. Douglass blinked, not quite sure what he meant.

"At...the cemetery," Oliver clarified. He pressed his palms hard into his lap, to the point where Douglass noticed the whites of his knuckles. "I haven't been to see it...yet, and I'd like to...if that's okay?"

Douglass closed his mouth and brushed his fingers through his hair in an attempt to wrap his mind around just how crazy a request his friend was making. *It's almost four in the morning, snowing pounds, and he wants to go to his mother's grave? Right now?*

Something happened.

"All right." Douglass shifted the truck into gear and began puttering down the road at an alarmingly slow pace, praying that he could make it the extra ten miles to the cemetery without falling off the mountain.

The ride was silent. The kind that Douglass recognized as that deafeningly loud nothing-noise that Oliver made when he was trapped in some form or fashion. It made the drive painfully uncomfortable all the way to when he pulled to a creaky stop at the edge of the cemetery gate.

Oliver got out before he even managed to put the truck in park and offered an uncharacteristically polite 'thank you' as he kicked through the snow to stand in the warm yellow of the headlights.

Douglass hurried to follow him, quickly throwing on his parka and stumbling out to catch up as Oliver stole a bouquet of fake flowers from another grave and made his way to the large granite headstone.

The boy was already there, staring at it in his insurmountable silence when Douglass walked up next to him. His face looked tired and awake at the same time, and Douglass could see the minutiae of Oliver's eyes scanning the words written on the bronze plaque.

"Do you think she ever loved me?" Oliver asked. His words were hollow, and his gaze moved from Marie's name to the downturned face of the bronze angel that sat on top of the headstone. It was a beautiful marker. It was a shame there was nothing under it.

"I do," Douglass answered, his eyes staying on Oliver and the way his fist clenched in subtle response. *He doesn't believe me.*

"How do you know?" Oliver countered softly. "How am I supposed to know? It's not like I can just ask anymore. It's not like she wouldn't just lie. There's *nothing there.*"

He tossed the flowers at the base of the headstone and quickly brushed his fingers through his hair in an effort to calm his nerves.

"It's okay to be—"

"It was too much of a coincidence," Oliver cut off Douglass's attempt to console him. "It was right before—right before I started. What if Theo was right? What if I made her leave? It makes sense. Too much sense. She was—she was *always* gone, Douglass. Even before now. Even before you or Jon were around. She was *always* busy."

Douglass dropped his gaze from his friend's, desperately searching for some sort of answer he could give. He didn't even know why Oliver wanted to be here. He'd been so adamant about not speaking about his mother. Not even addressing it. Or anything surrounding her.

"That doesn't mean she never loved you," he finally offered, though it was hollow, and they both knew it.

"What if she doesn't, though?" Oliver's voice cracked, and it grew higher as he wiped unwanted tears from his eyes. "She knew. She knew the whole time what I was, and she was gone. She always went away. She didn't want to be around me because she knew I was broken. I was too much."

Oliver forced out a little laugh, pressing his palms into his face in a futile attempt to quell his upturned thoughts. And all Douglass could do was stand there and watch him and try to figure out how to help him in any way he could.

"I—I probably made her leave…I probably broke her because of what I am—what I do. It was my fault." Oliver sniffled, settling on the horrific assumption as though it were the whole truth. "I don't know how, but I did something wrong. I did something, and it's my fault. It's my fault she got hurt, my fault Matthew hurt us, I was the reason we had to leave…if I hadn't—if I wasn't such a *fucking idiot*—"

"You're not—"

"But I *am!* I caused all of this, right? I had to. I was stupid, and I trusted Daddy—Matthew to-to-to not h-hurt her. If I hadn't been so stupid—if I just *kept my mouth shut*…" Oliver drew in an ugly little gulp of a breath, resting on the awful thought and all its finality. "It's my fault she's gone. *I killed her.*"

Douglass bent down, drawing Oliver's attention as he scooped up a large handful of fresh snow.

"What—what are you doing?" he mumbled stupidly as Douglass stood up and held it over his head, letting it drop right on top of him and causing Oliver's tear-stricken eyes to widen with surprise.

"Distracting you," he replied, offering a genuine smile that made Oliver's whole face turn more red than it already was from the cold and his tears. Douglass rested his hands on his friend's shoulders, making sure to look him in the eye as he spoke. "It's *not* your fault, Oliver."

"But—"

"Nope." He cut in, taking another handful of snow from the top of Marie's marker to throw at Oliver's chest before he could object. "Not your fault."

"But it is!" Oliver's face screwed up with indignation, and he scowled at Douglass, warranting another snowball to his side. "Stop throwing snow at me!"

Oliver dropped down, packing a solid ball in his hands and chucking it right at Douglass's head, who merely cackled at his bad aim.

"No, don't think I want to," he remarked, landing a hit on Oliver's shoulder just before he ducked behind Marie's angel. Oliver grumbled and huffed, blowing out a puff of condensation as he began mass-producing shoddy snowballs in an effort to get at least one good hit.

"You're only dodging good cause you got long legs!" He snuck around the grave marker, landing a snowball on Douglass's pant leg before he made it to the other side.

"No, I just have better aim." Douglass's head popped up from behind the stone, and before Oliver could react, he got a face full of fresh powder.

The boy's triumphant little giggle was cut short, though, when Oliver crawled over the marker and grabbed hold of his hands, forcing the kid to struggle against his maniacal effort to shove as much snow down his jacket as he could get.

It was fun and stupid. Even as Oliver managed to offset his balance and push him sliding backward in the snow, all Douglass could think about was the way his friend's entire face had shifted from that awful grief to a bright and competitive grin as he panted and fought for silly dominance. It was something he had missed dearly.

I missed you.

***

"Ha!" Oliver cackled, catching his foot behind Douglass's ankle and tripping him up. The boy faltered, his hands still clasped in Oliver's as his eyes widened and he dropped back into the snow, pulling both of them down with a thud.

Oliver situated himself comfortably on top of him, pressing the boy's hands into the ground so he couldn't break free nearly as easily.

"Sorry, *stick boy*, I win," he congratulated himself, easily holding Douglass down with his weight alone.

"Stick boy?" Douglass grinned and huffed, trying to kick his way out from underneath Oliver's iron-clad victory. "Unfair! I don't go around calling you short and stubby!"

"Unfair?" Oliver grinned and thrust Douglass back down into the snow. "It's not my fault all I have to do is *sit* on you. And I'm almost five feet now!"

He leaned down, reveling in Douglass's inane and hilarious struggle. "Just *wait*. When I hit puberty, I'll be taller *and* heavier than you."

"All right!" Douglass sighed in whole defeat and relaxed, a little hum of laughter wheezing out of him. "You win."

Oliver's stupid happy smile widened, and he let go of his friend's hands, sitting back and drawing in a slow, icy breath. Douglass panted below him, his eyes closed with a soft and content smile on his face that Oliver didn't notice turn into a smirk the moment he allowed him freedom.

"Rematch!" The boy shot up, and Oliver promptly grabbed his wrists and leaned into him, easily forcing him back down on his back and watching his eyes widen with startled glee.

"*How* are you so strong?" Douglass breathed.

"Dindet is *really* heavy."

Douglass gave another little sigh, followed by that sweet smile. It caught Oliver entirely off guard, and he froze in his thoughts.

This is nice.

Douglass is nice.

He's always nice.

Oliver watched him closely, the way he breathed, big and deep heaves that probably made it burn a bit from how cold the air was. Or how his curls had caught snowflakes and how they sifted around in his hair when he tilted his head up to look at the stars. Or at him.

He's such a good person.
All the time.
No matter what I do wrong or how bad I am.

"You gonna let go?" Douglass's voice briefly pulled Oliver out of his thoughts, and his eyes flickered back into focus on the boy's face. He was staring right at him, the creases of his eyes crinkled up with the tired smile on his lips, and in that moment, Oliver wanted nothing more than to kiss him.

"Oh, *shit.*"

Douglass blinked, only just barely noticing the look of visceral realization that flitted across his friend's face. Oliver's gaze dropped away, and his soft smile fell for a second, prompting Douglass to crane his neck and wriggle his hands to get his attention back.

"Everything okay?" he asked in that sickeningly genuine tone.

You can't do that. You can't like him. Not like that.

"Uh…yeah." Oliver dipped his head, loosening his grip on him as he folded down and rested his head on his chest. He was warm. So unbelievably warm and it was so unbelievably cold outside.

Oliver pulled his arms close to himself, holding on tight to his friend's jacket.

He was a friend. *Just* a friend. *Barely even that. A neighbor. That's it.* They *used* to be friends.

You can't hurt him like that. You know what happened last time. It won't work. You'll break him. He's too good, and you don't deserve good things.

"Thank you…" Oliver moved after a moment, prompting Douglass to rest his hand over his head and brush bits of snow out of his bangs.

"For what?"

"Distracting me." Oliver hesitated, taking a moment to wipe the stupid tear that rolled down his cheek before he lifted his head to look at Douglass. "I think…I think I'm ready to go home now."

Douglass searched his face for more information, more than what Oliver was willing to give, before his eyes settled and his lips grew thin with understanding.

"All right."

Ugly Money

I t was ridiculously late by the time Oliver got back from the cemetery. He crept into the home as quietly as possible, taking care to check both the couch and the attic to make sure neither Dindet nor his step-father were awake or, even better, present. Unfortunately, the latter was.

Oliver pushed the attic door open just enough that it wouldn't hit any of the mouse cages on the floor. Almost immediately, his gaze landed on the machine. It was nearly complete. No exposed wires or burn marks from failed tests. Even most of the blueprints had been shoved off to the side to make room.

He wasn't looking for the machine, though. Instead, he scanned the dark for his dad's laptop.

It was across the room, sitting precariously on top of old textbooks, and thankfully it was still unlocked.

Oliver snuck inside, weaving around all the excess tools, tables and cages until he made it to the small clearing right before the old futon and Jon, who lay kinked up and drooling on his lab coat.

He dropped down and quietly began fiddling with the windows in search of his father's bank access, desperately hoping that he could figure out a way to pull out what Jon had set aside from their settlement and get rid of Markus altogether.

Crap. Password locked.

Oliver grimaced, his eyes flickering back to his dad as he murmured something in Gujarati and rolled over flat on his face. *It could literally be anything. Or worse. Anything not in English.*

Rather than attempting to guess and risk locking both of them out of access, Oliver leaned back and closed the window, moving his thoughts to the only other option available. *His wallet.*

The boy watched his father, particularly the part of his coat that bulged around the pocket, indicative of it holding exactly what he needed. He waited and listened, struggling with his own exhausted desire to doze off from the rhythmic exhale of the man's snores.

Eventually, he got up the nerve to creep over and reach into his pocket, gingerly extracting the valuable chunk of sewn leather and immediately digging through it for all the cash available. He wasn't stupid enough to risk giving Markus access to his cards.

Hopefully, 735 in cash would suffice. *For now. Just this once. He—he probably won't even notice it's gone. He uses cards way more anyways.*

Jon snorted loudly, and Oliver's heart nearly jumped out of his chest. His head swiveled back to stare at him for a second or two longer, just to make sure he was asleep before he shoved the wad of cash into his pocket and silently snuck back out into the balcony hall.

"Oliver?" Dindet's voice forced the boy to stop, and his attention dropped down the stairs where she stood at the back door, staring up at him and dripping black sludge on the floor. "What are you doing?"

"I—" he hesitated, narrowing his eyes as his tired thoughts closed in on her, and a frown pulled at his lips. "It doesn't matter. And it's not like you really care anyways."

The alien blinked, and for a moment, her eyes flickered out the door to the tracks she'd made in the snow. "I'm sorry...I—I was—"

"What?" Oliver cut in, trudging down the steps and thoroughly avoiding her attempt to touch him. "Busy? You've *been* busy. I'm sure whatever it was. It was way more important than me."

Dindet followed him a couple of steps more, despite the visible exertion it took. It looked like she would turn into a puddle the longer she tried to move.

"What were you even doing?" Oliver added, hoping he had adequately removed the bite from his voice. She looked dangerously unwell. "You're melting all over the place."

The clown drew back and immediately dropped her gaze. "It's nothing bad—I'm fine."

You liar. Oliver's unconscious look of concern twisted up into an ugly little scowl, and he huffed. "You know what? Never mind. I don't care anymore."

"I'm sorry—"

"*Be sorry.*" He pulled his hand away from Dindet's second effort to reach out and took a solid step toward the front door to further their distance. "I'm tired of wasting my time worrying about you when you barely even acknowledge I exist—if you want to leave, then *leave.* You only came here to help with that stupid machine, right?"

"I came for you—"

"Right," Oliver cut her off again, rolling his eyes at her pathetic display of remorse. *She doesn't really care. If she really cared, she would have stopped Markus. She would have been there.* "I forgot—I'm just food. It's not like you actually want to be around me. You made that *glaringly clear.*"

"I don't—"

"Just forget it. I *don't* care."

***

"HEY!" Oliver belted as he trudged toward Markus. He sat in the corner of the courtyard among one or two of the other upperclassmen Oliver vaguely recognized from the orchestra pit. Though Cody wasn't there.

Instead, a girl sat eating her lunch with them. She looked to be in the same year as Oliver, and his eyes flickered to her and back to Markus, twisting into an enraged glare.

Oliver sifted through his pockets, pulling out the wad of cash he'd pocketed from Jon and tossing it straight at the senior's chest.

Markus blinked at him, a full second passing by before he responded. "Uhh, what's this?"

"I want you to leave me alone," he said, his anger cutting the words in his throat. "Don't talk to me, don't text me. Don't even *acknowledge I exist.*"

Oliver shifted his attention back to the girl, who by now was staring at him, slowly chewing her food. "Stay away from him."

"LOL, what?" Markus laughed, elbowing one of the boys to his side and pulling himself to his feet. His sudden height caused Oliver to shrink back instinctively. But he steeled himself in his anger and sized him up, despite their dramatic difference in stature.

The senior took the last drag from his joint and flicked the roach into the snow, leaning in and causing Oliver to tense softly, though he refused to drop his gaze. He watched as Markus pulled out something small and black from his own pocket. "You know what this is?"

Oliver glanced back through the foggy windows of the school where Douglass stood behind them, watching the encounter intently. He returned his gaze, only briefly looking at the black thing Markus held between his fingers.

"No?"

"It's a flash drive," the senior said, so casually. "Who was that friend you were talking about? Some boy, right?"

"Wh-what?" Oliver forced out a nonchalant little laugh. *This is a joke, right?*

"You mentioned his name once. Douglass? Tall, curly hair—hangs around you all the time." Markus continued, sneering at Oliver's dumbstruck stupor. "He's into you. I can see it. Head over heels, I bet. How *awful* would it be if he found out about your little secret? He would *hate you.*"

Suddenly, and without warning, Oliver felt himself stop existing altogether. Like some screaming, whirling monster had gobbled him up and left his body standing there in the snow, listening to this wretched human being speak.

He forced himself to blink, to look away. To finally start breathing again. Every word out of his mouth hit like a mallet. As painful as the way Matthew hit him. *He used you. And you let him. He tricked you. You. Were. Wrong.*

"Oh, you didn't think I'd set up a—what is it?" Markus turned to one of his friends. The smirk on his face felt like it sliced into Oliver's throat when he looked at it. "Oh, right…precaution."

"You…you didn't," Oliver murmured, desperate to get back inside his body so he could move his feet. *Run.* But that desperation was met with a torrent of creeping and terrifying pain in his chest, and it felt like all his ribs had been caved in from a deadly blow. "That's…that's illegal—"

"Only if I get caught," Markus cut in as he thumbed through the money. Oliver's gaze flickered up at him, then to the boys next to him. The grins on their faces. The senior folded up the money and put it in his pocket, and took one uncomfortably close step toward Oliver, leaning close to his ear so only he could hear his words.

"If you say a word about it, I'll make sure *the whole world* knows about our little movie."

He tried to smile, to hide how much it hurt to hear. A heartbreaking little laugh muttered out of Oliver because he truly and honestly didn't know how else to react. It was a big joke. He was just a big joke. *None of it was ever real, and how hilarious is it that you convinced yourself otherwise? Douglass was right. You are an idiot.*

"Blackmail works a lot better than bribery, *baby girl.*" Markus pulled away, looking down his nose at Oliver as he whirled away into abject horror. "Thanks for the cash, though."

Oliver smiled a little wider and blinked away the pointless tears in his eyes. *It was fine. This is fine. It was just—just a joke. This isn't happening…*

***

Oliver forced his way into the only bathroom he was allowed in, slamming the door shut and locking it tight before the weight and crushing physicality of his own thoughts compounded on top of him and sent him to the floor in a crumpled heap. He moved so much more than he thought he would. But that happened when he couldn't contain it all.

Every breath ached, and every thought burned. *What did you do?! You let him touch you. Let him hurt you. Let him trick you. And everyone will know. Those ugly words, all those rumors are true, and you're exactly what they all say. Exactly what Matthew said.*

Oliver grimaced, digging his fingers into his skull in an effort to get it to stop. God, it hurt. Like ice picks in his brain, an awful clawing that peeled back the wrinkles and left nothing but blood and viscera, spilling out his ears. Acid that burned his face.

His stomach twisted and knotted, and it felt like glass had been sliced and embedded under his skin. And hands.

Oliver forced his eyes open to stop how quickly his thoughts moved from his deception to his father's punishment. He needed to focus, to think about something else. *Anything else.*

But he *couldn't*. He couldn't get rid of it now. It was molded into the very fiber of his being, and when he opened his eyes, through the thin layer of reality, all he could see were Matthew's eyes, his scowl of rage. The look he made when he was trying to make sure Oliver never took another breath.

"Stop! It's not real," he begged softly, pounding on his head to make it go away. "It's not real. It's fine—I'm fine! Everything is—"

Oliver choked and scrambled, jerking away in an effort to get the feeling of hands and fists off his flesh. It wasn't there, but it hurt like it was. Bones snapping, twisting out of their sockets. And glass, everywhere. Inside him—he could feel it. Taste the blood in his throat, on his tongue, and that horrific burning. That ache.

Oliver screamed.

Trial and Error

How long has he been in there?" Jon spoke softly to the school janitor. It was well past the end of the school day. He'd spent most of it with Dindet working on the finishing touches of the molecular transporter. He only realized it was so late when Douglass came in the door going off about how Oliver walked out on him at lunch, and he hadn't seen him since.

"'Bout six hours now?" The janitor looked at his watch and quietly unlocked the door. "Tried making 'em come out 'bout five times today, but they keep locking the door again."

"Maybe if it's me, he'll let me in?" Jon offered a soft and hesitant smile, rapping on the door softly. "Oliver, it's me, Jon…will you let me in?"

No answer. No movement either. He creeped it open, taking care to slide in without letting anyone else see inside the bathroom.

Oliver sat on the floor, staring at the wall with clumps of matted hair still stuck between his tightly clenched fingers. He gave no indication that he even saw his father approach.

"You don't look so great," Jon crouched down, moving slowly and carefully as he drew near, paying close attention to the minute detail of his son's eyes flickering to him with a hollow and exhausted gaze. "You've been in here all day. Are you hungry?"

Oliver didn't answer him, but he did keep a keen eye on the snack bar Jon pulled out of his pocket. It was a rare kind. One that he could only find in India. One of his absolute favorite flavors, too.

Jon sat down next to him and set the snack on the ground between the both of them. He didn't expect his son to take it or even eat it. But if he did, that meant he could somehow coax him into talking.

"We were worried about you," he said softly, glancing down at his son as he stared at the food offered him. "You didn't come home, and I was worried something happened...it's okay to tell me if something happened, Oliver. I promise I won't be mad at you. I won't hurt you."

Oliver still didn't answer, but this time he moved, deftly taking the snack on the ground and tearing it open to eat. He was starving, and he looked it, taking massive bites that he barely even chewed before swallowing it down with tears streaming down his face.

"You really did a number this time round," Jon offered a gentle smile and tucked a piece of hair behind his son's ear. Oliver swallowed the last of his small meal, and the second his mouth was unoccupied, it dropped open with an ugly little sob, and he pulled in on himself.

"I'm sorry!" He cried, "I'm sorry, I didn't mean to. I know I'm bad. I know I did bad again. I—I couldn't make it stop. It wouldn't stop, and I tried. I promise. I did everything I could but—but—"

"Shhh, Oliver, it's fine." His father reached out, allowing him the opportunity to take the embrace he offered. Almost immediately, the boy clung to him, crawling into his lap with a desperate desire for that affection. That comfort that he didn't think he could get anywhere else.

"Dad—" Oliver choked on his words, burying them in his

father's shoulder. "I think—I…I'm broken…I don't think I can fix me."

Jon drew in a soft breath, unable to reconcile the desperation in his son's voice. *Something good. He just needs something good right now.* So he pet his head, slow and gentle, and said the only thing he could think of.

"We finished it…the machine."

***

"Oliver, will you plug these into the adapter?" Jon directed the boy toward a pile of plugs and wires that sat in the corner, trailing up and through the attic window out toward the powerline in front of their home. "Dindet, please rewire that cord to the grid. We need to have it last at least thirty seconds."

The scientist was busying himself, turning dials and setting up the DNA scanner. He glided from one end of the room to the other, tearing off a bit of the clown to mix up with a strand or two of Marie's hair he had collected from her brush.

He dropped the materials into a sort of suction tube that would hopefully track the right version of his wife and pull her through with the help of the properties in Dindet's matter.

As soon as Oliver returned, Jon had him run back to the power box and turn off everything except for the circuit that connected to the attic.

"All done," Oliver panted as he pushed through the attic door and kicked aside the blueprints.

His father nodded and pointed at the hundreds of flammable papers. "Put those out in the hall real quick. Don't want to catch the house on fire."

Once most everything in the attic was rearranged, the three of them stood in the quiet space, preparing themselves for the next, and last, step.

Jon pulled in a breath, glancing down at his son, then at the clown before he knelt down in front of the power board of the machine, flipping small switches until it made a repetitive ticking noise and whirred up with a high-pitched buzz.

The wide, satellite-like plates that faced each other sparked with loud, crackling electricity that made the three of them jump upon the first completed arc. Dindet flinched away at the sound of it.

Slowly, the arcs of light built a pattern, growing with intensity and filling the air with a static that made Oliver's hair stand on end.

Dindet rippled as she tried to fight against the magnetic pull of the semi-formed portal beginning to open up with a pulsating blue glow.

This is a mistake

It was working. Despite the flickering of the streetlights outside and the terrible loud noise it made. Oliver edged closer, straining to see what may come through.

Something is wrong.

Piercing, awful wails of agony struck alongside, shaking as something was beginning to form in the light.

It's not going to work

IT NEVER WORKED

Stop it

STOP IT NOW

TURN IT OFF

"Stop it! STOP IT!" Dindet shrieked, tearing past Oliver and shoving both him and his father aside.

"What are you doing?!" Oliver screamed through the noise. He wrapped his fingers around her arm and tried to pull her back, but she whipped around and pushed him away in her frantic effort to turn it off.

"She's scattered!!" Dindet glanced back at the

Terrible

Screams

The de-atomized ghost of what shouldn't be.

The alien clawed through the air, digging her talons into the power board as an agonizing jolt of electricity shot through her. And for a moment,

she caught a glimpse of

something

Awful.

The machine buckled and let out one last hideous screech before the power cut out, and the three of them were enveloped in darkness.

"No! No, no, *no, no!*" Jon scrambled for a flashlight and found a battery lantern that he opened up. He searched the room for his son, who had grabbed Dindet's shoulder and twisted her around with a furious glare.

"WHY WOULD YOU DO THAT?!" Oliver barked, pushing her hard toward the door. The clown stared at him, an idiotic look of confusion and fear on her face at his rage.

"She—she's scattered," she replied dumbly, backing away from the boy as he herded her toward a corner.

"Oliver—" Jon started.

"WE WERE SO CLOSE!! WHAT WERE YOU THINKING?!" Oliver threw his hands out in a violent attempt to hit her before his wrist was caught, and he was yanked back by his father, forcing him to stare up at the man with wild, enraged eyes.

"You are *not* your father." Jon's voice was low, and Oliver's glare flickered back toward the alien and then once more at the scientist. He stared at him for such a small amount of time, a look that was so full of hatred it made his father hesitate. Then Oliver wrenched his arm out of Jon's grasp and bolted out the door.

"She was scattered…" Dindet repeated, flickering through a rainbow of colors as she tried to explain to anyone that would listen.

She wasn't going to come back. She can't come back.

Jon dropped down to the ground, digging his fingers into his head to keep himself from crying out in grief. His thoughts whirled, swirling up into a black pit that dropped him truly down into the desperation he had staved off for months.

On some level, he knew she was gone. He knew it was a waste of time. He tried so hard to pretend otherwise.

"Find Oliver," he muttered, choking back his tears as he peered up at the clown. She stared for a moment, baffled and battered by his torrent of emotions, but nodded and immediately vanished from his sight.

Jon swiftly headed downstairs, grabbing his coat and keys along the way and going straight to his car. He veered out of the driveway only to be stopped by Chris, who stood frantically waving in the middle of the street.

"All the power went out! What happened?!" The man took a step back when Jon's fearful, teary eyes shot back at him.

"I need to find Oliver." Jon began to creep forward, and Chris walked beside him, his mind running rampant with questions before he came to the conclusion.

"He ran off?! I'll help!" Chris exclaimed, smacking the side of the car before sprinting back to grab the keys to his truck and careening out into the street to go in the opposite direction Jon went.

***

Oliver hit the pavement of the road, sprinting as hard as he possibly could, not looking or thinking about where he was going except that he just needed to leave.

He only slowed when the sting of asphalt made his feet raw and bloody, and he found himself several miles from home. In a daze, he continued off toward the only place he thought would be okay to be.

He came to a halt, staring dead-eyed at the large marble slab that stuck out of the ground, his mother's name inscribed into its bronze plaque.

"Oliver..." Dindet took a hesitant step forward, and the boy clenched his fist as a small threat to stay back.

"We were so *close*...she was right there," he said quietly, lowering his head as he tensed himself through a rack of sobs. "Why—Why'd you do it?"

Dindet averted her eyes, unable to respond, and he spun around, throwing his fist through her head in short vengeance.

"You were supposed to HELP!!" He advanced toward her as he clawed for her bean. "You said you came here for ME! To help *ME! Right?!*"

Dindet dodged his unstable attacks, taking a small retreat with every step backward while she grappled with herself to stay whole.

Oliver stumbled, grimacing as he stepped on a sharp stone and shot a glare up at her. *How could she? How could she take everything, EVERYTHING away from me like that?! And still look so stupid and confused?! How could she just lie to me like that? Trick me?!*

"We were so *close!* I was *so close,* and you took her from me! You took *everything!!* Now—now I'll never know!! ALL YOU DO IS HURT PEOPLE!" he screamed, "All you do is hurt me! And my Dad! And EVERYTHING!! YOU'RE A *MONSTER!!*"

The clown drew in a ragged mock breath at his words, and he could see the hurt in her eyes, but it didn't matter. *Nothing matters.*

"I don't want you here anymore." He straightened himself

and stared her dead in the eyes, knowing and relishing the fact that she could taste every ounce of his unbridled rage. "Go."

She flinched and opened her mouth to speak.

"GO!"

Oliver forced himself past her and headed back toward the cemetery gate. He needed her to wallow in despair. He wanted so desperately for her to deserve it.

***

Dindet stared at Marie's grave. For so long that she wasn't sure how much time had passed, but something inside her felt as though it had died, and the stench of it swelled and grew until it was all she could feel and hear and see.

In one breathless moment, she was entirely lost, swirling in the whipping black as all of her lashed out in desperate and futile attempts to contain that horrible thing.

You failed.

Suddenly, a terrible pain seized her, and the world turned as black as she was inside.

Chris trembled, dropping the taser in his hand as he stared down at the perfect cubes that scattered on the ground in front of Marie's grave marker. It was the first place he thought he'd find Jon's son.

His phone buzzed in his pocket, breaking his shocked silence, and he fumbled to retrieve it.

"Ye-yeah?"

Jon spoke on the other end.

"You found him?" Chris knelt down, picking up one of the cubes and hesitantly turning it in his fingers. "Good."

He nodded, "I'll head back—lemme just grab something real quick."

Bitter Fault

Oliver half expected Dindet to be standing in the living room looking as dumb as she was when Jon brought him back home. When she wasn't, he rolled his eyes and went straight to his room.

"Oliver—" His father started to reach for him, but the boy shot a quick glare at him and ignored the attempt. He didn't want comfort. He wanted to be mad. *I want that stupid clown to make sense for just once.*

He flopped face down on his bed and let out a muffled scream as he bit into a pillow. Eventually, he turned over and stared up at the ceiling while the lights flickered back on.

He could hear Jon downstairs, walking around until he heard the door to his parents' room shut, then he closed his eyes, clenching them tight to keep tears from streaking down his face. *I'm never gonna know now. And it's all her fault.*

It was dark out, and had been for a while when Oliver turned his head over to peer at his alarm clock. Three a.m.

He sat up and moved to his window to see if the clown was back yet. *She always comes back.*

If she was, she wasn't sitting on the porch, so he headed back down to the living room. He flipped on the lights and circled around the couch, throwing aside the quilt just in case she was under it.

Oliver felt a small pang of guilt as he glanced around the room. It felt odd that she wasn't back, popping in with a dumb smile and dragging him off to someplace she thought was fun as her usual apology. *It doesn't matter. It's good she was gone. She finally did something I asked.*

I don't need her. Want her.

He hesitantly turned toward his parent's room and crept toward the door to peek inside. Jon was lying on the bed, splayed out in an exhausted slumber in the dark.

He glanced back up toward his room for a moment, then snuck through the door and quietly crawled up into the bed next to his father.

***

"Where's Dindet?" Douglass caught up with Oliver as he trudged up the road toward the bus stop. He looked even more loathful than he usually did.

"Gone."

"What do you mean?" Douglass glanced at the gauze that peeked out under Oliver's sleeve, ignoring the sinking feeling in his chest. *She couldn't have left before the semester was over, could she?*

"I mean, she's *gone*," Oliver said, picking up his pace with a quiet mutter.

"Before winter—"

"YES, Douglass." He shot a glare at the kid, forcing him to drop the subject altogether. Douglass fell behind him, keeping enough distance so as not to tread on his already frayed nerves.

"My dad found a new conduit for his machine," he said softly.

"That's *great*," Oliver replied, though he wasn't listening. Douglass had absolutely nothing to say that he would want to listen to. In fact, he would have preferred it if this last week before school let out would pass without him socializing with anyone. What-so-ever.

"It's really cool, some kind of—"

"*I don't care.*" Oliver cut in gruffly, glancing back at him for a second before he came to a stop at the edge of the road.

Douglass squirmed uncomfortably, mentally going back and forth with himself on whether or not he should mention it at all.

"Is it because you ran away?" he asked tentatively, keeping his eyes on the ground just in case Oliver was glaring daggers at him. The boy didn't reply.

They stood in silence as the bus pulled to a stop with a squeal of its brakes. At that point, Oliver sucked in a preparative breath and turned to face him.

"Yeah…it was."

***

Sometimes, the cold, laminated wood of your composite desk is the only thing that keeps you present and tethered down to the world. That's exactly what it was trying to do for Oliver, but he simply, truly, didn't care. Not about last night, or Markus, or Douglass knowing about it, and definitely not the teacher raving about the trip to AKAN lab this Friday.

Douglass had forewarned Cassidy to prevent her from trying to console him, but he could already see that infuriating pity and concern on her face out of the corner of his eye when he turned his head. She didn't say anything though, which made it worse. Like when someone only asks you if you're okay because they saw you cry. Except backward.

"Oliver Jari—Jariwala to the counselor's office."

The boy's head shot up at the grainy announcement and swiveled around to the teacher, who shrugged and gestured toward the door. He stood up, furrowing his brow at what he knew was going to be a bad time, and headed straight down to the counselor's office.

The kid slumped down into the chair across from Mrs. Bradshaw, who, for once, wasn't nose-deep in student files.

"You called me?" Oliver had his attention more on the small window that faced the atrium and the crinkling brown vines that shook in the wind.

"It has come to my attention that things haven't been too great at home," she stated frankly. He sat up in his seat and turned his full attention toward her now, slow anxiety creeping up around him.

"W-what?" 'Who told you', was what he wanted to say, but he bit his tongue and let her continue.

"A fellow student's parent informed us of your runaway attempt and... I know how hard things have been for you after the death of your mother. So, the principal and I have decided a small counseling session after lunch every week might be beneficial."

No. This isn't happening. Seriously. This can't be happening.

"I don't want to," Oliver muttered, hunched forward and moving his eyes to the cup of pens on her table.

He'd done all of this before. Back when he and his mom left Matthew. He didn't want to talk to that dumb school therapist about things she could never actually get. He definitely didn't want to be *made* to talk to anyone.

Maybe that's what makes Dindet different.

She'll come back eventually.

Mrs. Bradshaw leaned forward, holding her hand out in a meager and unconvincing attempt to provide comfort. Oliver sat further back in his seat.

"I know things are hectic, and it's all right to talk to someone about it," she said, in that empathetic type tone that he knew was about two steps from a CPS call.

"I don't *need* to talk to anyone," he retorted, picking at his sleeves in case she saw his bandages. "Plus, I *already* talked to your stupid school therapist, and I don't like her."

I don't like what she makes me think about.

"It's your choice," Mrs. Bradshaw answered, standing up and heading toward the door to open it for him. Oliver got up and followed her.

"Then I *choose* not to," he affirmed, briskly stepping past her and heading straight back to class. He wanted to go home. He thought about doing just that.

Skipping out of class, sneaking out through the gym, and just walking back home. That would be a terrible idea, though, if he wanted to maintain the fragile illusion that everything was perfectly fine. *Everything is fine.*

Oliver quietly sat back at his desk and shot Douglass a hateful glare.

It wasn't his fault, but he wanted it to be. He ruminated in the strong desire to blame everyone around him, his dad for being so obsessed, Dindet for getting his hopes up for nothing, Markus for taking advantage of him, and Douglass for this stupid aftermath.

It was his own fault. And he knew it.

***

Chris tapped the glass of a large container, pressing the end of his pen into his lips while he studied the increasingly strange substance that morphed and floated inside of it. He pulled his phone out of his pocket and began recording notes.

"Substance seems to mirror the sample I borrowed from Jon, but it's significantly more dense." He recorded, shifting his attention to the other thing he picked up alongside the cubes in the cemetery. "The only thing it naturally responds to is this soft, oval-shaped object."

The scientist pulled on a pair of latex gloves and began inspecting the small, round orange thing. *I'm sure it's some kind of organism, algae, or a type of plant, maybe? It looks similar to the one Douglass had brought home a few weeks back.*

Chris hesitated, glancing back at a tray of scalpels in a quiet battle for the best way to go about understanding whatever this thing was. *Start with safer tests first.*

He plucked the orange thing from its makeshift stand and brought it over to the container, gently pressing it to the glass to see the reaction the gelatinous substance would have.

Immediately, the non-newtonian fluid splattered itself against the barrier, growing dense around the little ball before slowly fanning out like water rippling on a still surface.

"It seems to naturally attract the substance, but—" He stopped, pulling the bean away and heading over toward a D-cell battery. He set down his recorder and lightly pressed the positive end of the battery to the small organism, all while keeping his attention on the substance in the container. "Small currents cause the substance to contract."

Contract it did, the congealed mass balled up tight, aside from small spikes that shot out on occasion, trickling off of the black goo and solidifying into perfect cubes on the floor of the container.

Chris made his way toward his energy converter, grabbing a small magnet along the way and pressing that against the bean as well.

The black mass quickly lost its tight spikiness and lashed out for a moment before it completely liquified, a few small bits of it still hanging in the air like ash until they withered away.

"Magnetic current also seems to affect it." He set the magnet down with an apprehensive sigh. "The matter isn't enough to conduct...I've tried to parse out the sample I got from Jon, but after a couple of tests...every single trial dissipates it."

Chris rolled the small thing in his fingers, contemplating the decision he had to come to at some point. *This thing keeps all that matter collected and condensed—theoretically, if I threw it in there with a test, at a low voltage, nothing big at all, it could probably keep it from dispersing into the air.*

On the other hand, though, this is a monumental discovery, and if I claim it as a new species—if it is, I could reap the benefits of that…in a few years. I don't have the time, though. I need something now. I need to take care of my son.

Chris set the bean down on the counter, heading out of the garage toward the kitchen, and slumped down in the dining chair. The table was stacked with collection letters and bills. He had already nearly had a heart attack when the power went out. He thought it was due to his reluctance to pay for the electricity.

It wasn't reluctance. Or neglect. Missy was a fickle, expensive woman, and regardless of if he got majority custody, the settlement on top of the medical bills were breaking him down, and this was the only chance he had.

A breakthrough like his converter could grant him hundreds of thousands, the same way the transporter had for his colleague.

***

Dindet remained silent, out of herself, while her thoughts jumbled up around her. She could see the man when he left, tasting a concoction of guilt and worry that swirled up around him when he walked. She couldn't move though, not without the rest of her, and that was stuck in a jar. The room buzzed with a crystalized magnetism that kept her trapped and dizzy, and in pain.

She struggled even to make herself whole, and it didn't help that the scientist would return eventually to zap her unconscious.

She was a mess of colors herself, whirling and whipping purple terror and black, terrible nothingness, and inside all of that, she recollected an even worse thing.

A memory.

It was like everything was happening all at once, except only half of her knew what it was. The worst kind of dread drew up inside her and all she could do was sit there and wait.

257

The scientist returned, murmuring to himself quietly when he came to take her from the table and shove her into some other jar with a piece of her that, if it weren't so small, she could have escaped with.

"I hope this works…" he prayed quietly, turning over the jar for a moment before setting it inside his miniature electromagnetic disruptor.

The machine flipped on, and the clown heard a faint ticking noise, followed by some growing hum that evolved into a shriek as a bolt of electricity shot through her, and every particle contracted in horrific pain.

She wanted to scream. The agony of every last atom of her arcing lightning through her body was far worse than she could have ever imagined. And it wasn't stopping. There was no darkness after it, just terrible, horrible, *endless* suffering.

Gone

Oliver filed in line behind Douglass and Cassidy as the entire class climbed up onto the bus and sat down with another class from across the hall.

"Is your dad going to be there?" Cassidy asked, nudging him a little with her elbow. He rolled his eyes and pressed himself up against the side of the bus in a flagrant effort to ignore her.

"My dad is!" Douglass popped up from behind the seat and leaned over to insert himself into the conversation. "He's presenting his new machine to the board of directors today and said that if it goes well, he can show it to our class too."

"No one cares, Douglass." Oliver huffed quietly. Cassidy bopped his head lightly, and he shot a glare at her, which she returned in kind.

"Just 'cause you're in a bad mood doesn't mean you can be mean to everyone else!" she stated, smiling back at Douglass as a small apology to him.

The three of them settled down as the bus lurched forward and pulled out of the school lot. So it could drive a whopping forty minutes north to the AKAN lab.

Oliver didn't want to go back, really, and hadn't been back since before the accident. It was closed for a few months for renovations.

It looked different, sort of. The back left wing was entirely new, for reasons. The art piece at the central staircase up to the lab was the same, though, and Oliver drew in a quick gasp at it and dropped his gaze back to the pavement.

Cassidy butted him softly with her shoulder, offering a consoling smile.

"You okay?" she asked, slowing her pace to try to veer him further away from the entrance to maybe calm the nerves she figured he had.

"I'm fine."

"Right," she replied almost sarcastically.

He shot another glare at her and fell back into the back of the crowd to avoid her. He didn't need Cassidy trying to make him feel better about this place. She didn't need to make him feel better about what happened here.

Oliver busied himself and his attention by picking at the gauze around his wrist until it started tearing off. Only to pass the sculpture, and the lab entrance, and to ignore the tour guide that spouted science crap.

Something swallowed him up here, and it wasn't the fact that he hadn't been here since before his mom was gone. That bothered him, yeah, but he sort of missed her—Dindet.

It was a weird comfort that he didn't think about often and didn't think mattered until it was gone. He didn't have to deal with talking about how he felt or people asking him if he was 'okay'. She just automatically knew when he wasn't, and he didn't really have to say anything.

She'll come back…right?

***

Chris pulled into the employee parking and scrambled out of his truck, tearing the bungee cords off of the tarp and folding it aside to reveal his completed project.

He ran up to the back door just as Abadi and Kistle pushed

out of it, ready to help him pull the contraption onto a dolly.

"I'll need another for the container," Chris mentioned, gesturing at the large glass tube that held an undulating and unconscious Dindet inside. Kistle nodded and headed back inside to grab another one, and the three of them wheeled the converter into the back entrance of the lab to prepare it for presentation.

"That's the thing you were talking about?" Abadi questioned, struggling to sit the tank upright.

"Yeah—I found most of it Monday," Chris answered, hurrying to help the man so it wouldn't topple over. Abadi gave him a rather incredulous look before taking an interest in the substance he had found.

"You sure that'll work?" He glanced back at him, but Chris was already piecing together his machine.

"I've been testing it with low currents all week. It works great." The scientist waved off his concerns.

"Besides, it's just a trial presentation. Once the directors approve of it, I'll start working on a synthesized conductor to replace it," he continued, fitting the tank up to the electromagnetic plate of the machine and providing a little spit and shine to make it more presentable.

***

"We have the top minds of the country working on projects in all fields of science, but this is our crown beauty." *The super collider'.* Oliver mocked the tour guide's excitement and rolled his eyes.

All it did was smash particles together at a ridiculously high velocity. It wasn't even special, but because the thing was so huge and made the whole lab one giant circle, everyone assumed it did something incredibly important. *Next, he's gonna talk about the nuclear reactors.*

As if on cue, the tour moved down the hall toward the nuclear physics department, and Oliver trailed a bit behind the rest of the class, looking around at some of the things that had changed. The east wing looked about the same, aside from the new tile. So, he broke off to explore the wing his mother last was.

Oliver was familiar with the lab to the point that he remembered it perfectly in his nightmares, and there were plenty of places to hide if he had to. He didn't usually when his parents were here, but even the janitor recognized him, so he probably should have been more discreet.

"Erh...ehem." he overheard Douglass's dad clear his throat and folded himself against the wall to avoid his line of sight.

"I just know that when the board sees this thing, they won't hesitate to—Oliver?"

Crap.

Oliver scrunched up his shoulders in anticipation when the man's hand landed on them and pulled him away from the corner.

"Are you here with the school?" he asked, leading him down the hall, likely back toward that boring tour.

"N-no?" *Crap!* He panicked. Oliver mentally smacked himself in the face and peeked to see if Chris had bought it.

"Oh, Jon came to see my presentation then? That's good! I've been meaning to chat with him." He grinned, pressing his hand into Oliver's back and directing him left, down a corridor that led to the renovated portion of the lab. "I'm sure Douglass told you about my project, but I didn't think either of you would be ready to come see."

"Right, yeah—your, uh, energy converter?"

"Electromagnetic frequency disruptor, but, yeah, it's also an energy converter," the scientist corrected.

"It's actually quite interesting. I found this strange substance that works almost perfectly as a conductor—I'm temporarily using it to act as the conduit for my contained Tesla arc, and once the presentation is over, I plan on presenting that to the board too. You should really get a look at this." *So that's where Douglass got his talkative nature.* Oliver let out a reluctant sigh, rolling his eyes until they caught sight of what exactly Chris had found and put inside his machine.

He froze, staring at the floating, amorphous and starry black mass in its container as the scientist went ahead of him to excitedly show off what he had made.

Unmistakable. It was so undoubtedly her that it almost physically hurt.

"Uh, Mr. Furkin, I don't think that's a good idea." Oliver took a small step forward, glancing to see if anyone else might be around.

"It's a brilliant idea!" Chris argued, too caught up in his own excitement to notice his concern and worry. "I'll show you how it works real quick."

Oliver moved a little closer, catching a glimpse of Dindet's bright white eye that blinked away, and his heart dropped to his feet.

"Mr. Furkin—" He stopped himself, momentarily perplexed by a soft ticking noise that grew into a whir and filled the air as a terrible dread boiled up inside him.

It's going to—

For half a second, Oliver saw her come almost completely together, and then a large, white arc of lightning shot up from the plate underneath the alien.

A horrendous screech erupted from Dindet that echoed the one he heard in her nightmare.

Every bit of the creature contracted—or tried to—but the electricity shot out and darted off the glass and back into her spiking, terrified mass.

"TURN IT OFF!!" Oliver screamed through her cries, only for it to fall on deaf ears.

"I KNOW IT'S LOUD, BUT LOOK HOW MUCH POWER I'M PRODUCING!" Chris grinned, clapping his hands together before moving the dial up a little. "ALMOST 2.5

GIGAWATTS AN HOUR. IT'S REMARKABLE!"

Dindet's agonized shrieking grew louder, and it made Oliver's ears ring as his eyes flitted around the room. *Do something. Stop this. Move!*

He bolted to the machine, trying to yank the scientist back, but Chris's confusion prevented him from budging at all.

"YOU HAVE TO TURN IT OFF!! YOU'RE KILLING HER!" Oliver cried, pounding his fists against Chris's chest to make him move or do *something*.

The man only stared at him, deaf and baffled by his response. Oliver shoved him back from the control switch and accidentally hit the dial far too high, causing the alien to cry out even louder.

"It hurts! It HURTS!! Make it stop. MAKE IT STOP!!" a horrific and concussive wail tore out of the alien, and Chris swiveled his head around, suddenly realizing that something was very, *very* wrong.

Oliver ripped past him, straight to the tank his friend was being tortured inside, and desperately banged his fists into the glass as hard as he possibly could.

This is your fault. She was here the whole time, and it's all your fault.

Tears stung in Oliver's eyes until he could barely see what remained of the alien's mortified face. He pressed his forehead into the glass, frantically searching for some kind of solution to save her.

She was here because of him, and the horrible realization sucked every last bit of thought out of his aching head until the only thing that remained was a terrible, desperate whisper that pleaded to do something, anything.

Anything at all. Save her!

He lifted his head, numbly staring at the small spider web fractures he had made in the glass with his fists, and came up with a stupid, last-ditch effort.

Oliver crashed his head as hard as he possibly could into the glass, shattering a portion and allowing that awful screeching lightning to erupt into the lab and jolt up through his skin, forcing out a high-pitched yowl from the boy as he tore shards away in effort to pull Dindet's jagged body out of its prison.

The sight of it forced Chris out of his stupor enough to switch off the terrible machine, bathing the room in near silence. The only remaining sound was the creak of glass splintering and cracking under Oliver's shoes as he helped Dindet make her frail escape.

The clown crept through the shattered glass, dripping bits of herself like fresh blood down the broken pieces. It dried away after only a couple of seconds on the ground.

Oliver frantically tore away more of the shards and let her fall into him, staining his clothes an inky black as all of her matter began to float away into nothingness.

It was like ash, soft and so unbelievably fragile. *She is so fragile, and I—*

"No…no, no, *no…*" he breathed, dragging what was left of her as he fell back on his knees. She was melting all over him. She needed to go back together. He needed her to come back together.

"Y-you're okay," Oliver told her when bright, blank and white eyes tried to flicker open.

"You're okay now." More to convince himself of it than anyone else, and he almost believed it when bits of her tensed in a weak effort to stay together. She was trying. He could tell. She was trying so incredibly hard, but he could see that it simply wasn't enough, and she continued to melt and evaporate in his arms.

"Don't go…please—" Oliver choked on his words and clawed at the parts of her that spilled over onto the ground, desperately pressing them back into her, only for them to burst in his hands. It felt like blood. In his hands, spilling over. With shattered glass. *I can't—*

"*Please*, I'm sorry…*I'm so sorry*, I'm sorry. Dindet…" His words were the only thing he could hear, and they were far too late to mean anything now.

Oliver sat there, crumpling up as he tried to hold up the decaying corpse of his friend. But she continued to melt away until the only thing left was a small orange thing that dripped into his palms long after she had evaporated.

"I'm sorry...I'm so sorry, I'm—"

"Oliver..." Chris's voice stirred him from his loss, if only a moment long enough for Oliver to twist his head around with a quiet, empty look of utter shock.

"You...killed her."

"I..."

"She was my friend," Oliver said, almost too quiet to hear, but as Chris approached with a meager effort to console him, he bolted up and clutched the last bit of Dindet to his chest. "She was my friend!! And you KILLED HER!!"

Chris took a step back, lowering his hand as his eyes met Oliver's wild glare. For a quiet second, and that was all it took, he pieced together everything. "The foreign girl..."

Oliver stood up straight and brought his teary gaze back down to Dindet's only remains, "She's gone..."

Epilogue

"Amelis Behavioral Health Center." Poppy held the phone to her face, keeping her focus trained on the woman tied to a chair in front of her. "This is Miss Popiviolli speaking."

As the voice on the other line started speaking, she switched the phone to speaker mode so she could set it down and finish her work.

"Is Dr. Aguirra still there?" Jon's voice was soft but recognizable from the few moments Poppy had seen him at the lab.

"Unfortunately, no, she's recently retired from her position here. Why do you ask?" Poppy thrust her fist into the woman's chest, the same woman she knew Jon was trying to reach. And as he spoke, a lurch of black and starry matter flooded into Dr. Aguirra and caused her veins to tint with their shade.

"My son used to see her. For trauma therapy. He—recently he's been regressing and…there was a tragedy…" Jon paused, and Poppy could almost taste the worry through the phone. "He lost someone close."

"You're looking for psychiatric care?" Poppy forced the woman's gaping mouth shut with her glare alone.

"No, I mean—nothing too intense. He's never taken well to

therapy. That's why I wanted Dr. Aguirra. She's worked with him before—he's comfortable with her. You're certain she's retired?"

"I am." She placed a finger over the doctor's trembling lips and slowly pulled her claws out. "She moved across state, and I believe you're in need of someone local?"

"I'd really think it best if we could get Debra—or, or, does she have any colleagues she recommends?"

"Well," Poppy feigned a pause for contemplation, stepping back as she watched the woman she'd captured melt and congeal into an inhuman sack of flesh and meat. "*I* could provide the service you're looking for?"

"Are you qualified?"

"Very," she answered, "I was recently hired with Pineton High School as an on-campus therapist. Does your child go there?"

"He—he does!" Jon's voice raised with relief as the sound of a jet engine erupted in the background. "His name is Oliver. I can send you his information. He's not going to be in town over winter break, but—but I think it would be good to start sessions with the new semester?"

"Yes." Poppy lilted her voice, forcing a pleasant smile into it as she grabbed Dr. Aguirra's phone and took it off speaker. "I think that would be *grand*. And—what was your name?"

"Jariwala, Dr. Jon Rhun Jariwala, my son is Oliver."

"I look forward to working with you, Jon. *And* meeting Oliver." She ended the call, her attention turning to the boy that had quietly entered the room during the conversation.

The boy shook against his will, and in so much delicious suffering that it made the mime's stomach growl as she forced his tremored hand to raise, dropping something small and black into her palm.

It sank into her, safe and sound within her matter, and she raised her gaze, offering some false and sweet smile to the high school student that stood there, tears rolling down his cheeks unfettered and ceaseless.

"Thank you, Cody." Poppy lifted her chin, addressing someone new now, "Mr. Tarsul, please prepare room 224. We'll be receiving a new patient soon."

CPSIA information can be obtained
at www.ICGtesting.com
Printed in the USA
BVHW050009170123
656385BV00011B/79/J